ECHOES FROM
THE EDGE

**James van Loon and
Paola Bortolotti**

Oxford Publishing, Sweden

TO FABIO CRISTIANO

ISBN 91-970984-5-0

The authors

James van Loon, author of the novel *Double Journey*, chose many divergent paths in his artistic journey which spanned from a brief career as a radio disc-jockey in his native America to an introspective experience as a monk in a monastery, followed by studies in philosophy and psychology. His peregrinations took him to the cobbled streets of old European towns speckled with cafés and real characters where he nurtured his passion for writing. He has been lecturing on social narratives and the symbolic systems of fiction and film at universities in Italy, Spain, Germany, Sweden and England, where he how lives writing, lecturing and practising hypnotherapy.

Paola Bortolotti, winner of the Joseph de Whitt Literary Prize, is not only a writer of fiction, but also a professional translator. Her passion for the arts pervades her outlook on life and has grown from her various involvements with the arts, as a model and porcelain artist, fiction writer and literary translator. A compelling fascination for the 'other', identified as different from her familiar cultural habitat in Italy, has taken her to various parts of the world and total cultural experiences as a keen observer of people in Germany, Greece, the United States and now England. Her latest creation of beauty is her son, Fabio Cristiano.'

If the world were clear
we would not need art.
Albert Camus

ONE

A VIKING

The Viking ship, not a flutter in its sails, rested, its oars motionless, the sea-reach to interminable waterways far from its anchorage at this Scandinavian exhibition. The tanned sails stood still, but they gleamed with the varnished spirits of past travels.

I stood there next to a spirited young man, who I later learned was Michael, an art student, attending a course in Scandinavian art history. As we were reading a display about their pagan rituals, Michael turned towards me, 'Did you know that when Christianity was brought to Scandinavia the Vikings thought Christ was a pale god in comparison with their gods? However, it was the Church that actually made Christ a pale god because in reality, Christ was probably a very passionate young man!'

Looking at the depiction of Thor, the Viking god in full battle array, I asked Michael if he believed in God.

'Sometimes I think God is a myth like the Viking gods,' he replied with determination.

'What is this myth? Just a myth?—or is Christianity something psychologically much deeper than pagan myths?' I inquired, intrigued by his statement.

'I think myths—are symbols of the collective unconscious,' he answered as he stood in a trance and gazed on the bow of the boat that faced seaward. I could tell his mind was elsewhere, far from there. Although endowed with classic Mediterranean features, dark wavy hair, a straight Roman nose and olive skin, the art student possessed the aura of a Viking with his rather tall and muscular frame. With a Viking voice between bass and baritone, he began to talk about stories in Nordic mythology as if they were his own memories, stories that evoked the great spirits of the past, stories of the

Vikings' great courage and battles against the underworld. I found this exciting since it was my doctoral dissertation on the psychology of Nordic mythology that had brought me to this exhibition at the University of Denver. I was impressed by his deep knowledge of the dark Nordic myths suggesting a somber nature quickly disproved at times by a mischievous smile and eyes shadowed by raven eyebrows.

I soon realized that Michael was not an ordinary student, but a seaman, a wanderer whose mind appeared to have sailed to the farthest stretches of the Earth. Many minds are the stay-at-school type, but his certainly was not; he was definitely not typical, and he had a propensity to spin ideas like his connection between Viking pessimism and Sweden's high rate of suicide today. His words plunged me into a ferment, a desire to study his unusual mental connections, and while deep in my thoughts, I finally reacted to the new ideas he was sounding with the voice of someone interrogating an echo. Maybe he had thought I was a sounding board, or he was talking more to himself than to me because I probably seemed to be only reading the displays, but I was definitely listening as there was some puzzling, abstruse or teasing connection between his ideas as he interwove mythology and Jungian psychology, revealing a relationship between the Nordic myths and his mind. Later, I was to discern that the Nordic myths and Michael's mind had a different reality. His remarks were often surprising, and I sometimes had to accept them in silence so that I could think about them as he set my mind searching. We talked about the Vikings and their need to be courageous in spite of Evil that would inevitably conquer Good. He enlightened the darkness of Viking yesterdays, but at this point I didn't realize that I would be drawn into Michael's metaphors of madness.

As we gazed at maps of the Viking conquests stretching to Rome and beyond, Michael said, 'Someday I hope to travel to Scandinavia. It's amazing how they traveled so far—even to America—in these simple boats, and it must have shocked everyone, especially the Anglo-Saxons, when they attacked naked.' The thought of the English reaction struck me as original and very amusing.

We moved from one display to another; Michael ran with intense movements mimicking an attacking warrior as he rushed towards me. He wasn't just looking at an exhibition of straightforward facts as I was, he was becoming emotionally involved, and nowhere did he stop long enough for me to get a specific impression of him or the different exhibits, as he and the displays seemed to merge.

Standing before a depiction of Viking tribal life picturing a family bathing together in a forest lake, Michael burst out in a praising tone, 'A Viking woman in the eighth century could easily divorce her husband; she just had to put the man's shoes outside the front door and that told him and the village that she didn't want him anymore. Scandinavia has always been a progressive place.' Twisting his head to the side and cracking his neck, he continued enthusiastically, 'In fact during the Viking times, the more intimately a man touched a woman the lower the fine was. For example, if one touched her wrist, one had to pay four ounces of silver to the magistrates, but if one touched her breast, it was only one ounce.'

'Why is that?' I asked, puzzled by the apparent paradox.

'They assumed a woman probably wanted it if she let a man go that far,' he explained, in a natural tone.

I couldn't help thinking that they must have been sexually generous people, an idea I found amusing, and considered making a joke, but I sensed Michael wouldn't take my idea humorously as he seemed to have an unusual attachment to the Vikings; they were almost alive to him.

Finally a bell sounded and we were ushered out of the closing hall into the cold and foggy darkness—a darkness of the modern world devoid of Viking fires. The images encompassing the stillness of primeval forests were suddenly replaced with rock music from the dorm windows and drunk students on the campus, but my inner self was still obsessed with the Vikings and our discussion. Our continuing conversation led us off the campus to a popular student café hidden in the fog. Once inside, we took a table wedged into a window recess facing the street, ordered beer and sandwiches, and as we talked about the exhibition, I could see two Michaels—the one at the table and the other a dim, surrealistic image of a seaman in the window. There was an ebb and flow in the conversation that carried us far beyond the small table—the thoughts, words and laughs swelled and swept us farther. I was sailing with a Viking, and it soon became clear to me that Michael, in his quest for the fullness of life, devoured new experiences, new people, new impressions.

After this first encounter, I met Michael on several occasions at different university cafés where in his spontaneous way, he put the pieces of the puzzle of himself together for me. Michael considered himself an artist and wanted to see life as Manet's impressionistic picture of a perpetual picnic—in spite of difficulties. By living with his parents he had no rent to pay, although the price was the constant battle with them. His father, a successful businessman, had told him he was either going to study business or learn to stand on his own feet. His father had worked hard for many years building up his own company producing and marketing bathroom fixtures, and he had strongly hoped Michael would take over his company when he retired. Michael's mother, who came from a well-to-do family, expected no less than success from her husband and children. Although his parents always spoke proudly of his charming, outgoing personality—perfect for marketing and management—Michael was a natural free spirit with an intense interest in the arts, at first acting and painting. Later he wanted to be a writer, but he admitted that was due partly to the attractive writer's lifestyle, sitting at cafés and pubs and discussing intellectual themes late into the night with some good wine. He had a year left before deciding on his major; however, if he insisted on studying art or literature, his parents had plainly told him he had to move out. For Michael, his parents represented a form of bondage that hindered his own emancipation and actualization as a young man.

4

Michael had a part-time job working on stage sets for a Denver theater company, and every once in a while he'd sell a painting, or a portrait of someone sitting at a café or pub. He could have saved some money if he hadn't frequented the cafés and pubs so regularly and had limited the number of classical concerts he purchased tickets for. He moved from one musical and literary festival or art exhibition to the next, as life became one long festival. He enthusiastically disclosed his belief that life was to be savored and enjoyed; it was a fabulous gift from God.

The following week we ran into each other at a student wine bar named *The Chapel*. The blue-green atmosphere of its interior was provided by the sun shining through the engraved window panels which resembled stained glass icons in a Greek Orthodox church. The customers talked in a low voice, as in a chapel, and Michael, in gray tweed trousers and a sage-green sport coat, sat in a little cubicle, like a confessional, writing something he was eager to show me.

'Jason, I'm writing a report on a study for my social psychology class,' announced Michael enthusiastically. 'The university does so little to help the disabled students that I thought a study might convince the administration to do something to ease their hardships on the campus!' Excitedly, Michael continued, 'The university medical center lent me a wheelchair, and last week after the heavy rains, I wheeled myself along the sidewalk on the west end of the campus by the library. I was speeding ahead when I caught up with a young woman, also in a wheelchair.' Michael moved his arms in circles as if his café-chair had been a wheelchair, shook his dark hair out of his face and continued, 'We started talking without looking where we were going, and we ended up in a muddy section where the sidewalk was being repaired. Suddenly, we were absolutely stuck. As we struggled in vain to maneuver ourselves out of the mud for about ten minutes, hundreds of students must have walked around us not one of them offering to help. I really felt sorry for the woman next to me. She was really helpless.'

'Did she know you could walk?' I asked intrigued,

knowing I could never do what he did.

'No, I hadn't told her because I really wanted to pretend being disabled. Besides, the study has more validity if people are debriefed afterwards,' Michael said with the self-assurance of a psychology researcher.

'Anyway, seeing that no one had offered to help her had really made my blood boil, so I suddenly stood up and lifted the young woman in her wheelchair out of the pothole and onto the good surface of the sidewalk. The shock on her face was mild when compared with the other students' astonished looks as they watched me lift my own wheelchair too. They were still staring at us in disbelief as we wheeled away. After hearing all about my study, she found it very interesting and asked me to give my study to the university newspaper for publication.'

Imagining the students' faces was intriguing, but I found that the emotions in his news article moved me even more than his guts did. As we discussed our likes and dislikes, some similarities between us emerged: we both liked descriptive authors like Gass and Styron, were stirred by the music of Sibelius and Grieg and were fascinated by the paintings of the expressionist Edvard Munch.

The following week, I saw Michael at several of the lectures on the Vikings held every evening at Myers Hall. After the last slide of the Friday lecture depicting a Viking family sitting in a house around a fire, we left the hall and walked towards the parking complex. Suddenly Michael asked, 'Would you like to go to a party? To celebrate the exhibition, the Scandinavian language department is having a masquerade party and everyone has to dress in the spirit of Nordic mythology. Are you interested?' Even before I could answer he continued, 'I've got some gunny sacks, strips of leather and some aluminum foil to make helmets in my car.'

On the way to our cars, we noticed a church where, surprisingly for a cold Friday evening, a wedding party was gathered. A line of men were waiting to kiss the bride.

'Jason, she's a beautiful bride, let's get in line for a kiss!' suggested my friend in a spirited way.

'You know her then?' I asked, surprised.

'No—but that makes no difference! Don't you want to kiss her?' he insisted, as if it had been the most natural thing to do.

'Sure—but I couldn't do that!' I answered in disbelief

'Okay, just wait a minute!' said Michael in his naturally confident tone, walking self-assuredly toward the party.

As Michael stood in line, all the men's eyes on him didn't deter him from waiting for his turn. When that came, I was amused to see him receive the longest kiss of them all. Finally, with a mischievous smile and a jovial swinging of his arms in the air, Michael left the wedding party, and we continued walking toward the parking lot.

I followed him in my car, while sparks flew out of the exhaust pipe as Michael's rusty red Volkswagen chugged down the busy street. I parked behind him at the department of Scandinavian languages and then joined him in his car to help him make our costumes. Deftly and artistically Michael crafted two Viking helmets out of thick aluminum foil. Insulated from the crisp Colorado cold, we tried to change clothes inside his warm car, which turned out to be too small for that purpose, and we both had to get out. Standing outside the car in our underwear, in a flash I realized that by shutting the door, Michael had accidentally also locked it from the outside, leaving the keys and our clothes inside. Realizing this, my companion started laughing as he crazily jumped around, barefoot, in the cold. A spontaneous burst of contagious laughter warmed me.

At his suggestion, we ran clumsily across the silvered street and straight to the party hoping to find a wire clothes hanger to pry open the car door lock. In the frosty air, the thin luminosity created by the moon emphasized the contrast of my bright white skin and Michael's darker skin, as we ran quickly over the frozen grass sliding down the slippery sidewalk which lead to the department building.

We rang the bell and stood there, jogging on the icy porch, laughing and gesticulating crazy messages to each other. A young woman opened the door, but at the sight of us her friendly expression turned into one of shock. She then appeared to suddenly realize that we had come nearly naked like the Vikings. Michael with his muscular body didn't need to feel uneasy, I, on the contrary, was quite embarrassed and hoped no one from my department would see me standing there in my bikini Jockeys. Judging from the students' laughter, surprise and welcome, we must have had the appearance of being held there captive by a spell. Animated by an obvious excess of beer, the dizzy festive faces of the students stared at us. If only I too had been a little inebriated, that would have eased my embarrassment. A burst of yelling and a hundred hands clapping overpowered the already loud music, but this did not startle Michael, who in response leaped towards the party, howling even louder, spinning around and screwing his face into expressions of attack at a group of laughing women.

Within seconds he was in charge of the party, the leader of the Vikings, and had it not been for his dark brown hair, he might have been Erik the Red. Watching Michael and chuckling nervously, for a few seconds I forgot that I wasn't wearing any clothes. When I realized that I was nearly naked, I wondered if this was the way the Vikings had felt. 'No,' I thought, 'they must have felt more like Michael.' I could feel the warm flames of embarrassment engulf me especially as my eyes met the dean of the psychology department.

With borrowed bathrobes, slippers and a clothes hanger we retreated from the party, managed to open the car and retrieved our cold costumes and clothes.

'Sorry about locking the doors!' apologized Michael. 'That car was coming down the street so fast, it would have smashed the door if I hadn't quickly slammed it shut.' Before I could say anything, he continued, 'You looked really embarrassed when that female professor saw you in your fruity looms. I think she liked you!' His observation momentarily boosted my spirits, and we invaded the party once more.

Inside the warm party, I kept feeling that the women were looking through our burlap bags, and I still felt naked. Maybe this was the way women felt at a party when men looked at them. I hardly had enough time to peer into my thoughts when suddenly two women approached us: one of them walked resolutely and barefoot over the hardwood floor with a splendid self-assurance. Her tanned thighs moved energetically in a deerskin dress which barely covered her from her thighs to her breasts. What a contrast with the skinny physique of the other girl, whose unripe appearance made her look like her younger sister. The more mature and attractive one asked Michael to dance, which left me feeling odd as I just stood, silent, next to the waif. To break the tension I invited her to dance. Strangely, even though I was older than Michael, he had attracted the more mature-looking of the two women, and although my partner said she was a freshman at the university, I had the impression of dancing with a little girl. But suddenly my thoughts changed as I started to wonder if my gunny sack would fly off at the first good shake. My dance partner then told me how she found my friend very attractive, which didn't help my feeling of inadequacy.

Michael's masqueraded maiden was Laura, as I later learned. She was incredibly beautiful. Her eyes of deep forest-green, a gleaming cascade of dark hair fell on bare, salacious shoulders which shook voluptuously as she molded her movements to the music, the stretching deerskin tugging on her skin to hide this voluptuous 'Viking' woman. Being barefoot emphasized her primitive image, and to keep my eyes off her for a longer period of time was beyond my control. My partner started talking snidely about Laura, and I fretted and took to arguing with myself whether or not I should tell Michael, but I finally realized that my talking, or indeed any action of mine would be dismissed as a mere futility since Michael seemed to be a man of his own mind.

At the end of the Viking fete, Michael grabbed my arm and pointed to a woman leaving the party with a young man, 'That's my sister Shelly.'

She possessed attractive features similar to Michael's, except for her blond hair, and I wished Michael had introduced us, but it was just as well he hadn't since I wouldn't have known what to say to her.

Two weeks later at the university library I ran into Michael, and he proudly presented to me a novel he had begun writing. I was surprised he had started writing a novel, something I had always dreamed of doing. Since he let me read it, I periscoped for a desk at the end of the stacks where it was quiet. His manuscript, written in a style even more dynamic than my own, laid bare his perceptions, thoughts and feelings about his relationship with Laura, whose name, as well as his own, recurred throughout the manuscript. Until I understood why, I thought he used too many adjectives.

As a writer, however, he was truly adventurous. Like a Viking he sailed off the edge of the printed paper to touch the reader. My writing, not as risky as his, was rather like the sailing of a sailor on a ship inside a bottle, safe and controlled, but sailing nowhere. I was afraid the world was flat like my paper and I could fall off the edge. Michael rendered a 60's tone in his story titled *Echoes From The Edge*. He once revealed to me that he had a penchant for that era flavored with Beatles' music and existential philosophy.

Echoes From The Edge

On the Denver University campus, Michael, with a nervous appearance, kept watch for Laura's presence in her dorm window. He tramped back and forth between the residence hall and the students' wine bar across the street gazing fixedly from the brick lane below, in the hope to see her face through the window. Michael had a particular passion for Laura's mouth and eyes. Her elongated eyes, more like the eyes of a puma than of a girl, gave her an animalistic look. Her large mouth tantalized him. It revealed a primitive dimension of her nature, something savage and spiritual at the same time. Her full lips had already seduced him at the Viking party. Even though she had uttered very few words—she didn't need words—the mere unfolding of her lips, promising a primeval storm, had bewitched Michael. He now wanted to know that promised storm, diving deep into another dimension. Finally he convinced himself that he had nothing to lose by surprising her; he entered the sorority house, climbed the steps two at a time as if he was summiting Pikes Peak and knocked on her door.

Through the doorway, opened slightly ajar, Michael had a glimpse of Laura's face, wearing the wild-eyed look women have when they have just awakened, framed by tousled hair.

'This is a surprise,' she said in a sleepy voice, keeping the door only partially open. Through the door slit as looking through a tunnel, Michael's senses were drowsed by the dimness of Laura's nest, the incense wafting in the air, the marijuana music. Though the shades were drawn, Michael still had the fleeing impression of a bohemian decor with posters patching the walls with expressionistic forms and colors.

Michael's eyes met hers, beckoning him to enter, and with some hesitation he stepped into the room, almost slipping on a throw rug. If his movements revealed a certain awkwardness, her body dressed in a karate bathrobe bared the self-awareness of her seductive strength, accentuated by a pretty mouth, large, soft and of a vibrant pink which kissed him on both cheeks, something she had learned while living a year in France.

'Don't you have a class now?' she inquired. Her luxuriant black mane she did not know how to arrange. She used no make up, her sensuality came from deep inside. There was a mystical quality to her.

'My lit prof is boring, and I was curious about your

11

writing.'

She poured two glasses of French wine, handed him her latest poem, and, after a slow sip, disappeared into the bathroom for a shower. Michael sat slumped at the kitchen table, trying to understand this writing which bewitched him, as did her beauty and that unusual mind which had won her a scholarship to the university. He wished he could grasp the meaning of Laura's poem about red cloth.

Postcards, the limitations of vision—
        mirror the distortions of imagination.
Photographs, the doors to love—
        open with awareness.
Red cloth, the hymen between love and fantasy—
        creates life.
The mind, between the reality of actions
        and the limitations of vision—
Distorts mirrors and reflects God.

But her poetry didn't make any more sense to him than did his dreams about this unusual woman, and his thoughts soon wafted to their lovemaking after that dance, where he had first seen her. The sensation that emerged from these images took the shape of a question: had their lovemaking forged a connection between them?

Suddenly, she emerged looking even more tantalizing than before as she walked with a teasing seductiveness wet and barefoot over the floor. Her legs made a quick rhythmic movement from the ankles up along the curves of her calves and thighs, with voluptuous vibrations that disappeared under her karate robe. She snatched the drink from Michael's hand, drank a sip before placing it on the book case, and throwing her arms around him splashed his lips with wet wine kisses.

Somewhat inebriated from the wine, and challenged by

12

her suggestive signals, Michael mimicked the karate master, making chopping movements with his hands. In playful response she kicked her long leg towards Michael, who grabbed it and, as if wanting to stamp an indelible impression of his body on hers, he pulled her tight against him. Kissing her neck he imagined an exciting and licentious scene of conquering her as he stroked her legs, and pulled her robe up exposing more of her thighs and giving a shadow of a bit more. Stripping her robe off, he unveiled the sculptured figure of a martial arts instructress with long thighs and firm breasts, and in his strong, well-defined face, his ignited eyes glowed like hot coals.

He shook the thick brown hair out of his eyes as if to have a better look at this woman, the color of whose nipples and eyes fashionably matched the brown of her karate belt. To extinguish his stare, Laura wrenched him close to her. Michael forced a long kiss deep in her spirited mouth, and he felt her nipples harden against him. In a tantric trance his kisses moved over her breasts and down her silky stomach to her protected parts. Laura threw back her intoxicated face framed with flowing black hair and her panting matched the undulating rhythm that vibrated her body like violin strings.

Drawing him towards her lips, their mouths joined together in Zen unity until the kissing turned into biting and, in an aggressive stance she violently tore off Michael's clothes without any kind of restraint or pretension of propriety. Their strong bodies folded into each other on the floor in harmony as they exercised all the physical vigor of their youth. The rhythm of their bodies imposed a union of yin and yang, giving and offering, and their bodies never tired in their measured movements. In this frenzied fever of fun, his teeth bit softly on her vulnerable nipples. She threw back her head, and her panting mouth gave Michael the impression of being in nirvana.

He observed not only her karate facial expressions of serenity and self-determination, but her naked strength as their playful fighting match of many minutes brought them both to the verge of complete vibrations. Laura was beautiful with all that black hair.

These were the last words he'd written in this chapter of his novel describing this naked woman in his arms, a fabulous story, which still made me somewhat jealous.

The following weekend I intended to give Michael his manuscript and my comments at a student alehouse, but first I went to watch Michael compete on the university swim team, where his talent as a swimmer would have made fish blush with envy. Yet he wasn't happy when we met at the student pub, named after the school colors, the *Crimson and Gold*, a pub converted from a small warehouse.

Michael sat with a sad face which lit up as he saw me. 'Jason, thanks for coming tonight. We're now the conference champions, but big deal! My parents didn't even show up! They've got more important things to do! I'm tired of all their petty materialistic values—I feel my spirit crushed. I have often thought of entering a monastery to find expression of my spiritual values. You know, Laura never came to watch us as she had promised.'

I poured Michael a beer and tried to cheer him as I said, 'Maybe Laura wanted to come, but something happened. Maybe she had to study for finals.'

'Maybe it happened that someone else asked her out!' he echoed bitterly.

'Quit thinking so negatively! Besides, you swam great tonight,' I commented with true admiration.

Michael chugged a full glass down then added in a frustrated tone, 'Usually, swimming is good therapy for me, but tonight I'm just pissed. I'm going to quit! Jason, it's difficult trying to study, swim, paint and live with my fricken' folks.' Cracking his neck to the side, he continued, 'My dad really pissed me off last night. I found out that he had thrown out all my paints, and I almost hit him—but he was drunk. He's a bastard! He's against my painting even though I'm good at it.' His face lit up for a second as he

14

added, 'I won first prize with a painting at our high school art festival last year.'

'I know you're good, even though what you paint is spiritual porno,' I said trying to get a laugh from him.

'Porno is in the groin of the beholder, you idiot!' Michael laughed as he pounded his empty mug on the table.

Still trying to raise his spirits, I asked him, 'Who gave you the flowers for winning the meet tonight?'

'No one, I bought these for Laura, but I don't need them now. You're getting together with my sis tonight, give them to her ... I wish I knew where in the hell Laura was this afternoon. We had fun all last week. Monday we saw the new Swedish film,' and before I could ask him about it, he continued, 'Tuesday after classes we drove to the mountains and went ice skating. We fell a lot, but it was fun having her fall on me. The Homewood Lodge has a great fireplace and we talked about my novel.' Again, before I could ask him about his novel, he excitedly continued, 'Wednesday I found a love poem from her on my windshield. Jason, she's too good to be true; but I don't know if I can really trust her. I really don't trust anybody. I don't even know why I'm talking to you like this,' Michael said, as if drowning in his beer. After a swallow of the Coors I had just poured him, he resumed, 'I guess I wouldn't be so pissed off if Laura had been at the meet this afternoon. Anyway, I'm really glad you came.'

A silence of a few seconds was the only time I had to think of the best way to comfort him. Michael licked the beer foam off his lips and continued, 'Besides the monastery, sometimes I think about moving to Europe, maybe to Prague or Munich, to find cobbled streets, cafés and jazz dance studios. I've heard of a large commune of young writers and dancers in both cities. A new place would give me new visions, new smells, new tastes, new touches, a new life. On my own I could live more like an artist—I hate living with my folks,' Michael maintained bitterly as he poured more beer from the pitcher.

'Come on, do you really think chicks are better if they speak Czech or Bavarian?' I smiled. Suddenly I feared losing a

15

very interesting friend. 'The only difference you'd find is that they drink real beer. What about your studies?'

'My grades are terrible. In high school I could escape from home with my swimming and my schoolwork. It's crazy, last year I had the highest grades in my class and was Valedictorian, and now I'm flunking most of my classes. It's not an escape as it used to be.' He rose. 'Hey, it's late. I've got to go. Thanks for coming.'

I watched Michael walk out of the smoky pub and into the bright street, and on an impulse I followed him. Shining between the rows of dorm buildings, the last of the late afternoon sun sketched Michael's silhouette in pencil-point clearness. His jagged outline of sun-blazed jeans and jacket and mussed hair emphasized the unsteady movement of his gait, which jerkingly punctuated the stone sidewalk, listlessly following the trace of his brooding body down the walkway along the student fraternity and sorority houses. Just before I caught up with him, he stopped in the shade of a dorm building and, looked around as if looking for his lost shadow. Suddenly, he entered a doorway, quickly climbed the stairs and knocked on a door. I supposed it was Laura's, as this place matched his description of her address. There was no reply. He turned nervously around, acted as if he didn't see me, slowly descended the stairwell and walked across the street to the student hangout—a place of consolation.

In pursuit to hearten my friend, I caught up with him as he stood in the busy entrance of the wine bar, wallpapered with medieval monastic motifs. Through the yellow-azure tobacco smoke, incense-like, the highly polished wooden bar appeared like an altar of gold. Lights shone on the aligned bottles giving them the glow of lit candles. The clinking of the glasses handled by the bartender resembled the liturgical bells of an altar boy. Unlike a church, the wine bar was crowded, and as we took the only empty pew by a window and watched an exceptionally lively liturgy, I could perceive that Michael was in his own world, deaf to my homily.

Staring out into the darkness, he could see Laura's dorm window on the second floor of the building across the street.

The light in her room stood out against the deepening darkness. Suddenly he blinked in disbelief as he saw a sailor with her. His face turned into a wrinkled mask of pain as he drew his strong hand through his dark brown hair. The two figures moved abruptly out of sight, and the window became a blank screen. Michael looked around the place and pulled at the scarf, tight around his neck. At a candlelit table in the opposite corner, a young couple kissed, their faces melting together in the light of the flame. Michael's face darkened.

Sitting with his wine, Michael, as he later told me, had imagined the sailor undressing Laura, pulling off her clothes like lowering the sail on his boat, and there would be the crack of canvas as he emerged bare from his dirty, stiff clothes and then he would jab at her like the waves against a pier. He could almost hear the groan of the man's groins like the moan of the sea, and these meditations exhausted him. The incessant talking at our table generated an unbearable noise in his head; he stood, pushed himself around me, walked out of the wine bar and crossed the street to the dorm.

Scrambling to the second floor landing, he pushed open the unlocked door. Laura quickly sat upright in her bed, breaking the embrace of a young man and emerging from her turquoise sheets like a dolphin breaking out of the water. The naked man jumped out of the bed and grabbed a tennis racket leaning against the wall, but before he had a chance to swing it, Michael hit him hard and knocked him to the floor.

Later I met Michael, and we hoofed it to the *Crimson and Gold*, where the drunken students gave the appearance of a large family quarrel, mirroring Michael's quarrel with himself. 'Women tempt me with their bodies and then destroy me with their minds!' he blurted out. Drowning his anger and hurt with the brew from Colorado spring waters, he kept giving me over and over all the details of his encounter with Laura and the sailor. In disbelief, he then gave me his explanations, but I couldn't comfort him. I'll never forget the look on Michael's face—the angered profile taut—so taut that he shivered. His eyes were sick with hurt and anger; his whole body seemed on the verge of explosion as he moved his beer mug around in a circle on the table between us.

We were to meet the next day at the *Crimson and Gold*, but he didn't come. As suddenly as he had sailed into my life, he now sailed out of it; he disappeared and I didn't hear about him for a very long time. During the Christmas holidays three years later, I received an unexpected package from Sweden which I took with me to the small café where I usually had my coffee and danish. The package contained a manuscript and a letter from someone named Urban.

Dear Jason,

I'm a psychiatric intern at the Ulleraker Mental Hospital where Michael has often spoken of you and mentioned that your book on Nordic mythology was being published. He doesn't know that I'm sending you a copy of his manuscript, but I thought your contact could be helpful. It seems you two were friends.

I'm very concerned about Michael who is totally consumed with the Vikings. His splintered personality is very much exemplified in his writing as he is both the omniscient writer of the story as well as the projected protagonist. Lacking a sense of identity, he writes of himself in the third person, and, as is typical of schizophrenics, he sometimes has shallow, abbreviated and emotionally flat descriptions of himself and the other characters. Their utterances are paranoid projections of himself.

Michael fragments one idea from another; nothing flows. As with a person experiencing multiple personalities, time runs in circles for him; he blends different experiences into one happening. I'm hoping that, as a friend of his, you can help me to establish better contact with him. Please write to me soon. I'd appreciate your support.

Urban

Had Michael changed so much? Where was the man who had dared to stand in line for a kiss at the wedding? Where was the man who had conquered the guests at the Viking party? I began immediately to read Michael's manuscript in which he portrayed himself running across the pages. Was this scream of consciousness, called *Echoes From The Edge,* the schizophrenic expression of an artist who had gone over the edge? Reading his metalanguage heavy with metaphors and similes, I began to understand that much must have happened since our consuming discourse on the Vikings. Urban and I apparently had experienced Michael's personality very differently or had my perceptions of Michael been erroneous? I wondered now if Michael had seen himself at the Viking party in the same way that I had seen him. Had Michael been playing with my mind? Or is this fellow Urban trying to taunt me? Why would he write to me? Is this a Viking game?

My research had at that time led me to the psychological interpretation of the deeper meanings lying under the surface scratches on the Rune stones. Now I began deciphering something much more baffling and mysterious than those ancient writings, as I started discovering the relationship between the archetypes of Viking mythology and Michael's mind or possibly Urban's mind. Reading this novel persuaded me to share with you his manuscript which contained a complex world where shadows took form as reality. This book started on page twenty which meant that either the first nineteen pages were missing for some reason, maybe Urban knew, or that possibly the numbers two and zero had mystical value, like symbols in the Mandala and Sanskrit circle which I had seen in Michael's art work. This is what I read in Michael's original and possibly unedited words.

TWO

ECHOES FROM THE EDGE

* * *   Michael's Manuscript   * * *

Through the etched ice ferns on the window of the police car, the young man's captured eyes watch the rain gnaw a hole in the frosted pane, revealing not only the pounding sleet, but the depressing gray buildings of the mental asylum. As the patrol car suddenly stops, like the young man's heart, the overpowering officers jump out of the vehicle, and stretching their huge heads and hands into the back of the car, their large arms drag Michael out of the patrol car and into the lobby of the mental hospital's emergency ward. Half intoxicated, Michael struggles to wrench his arms away from the officers' grip, as they with difficulty drag his muscular body toward the reception desk. In a tug-of-war, he struggles to take a stance in his carpenter overalls, but the two overpowering policemen yank and heave him across the room. Scrimmaging with the two hulking angry officers, he fears they are going to drag him across insanity's thin line.

Michael's moss-green eyes jerkingly probe his new environment, a reception room where purple plants appear to glow radioactively in the drab lighting, a suffocating synthetic summer atmosphere and the warmth one would find in a nuclear reactor. A reception nurse, her carved cheekbones prominent like sharp blades, meets Michael's blurry eyes as she moves outside the caged window through a sliding door, and two male assistants, conscious of their strength, inherent in the stiff movement of their upper bodies, take him from the policemen's hands.

The nurse, reaching for a pen, pulls back her white hospital coat like a flasher and with unlimited personal questions fills in Michael's admittance form. He impatiently answers most of the questions until he can't see the relevance of asking about his marital status.

20

'Why is that important?' he smiles, 'unless you're interested in a date!' His remark falls unheeded by the nurse, and Michael is hauled by the ward-aides to the side of the austere room, where he stretches his neck to the side until it cracks, then shakes his dark hair away from his angry eyes and ferocious features. One of the assistants, in a tight unbuttoned nurse coat over his strapping shoulders, pushes the illuminated elevator button, while Michael glares at him and then gazes at the ceiling. If only a cool sprinkling rain from the ceiling would water his sweaty face, the jungle of plants around him, and have pressure enough to wash their huge hands off him. The water would be a refreshing relief from his overheated, shocked composure, but, adding to his frustration, nothing happens save the elevator doors sliding open like anguishing, clanging prison doors. Inside the elevator, with the stern nurse, the assistants let go of his arms. Released from their grasp he bends his neck again; the sound of the cracking vertebrae, accentuated by the silence of the lift, seems to say that they can hold his skin but not reach his bones.

Once the elevator's powerful pull stops on the third floor, Michael emerges from it wide-eyed, slowly following the silent nurse, feeling a senseless animosity from her. *Maybe she's angry at my allusion to a date, but her questions were dumb.* In the fluorescently lit corridor, the nurse raps on a door; from the other side comes a sound of clogs dragging across the room, and an old psychiatrist, Dr Svensson, with a long parchment-like face under mussed thin hair, opens the door. Anger and fear wind their way through Michael's trim body; his muscles tighten as he looks at the craggy-faced doctor, whose foul breath, through his long pointed nose, is more poisonous than any words he could have said; Michael backs away from the stench, bumping into one of the Viking assistants.

Emotions seemingly in line with his mind earlier this morning, now travel into knots as his dream of Sweden is jolted in this sudden stop at the mental hospital. Feelings from his last week in Munich intensify the subtleties of gray shades and silence in this mental hospital, lurking like monsters in his subconscious, and Michael creeps into his own mind. *It was wrong leaving Munich after what happened there.* Bolting towards the door he pushes himself past one of the assistants, until the other ward-aide catches him and yanks his arm behind his back with an arm-lock. The psychiatrist with quick, awkward movements fumbles for a needle in the medical cabinet.

The muscular men suppress Michael's fighting fists and lower his trousers as the sallow-skinned doctor injects him with a hypodermic syringe; Michael's fine facial features quiver with the fear that the needle, like a bayonet, will make him an easier prey to the doctor. The aged psychiatrist, famous in Sweden for his earlier research on laser lobotomies, tired and seemingly irritated by being awakened in the middle of the night, reads the police report and then the expressions on Michael's face, the expressions of a mad lad. His ice-blue eyes travel in a strange way all over Michael, carefully avoiding his angry eyes; he then continues to read the officer's report.

His trousers around his ankles, his knees resemble reflections in rippling water in the corner of the room furnished with a functional modern desk, decrepit chairs, a rickety table and lamp with a dead bulb. As the doctor hisses a few words to the nurse and assistants, Michael yanks up his pants for added protection before the ward-aides wrench him out of the room without a word. The assistants' shoes squeak in the silence of the corridor as if screaming at the weight of their bulky bodies, as Michael is carted off to an austere room in an adjacent ward. Inside the quarters there isn't much to inspect: two beds, two desks, a sink and metal mirror; everything strikes him as foreign, and he can't believe this is happening to him. Slumped on the bed, his eyes closed, tired from the medicine, he falls asleep; in his dreams he screams at God.

The next morning, a very haggard-looking Michael lies in his bed and scrutinizes the cracks in the high ceiling which loom like thunderbolts ready to strike at him. Disoriented and trapped, he quickly camouflages himself in his hospital pajamas and walks over the cold wooden floor toward the window to find safety in something he can recognize. From his window, through the double glass panes, he casts his eyes over the valley and the river Fyris bathed in icy fog, the stillness of the air unbroken by sounds of airplanes or traffic; suddenly, the dragging sound of feet in the corridor awaken him to the reality of the mental hospital. This realization turns into an electrical shock, his large green eyes endeavor to escape, gaping in both directions out the window, his thick, dark hair shifts from one side to the other of his imprisoned face as he cracks his neck and contemplates cracking the window. *These metal window frames are like bars, but who would want to escape out there. It doesn't look a damn bit inviting.*

Outside, down the river from Uppsala, with everything freezing, he dreads himself shriveling and shrinking in his oversized white pajamas, as the fir trees do from the cold climate. The snow storms of Sweden sounded exotic while he was a student in Munich, but now, in Uppsala, it's just frigid, wet, and depressing. As he undresses, his muscle-toned body quivers until he quickly pulls on the brown woolen slacks and Norwegian sweater he had bought when he'd first arrived in Uppsala on a train.

Suddenly, snoring erupts from the other side of his room; Michael shivers at the sight of a face appearing from under a mountain of blankets on the other bed. He immediately notices a collection of underwear—patterned in a blue and yellow Swedish flag design—hanging from a chair, the man's bed posts, desk, and even the night stand. *That guy is either very nationalistic or he goes through a lot of underwear. I can't believe it—they're even on the door knob.*

The lights in the ward, bright and jarring as a Tivoli park at night, blind him as he opens the door. In the corridor, he rapidly glances behind him to the sound of footsteps following him, thus getting an eyeful of a huge patient. Very broad, like a bear, he advances towards Michael. Although he keeps his head half lowered to hide a scar on his face, Michael sizes up his stature, even more towering if the man only straightened his posture and lifted his head. But he keeps his head down partially as he threatens Michael, 'I'm going to kill you, you foreign bastard!'

These words, daggers of hate, stun Michael. After watching the man's drug-dazed eyes and slow movements for a few seconds, Michael hides any sign of fear by yelling, 'Get off my back!'

Before any response can emerge in the giant's deep-set eyes, Michael hastens down the corridor towards the dining room where his exhaustion is exposed by the glaring light. In spite of the spooky amusement park appearance of the room, emphasized by the naked light from the ceiling fixtures, Michael feels safer in the presence of other patients even though their strained faces give the impression of sitting scared in a fast-turning ride. *I hope these people aren't all as crazy as that guy with the ugly chin. He's too doped to be dangerous. But I'm gonna get the hell out of here.*

Finding an empty table Michael pours and guzzles a cup of strong coffee while watching the ugly-chinned man carry his breakfast to the next table, where he stares at Michael and chews his toast, crushing the sticky toasted bread to pulp. The man, he later learns, is Bjornson, nicknamed by the other patients 'Scar' because of a long, straight scar on his right cheek, like a bookmark in a disturbed biography which includes his life as an artist and glassblower from the south of Sweden. The scar is the result of a violent encounter with a Turkish immigrant whom Bjornson found in his wife's bed. The Turk slashed him with an art piece—a broken glass dildo—to protect himself, and now Bjornson, locked not only in a mental hospital but also behind his scarred face, expresses remembrance of freedom and foreigners.

Late for breakfast, Brigitte, a slender young woman with corn-colored hair, rushes into the room; her eyes quickly scan the space stopping at Michael's table. Michael stares at her lipstick, thick around her mouth, bright as a fluorescent road-sign. She swings her bottom onto a chair opposite Michael, providing a buffer between him and Bjornson's hateful stare.

'I didn't know what dress to wear!' she chirps deliriously, squirming on her chair.

'I couldn't understand everything you said. Can you speak slower?' Michael inquires in a low voice, afraid his uneasiness will show and be detected by the threatening man.

'I'm late because I didn't know what dress to wear! Do you like this one?' she asks flirtatiously.

Michael glances at her dress and notices that she's not wearing a bra. 'Yes, I like the color green.'

'What's wrong with my blue one?' she yells, leaning over the table.

'Hey, I just got here. I've never seen your blue dress!' replies Michael, taken aback and totally confused by her reaction. 'Anyway, if you wanted to wear the blue one, why ask me?'

She just peers wide-eyed at Michael for a few seconds and then asserts in a lower voice, as if revealing a secret, 'Every time I wear the blue dress, every man I meet has an orgasm.'

'I wish you'd wear the blue dress then,' Michael replies spiritedly, continuing to avoid the stare of Bjornson who walks by their table.

She doesn't find his humor amusing; his American wit contains a deliberate barb, an ill-disguised wish to have a pleasurable situation rather than this threatening one. *I wonder what happens if that guy's medicine wears off.* Suddenly, Brigitte's face appears preoccupied and she vanishes without eating her breakfast. Some patients peck at their food in silence; Michael remains glued to his table thinking of the ugly man's words. *He's too crazy to be dangerous, and I'm sort of relieved that she's crazy because she is a real looker. I can't get involved with any more girls. They tempt me with their bodies and then destroy me with their minds. Grass is always greener on another girl's legs.* His thoughts switch to what happened a few days earlier in Munich, when Lena, a blond emaciated nurse, enters with some pills. Michael's dark pupils seem to reach out from the whites of his eyes as he says, 'What's wrong with the guy with the large chin? He keeps threatening me!'

25

'There is no one on this ward who is dangerous!' she reassures him. Rigid in her white coat and antiseptic mind, the nurse's heart is immune to his emotions. The pills sedate some of his thoughts and his desire to shriek out the terror that scares him deep inside. Lena leaves, and he's left to stare out of the dining room window. The tablets have numbed him, leaving his body helplessly sitting at the table, much as a sick bird huddles on the scrawny and bare tree branch outside. Suddenly he thinks the bird grins at him, only to realize that birds can't smile. Like the stars placed on his forehead for learning his catechism in grade school, the pills of this institution restrain and dwarf his individuality, reducing Michael to a catatonic body on a chair with thoughts and feelings more foreign than the new country.

His eyes move from the smirking bird to the sound of coffee dripping slowly through a Swedish filter. The sound of rain pacified him always as a child and now the sound of the coffee dripping slowly helps him to forget the smirking bird; his experiences become thick like the coffee as he hears each drop bang into the pot; the noise suddenly rattles him, and the strange smirking bird shatters his senses. Some of his perceptions in the dining room appear heightened. The walls in the room seem whiter than the snow outside, and the furniture becomes thick and black like his coffee; these images then change: now the furniture looks white and the snow black. Just looking around exhausts him in spite of the caffeine he is certain of tasting—not the coffee—and with his finger in his mouth he tries to touch the caffeine, wondering if the drug would slide down his tongue and make shrieking sounds inside his body. Suddenly he thinks the pills dispense these crazy perceptions. His thoughts then flash back to a college textbook stating that the psychiatric staff of mental hospitals were addicted to the patients taking drugs and that's why all mental patients were doped. The only stimulant he wants is coffee, a drug he desperately needs in the morning, and even more in the afternoon here in Sweden, with coffee break time at three in the afternoon, when the dark universe of night begins.

As the last of the patients move into the dark corners of the ward and their minds, Michael stands to find Lena, and starting to walk, he perceives even more the effect of the pills, and it seems to him that he is walking in water with slow and heavy movements. Taking each step, he fights the liquid environment around him, fighting a strange undertow, a tug to another world; he can feel he is drifting from reality. Fear comes to his eyes but he changes that quickly since he is certain of receiving more medicine if he manifests any more problems; further, he can't let the man who threatened him see his confusion.

At the other end of the corridor, music starts to spill out of the common room, and as Michael enters, the patients appear as a quiet audience for the stereo playing the music of a long-haired band, and the vinyl-covered armchairs grunt sick noises each time a patient moves in them.

All of a sudden, the breakfast woman, Brigitte, races into the room towards Michael in her cornflower blue dress, pulls back her thick blond hair and coos pouting her sensuous blue lips, 'How—does—it—feeeeel?'

'What—? Ooh—it feels good, thank you!' pants Michael, noticing her long nails—shaped, buffed and painted sky-blue.

Brigitte laughs seductively leaving Michael with the impression of a blue streak as she vanishes from the room, and he suddenly realizes that she looks somewhat like his sister Shelly. His thoughts are soon jarred by a woman who walks back and forth in the room like a caged animal. The skin of her face is drawn tightly over the bridge of her nose—away from her large, primitive eyes, the pupils of an animal held captive. Each time she passes Michael she grunts, 'What's your name?' without waiting for his answer. Finally she stops pacing and, peering through her wild black hair, asks, 'What's your name?'

'Michael,' he replies in a louder voice.

'Michael—!' she exclaims, pensively. 'That's the name my mother gave one of her children. They didn't know at birth what sex it was.'

27

'That's too—' he begins.

'The doctor was old and had forgotten the differences between boys and girls, you see,' she tries to explain to Michael.

'So, what do you have, a brother or a sister?' Michael asks, his lips twitching.

'We still don't know.' Before Michael's lips can unravel, she continues, 'Did you see the new male attendant? His face was all red, but I couldn't decide whether it was sunset or sunrise.'

Michael refrains from erupting into a spontaneous laugh, he looks at her and walks away—away from this woman who lost her baby named Michael, her husband, and her parents in a tragic boating accident. Michael doesn't yet know about her calamitous past. He stands up to leave the room, but is stopped by the sight of an oriental-looking rug on the floor before him. The hypnotic pattern woven on the floor suddenly turns the rug into an exhausting, dense pathway; he can't decide which way to walk over the rug, as some of the patterns look like a mountain range, he's just not sure. These new doubts keep him walking on a tightrope; the balance between appearances and reality often tips in one direction or the other. Whether the ward is dense or hollow is not clear either. With a tormented mind, he finds it safer to walk around the rug, directing his steps toward the lavatory, a corner of sanity.

After sixty minutes in the toilet stall, fearing the ward assistants will come looking for him, he finally decides to leave. As he nervously reaches for the latch, he clumsily knocks down the dispenser of toilet paper and the paper rolls under the door into the next stall. He tries to retrieve it but it keeps unraveling. Reaching under the partition into the next stall, he is surprised to see two shoes. Before he can pull his hand away, he feels a caressing touch.

'Let go of my hand, and give me the damn toilet paper!' Michael yells, disgusted.

A hand gives him the roll and the patient shuffles out of the lavatory with a disappointed sigh. The restroom has been

28

no sanctuary, and Michael enters the corridor determined to get away from the crazy people in this hospital.

The hollow eyes of Lena look over her tray of pills as she stands in front of the nursing station; Michael drags his feet to reach her, and as he gets closer, he sees her tightened face and wonders if her scalp grasps her hair like a migraine.

'When can I get out of this crazy place?'

Lena's answer vibrates vigorously, like an attack, 'This is not a locked ward so you may leave it, but not the hospital grounds.'

'Yeah. Well—I'll probably be leaving before the weekend.' Michael blurts out, and gives her a zany grin.

'You're kidding!' she snorts, stunning Michael.

'No, I'm not,' mumbles Michael.

'The doctor will answer all your questions!' she advertises with sarcasm, turning her back and leaving him standing petrified near a window. A new pretty patient with chipmunk cheeks walks by, mumbling 'Twenty chocolate chip cookies would be the perfect breakfast!'

Michael stares out of the narrow prison-like opening through which the sky is compressed and limited, and his masculinity is paralyzed inside him; he stands an hour at the window and sees nothing. In the corridor, Lena commands with dissonant words that bristle Michael's hair, 'It's time for art therapy.' The patients parade slowly down the corridor towards another ward except Agnete, the woman whose dead child was named Michael. She is constantly in a state of motion pacing between the front and back of the group. War wages inside her; there is no peace in her life as she runs the tightrope corridor of her anxieties and abandonment. In the art therapy room, she suddenly stops dead in her tracks, pulls at her Palestinian scarf which seems to choke her, loosens it and throws it on the ground. Clothes, as well as the mental hospital, hold her prisoner, yet the pills don't suspend her activity. The entire therapy room is colored by Agnete's strength; she squeezes the oil tubes with a frenzied might, throws black on her canvas causing explosions, then various reds quarrel with the black, and the resulting streaks take the

29

appearance of entwined desolation as harmony and equilibrium are annihilated in her art. Her dark, dull hair appears as unruly as her painting; no brush could tame it. Watching the storm of her creation, Michael feels emotionally drained, and even though he's been in the art room only a few minutes, he is already preparing for flight, investigating the topography of the studio. Michael is afraid, yet fascinated by Agnete's energy—even though it is manic—and longs for this strength himself, the one he used to feel.

The art instructor is a woman with straight stringy hair which needs shampooing and drab, oversized Bohemian clothing. She gives no specific directions—which Michael desperately needs. His eyes return to Agnete's picture. Aghast at the damage on her canvas, Michael moves his chair farther away from Agnete and the vibrations she is creating in the room. He looks to the other side of the room and sees a voiceless woman screaming; this soundless expression of anxiety in the room permeates Michael who feels lost in the art therapy, unable to participate in it, or even care, as if the crazies here were not at all present. The patients are pictures like the drawings they are painting—with shadows replacing facial features. The American's canvas remains blank ... The art therapy class comes to an end, and depression splashes the room as well as the canvases, while gloom floods Michael's mind. *Agnete is so primitive and burns up so much energy. That's probably why she eats all the flowers in the ward. I've got a headache and I need a cup of coffee to wake me up.*

The wind screams and runs around the old building as Michael walks through the snow squalls to the café situated under the chapel in the next building sunken into the snow; winter spits on his tortured face. He stoops as he walks into the low ceilinged café where the odor of the fog mingles with the smells of coffee and danish rolls. The gloomy and grim faces stare at him with expressions weighted with melancholy—the very opposite of the café faces he knew so well in Munich. The sipping of hot coffee and biting of crusty rolls all around him are disturbing loud noises, but the need for coffee to counteract the medicine and the need to get away from the ward constrain Michael to wait for his turn.

Michael orders a coffee, and the American accent in his words arise the curiosity of an elderly, well-dressed lady who also stands in line. The wrinkled woman and her granddaughter, Brigitte, the patient with the blue dress, follow the American to a secluded table by one of the windows.

'May we join you?' the elderly woman inquires politely.

Michael sizes them up then slowly nods.

'Are you from America?' asks Teresia, Brigitte's grandmother.

Before Michael can answer, Brigitte addresses him, 'How am I doing?' Then she leans forward waiting for an answer.

Old Teresia relaxes Michael's confused face by asking, 'How long have you been in Sweden?'

'Three days, and two of them in this avant-garde place.'

Teresia just glances at him with an expression of nothingness as she and Brigitte sit down. Suddenly the table is invaded by a third woman, heavy-set, with a pinched face and quivering hamster nostrils. Michael is at first oblivious to the impact of the intrusion but soon notices the obvious tension between Brigitte and the woman.

'Brigitte, why didn't you call?' Brigitte lets her eyes dart from the American to the intruding woman, who is her mother.

'Mother, I wanted to call you last night, but the phone on the ward was busy all night.' Immediately she charmingly peeps at Michael through her thick hair until her mother interrupts again. 'Why didn't you call this morning?' pursues the woman.

'Mom, I'm a grown woman now and I have my own—' Brigitte begins her harangue, but the words die in her throat as her mother charges with hers.

'Brigitte, this hospital is a place where you are to learn to be responsible and get to—'

Michael gulps down his coffee, afraid the threatening woman might grab his cup.

'Mother, stop worrying about me!' she declares as she lights up a cigarette to support her newly found energy.

31

The American starts thinking of his own mother and the time she had yelled at him while sitting at an outside café in a small western town. He can still remember her words, pungent as the horse piss which ran between the tables from a horse and cart standing next to the café. She reprimanded him for wasting time with his art instead of responsibly pursuing business classes.

Brigitte's mother turns her acid face toward the young man. 'Who are you?' she yells.

Still deep in his thoughts about escaping from the place, Michael doesn't answer her.

'Mother, don't worry. I can take care of myself. Besides, Granny was with me before you came,' she says behind her screen of smoke which she exhales all over the table.

'Who is that man? Have you met someone on drugs?' continues the mother, aggressively.

'No, Mother, it is—'

'He hasn't been doing funny things with you?' she asks, her pitch rising.

Grandmother Teresia loses her patience, 'Brigitte is a grown—,' but the twitching mother continues to probe the young man, 'Who are you?'

'My name is Michael,' he finally answers, calmly.

'You have an American accent. Are you a patient here at the hospital?' she continues.

'Oh, what's the difference, Mother?' whines Brigitte.

'Brigitte, I want to know. Your father and I—'

'All right. Yes, he is.'

'Don't be fooled, Brigitte! American men are in Sweden for only one thing!' admonishes the mother.

'RELAX!' exclaims Grandmother Teresia emphatically, trying to end the arguing. But Brigitte's mother doesn't relax and continues to press Michael instead. 'Why did you come to Sweden?'

'I came here because it's such a boring place!' returns Michael, unperturbed.

'Brigitte, I'm only going to ask you once more, did he try anything funny?' she pries relentlessly, seemingly expecting a positive answer.

'NO, MOTHER, for the hundredth time—' yells Brigitte in exasperation.

'I bet he's tried it a hundred times!' she continues, convinced by her own words.

Finally, Michael stands up and blurts out, 'Leave the girl alone, you bitch!'

'I won't stay here listening to your insults!' she stands, her nostrils quivering. 'Brigitte, I'll have to speak to your father. He's not going to like this American. And you call me the instant he tries anything funny. Do you hear me?'

Brigitte's mother leaves the heavy air of the café, followed by her angry shadow. *I hate that menopausal bitch.* Looking out the window, Michael sees Brigitte's mother now fighting with the storm outside.

The other patients, who have been staring at Michael's table, now resume their activities. Apologizing to Michael, Teresia explains, 'The only thing Brigitte shares with her mother is the same psychoanalyst.'

Brigitte digs into Teresia's purse, pulls out a mirror and peers into it. 'Grandma, do I look seductive to men?' she inquires, interrupting the conversation between Teresia and Michael. Without waiting for an answer, she turns away, runs her tongue over her teeth and puts the mirror back into the handbag.

Teresia glances at her watch and decides to take the next bus into the city at two o'clock. Standing to leave, she smiles at Michael, 'If you want, you can come to my home for dinner when you leave here.'

'Thank you—. I also have to run. I've got a meeting with a psychiatrist about leaving this place,' he replies in a hopeful tone.

Michael hurries from the café through the snow blizzard back to his ward while thoughts of leaving the hospital keep him warm. Inside, the snow trapped in his hair and on his woolen coat melts and drips to the floor with his perspiration as he stands a few minutes outside the psychiatrist's office.

Lena steps into the corridor and notices Michael waiting

outside the doctor's door. She yells sarcastically at Michael, 'In Sweden, you have to knock on the door!'

'I did, but there was no answer,' Michael responds, irritated.

Leaving Michael with his thoughts, Lena turns to search for the doctor. *I hate that bitch! This place is weird. The doctor will probably ask me dumb questions like, 'how often do your friends go to the toilet?' I can't stand this crazy place and the bitchy attitudes. It's just like the monastery.*

After searching several rooms, Lena finds the psychiatrist in a room at the end of the corridor where an old bedridden woman yells at the nurse.

'Wake the doctor up. I wanted him to change the TV program, but he wanted to watch the ski races, then he fell asleep, and now he's snoring. Would you change the program and take him with you?'

'You have a scheduled time with the American,' says Lena, shaking the doctor.

The mussed-haired psychiatrist leads Michael into his office, furnished in the same fashion as Freud's old office in Vienna with an upholstered couch and copies of Freud's famous patients placed on the book shelves in front of the bound volumes of psychiatric reports. The whole experience suggests a documentary film with all its gray overtones. Without a movement of his slate-colored eyes or a word from his immobile stern face, the doctor pastes electrodes to Michael's forehead and then ambles into the adjacent room separated by a one-way mirror. Michael's eyes can inspect the small room, part video studio with much electronic gadgetry and part library. His heart jolts as Lena's deep set eyes and stiff face, come into view. She sits in one of the Swedish modern chairs clustered around a coffee table, her face taut as if exposed to a strong wind. The rage he felt when the doctor wasn't in his office for his appointment has died as wind storms sometimes do, inexplicably, and he fears losing control over his emotions and thoughts. The doctor wasn't in his office when Michael knocked earlier, so Michael wonders if he left the hospital café at 11.30 this morning, maybe it was as late as 1.30 in the afternoon; he knows he switches mornings and afternoons sometimes, and even night and day are confusing. He remembers looking at Brigitte's watch, *or was it her grandmother's watch, and maybe her grandmother goes by an older time.* Michael believes he is right and the doctor was late. *Let's reconstruct the morning: I walked five minutes from the café and it took me five minutes to take off my boots and coat, and that's a total of ten minutes and I left at 11.15. I was definitely early for my appointment, I wasn't late. The doctor needs a time management course, but maybe time goes faster than I think—even my pulse feels fast.*

Pushing his chin with his hand he cracks the bones in his neck and ruminates of the bridge he tried to jump from and realizes now that he is bound together with Lena, in a Siamese twin fashion, to prevent him from trying again. Pens jerk on a moving strip of paper as Dr Svensson and Lena watch the EEG tracing. The psychiatrist instructs Lena to draw serum to measure the blood levels of the medication. 'How was the electrolyte balance in the first blood sample?'

Lena answers matter-of-factly, 'The electrolyte balance was unusual as in our old paranoid patient, Svendahl. Isn't this interesting? Even though an electrolyte balance can't indicate paranoia, the police report said that Michael might be paranoid.' The tone of her voice becomes heated as she continues, 'That's what bugs me. Why did the police bring the American here? He doesn't even have a Swedish residence permit. His passport says he's been living in Germany—. They should have sent him back to Germany. Dr Svensson, that's the reason our taxes are so damn high. We pay to take care of all the damn foreigners who want to come here.' In his gruff voice, Dr Svensson agrees.

Directly following his analysis, the professor—with his nineteenth century psychiatry—fetches Michael without explanation into the auditorium where he is lecturing to aspiring psychiatrists. Standing next to the professor's desk, Michael's thoughts about being released become muddled as the nurse brings in Svendahl, an old, demented patient with unkempt hair and dark eyes circled with rings like bruises. To

Michael's shock, the psychiatrist points at Michael, who, dark-skinned and wild-haired, possesses the very appearance Swedish psychiatry students expect from a mad person, and says in his valium voice, 'This young man is at the beginning of the disease—' then he points at the lobotomized inexpressive creature, who is too far gone to comprehend, 'And this man is at the end of the disease.'

After looking first at the drooling, sick man and then at the doctor, Michael attempts to flee from the room in his heavy boots as if they were the hoofs of a centaur. The nursing aides struggle to hold him, avoiding his fists and all the ugly Swedish words he can locate in his head. Another doctor scurries onto the elevated platform, gives him an injection, and the American is soon asleep.

Michael wakes from a dream frightened, remembering the prophesying words of the psychiatrist. *When am I going to get my act together? I can't take this therapy scene anymore! I've got to get out of here. This is like the monastery.* After pulling on his jeans and jean jacket, Michael rushes to the window which looks out at the Swedish landscape, but the serenity of the natural setting doesn't calm his fear of the doctor or of Scar, the mad patient. The heaviness of the pills weights the destiny shown by the psychiatrist, a man who reminds him more and more of his father.

As Michael paces around the room, he moves with a quiet hate in him, as if he had just killed his parents and were carrying their fresh graves within himself. He considers escaping, but he wonders how far he could travel in this strange land before the police would apprehend him again, as the pills which force their way deeper into his mind and tie him down.

At the desk, Michael unties a leather strip holding several letters, which he sorts until he finds a letter from his sister Shelly in Denver—an old letter which Michael still keeps because it shares his hate for their mother's moods and the occasional drunken explosions of their father. On the back of a postcard from Uppsala is the address and phone number of Urban who had lived in Munich. *As soon as I get out of here I'll call him.* Ideas from the postcards and letters don't wander in and out of his mind but possessively march in and control his thoughts.

With the warm air of the radiator the eczema sores on his arms itch as do the scabs he hides under a long sleeved shirt; he pulls off his jacket and his scratched arms are raw as the itching feels savage. His mother's complaints about his scratching and the bloody sheets still ring in his ears, and his fear, which sticks and itches like his eczema, lies under his skin, where he can't get at it. *Maybe Mom was right, she always said I belonged in a loony bin.*

His thoughts are interrupted as Lena, gaunt in her white uniform, steps into his room; Michael doesn't even glance at her but his heart shrinks from the mere perception of her in the corner of his eye. She imparts to him the invisible treatment—and he senses her hate. Indifferent to the walls and the stale smell of the ward, Michael's good looks have faded into a haggard mask. His eyes, once dazzling with his mother's humor and beguilement, appear dazed, filled with that same futility present in the pupils of cancer-stricken patients. As Lena dispenses his pills, his arm moves slowly, lightly, as though all energy had been drained with his sanity, desires and even his hunger.

Carpeted with thin rugs and as colorless as a shadow, the empty aquamarine-blue dining room is depressingly quiet. Suddenly the volume of nuttiness is turned up as noisy patients walk in muttering, snarling, crying, shrieking. As Michael squats down at a table away from the noise, Bjornson rushes naked into the room around the faded brown tables like the cock of the ward. *I knew that guy was a mental case. I've got to get out of here, they've got no reason to hold me. They're trying to make me believe I'm sick like these idiots.* The others hurry out of Bjornson's way like a herd of scared sheep except Agnete who, grabbing a plant, threatens him if he approaches her. The man grins grotesquely, sits down and in his clumsiness knocks over a milk jug, which only increases his laughing; he leaps back in his chair to avoid the streams of milk mixed with his sperm which dribble to the floor between his legs. With an unbelieving, incensed look, Agnete throws her potted plant between his feet and calls him a 'beast' wearing the expression of a sane stranger among the lunatics on the ward. Michael would discover later that once the State Employment Agency in Uppsala hired Agnete as a nursing aide for the same ward, not realizing that she was a patient momentarily on leave from the mental hospital. Doctor Svensson walks in with his aides towards Bjornson, and the noise decreases like the dimming of house lights at a dinner theater. Svensson directs the scene and the aides throw Bjornson a sea-green hospital robe.

Dinner consists of blood pudding. Michael touches it with his fork, but then he can feel the blood itching up his throat, bringing him on the verge of vomit; Michael pushes his plate away and waits for dessert and coffee. Brigitte has not arrived and he wonders where she might be. *Maybe she knew what we're eating tonight but I miss her crazy conversation.* The noise of pulverizing Bjornson at the next table disturbs him even more. As the patients finish eating, Bjornson, in his drab hospital robe, treks to the other side of the dining room to talk with Lena. Michael can't hear what they're saying, and it rattles him that Lena's sunken eyes and Scar's protruding chin point at him. After Bjornson disappears into the dark corridor, Lena walks by Michael's table, ignoring him until he shouts, 'Where's Brigitte tonight?'

'She's been transferred to another ward,' Lena announces in her usual unfriendly manner.

'Why is that?' Michael queries, alarmed, straightening himself in his chair.

'You're kidding?' she snorts back. 'She had too many problems for this ward. She'll get more help in 112.'

Another patient, a little middle-aged gray man sitting opposite Michael informs him, 'After she attempted suicide with a broken glass, it's plastic glasses and utensils for the rest of us on the ward—I guess it's picnic time!'

Michael doesn't find this place a picnic, and it's even

more of a hell without Brigitte. *She was the only one in this shitty place who had shown any friendliness. It's just as well, I think I was getting to like her a little too much. I've got to keep my mind busy.* While leaving the dining room Michael notices his roommate, gray as a stone with a gray stocking cap on his head. 'Hi, how ya doin'?' Michael asks. The granite face doesn't respond. *God, this place is depressing.* Michael walks to the desk in his room where he starts writing, which gives him peace, something he has done since grade school when he won a prize for a short story he dedicated to his mother. He feels angry remembering that he had found it in her wastebasket. Struggling to be an artist in an indifferent world, Michael asks the orderly, a student of literature at the university, to read some of his writing, the beginning of a novel. *I'll get more response from him than from Lena. She'd only say, 'you're kidding.' She's a bitch.*

The young student encourages him as he reveals, 'Froding, the Varmland poet, wrote some of his poetry while he was here at this hospital.' Michael starts wondering whether this hospital specializes in poets and novelists or perhaps poets and novelists specialize in madness? In any case the ward assistant's words can't reach Michael, who sits motionless until the sun goes out.

THREE

MAN BUILT ON SAND

Through the etched ferns of ice on the window of the hospital café, Michael watches the sun gnaw a hole in the frosted pane. Not only does it let in rays of light but suddenly Brigitte's face as she stands looking in at Michael and motions for him to join her outside. He stands up and wonders if someone else has been running with his feet. *Maybe I'm a multiple personality like Brigitte.* He pulls his tired legs to the door; outside, he squints into the light cerulean smoke of morning. Her pupils show she's scared, but she smiles as she asks, 'Do you want to take a walk with me?'

'Where can we walk?' Michael queries, dismally looking around at all the gray buildings.

'Down to the river. We can't leave the hospital grounds—but I need the sun. In my new ward we have a caged bird, and I must have caught a cold from the crazy bird.'

Standing, waiting in vain for a response from Michael, Brigitte—clad in just a light jacket and tight jeans—shivers in the freezing weather. Michael's snug jacket reminds him of the straight jacket they used on him the first night in the hospital, after he started swinging his fists. The collar of his jacket bites into the sores on his neck, but no movement nor twist of his body relieves the pain. It is a reminder of his near death, the wearing of a wooden tuxedo.

Michael follows Brigitte's lead through a small forest, down toward the frozen river where among the trees, large boulders resemble the kneecaps of Swedish mythical giants sleeping under the fairyland blanket of snow. While the sun shines, winter delays in its further attack providing the landscape a chance to catch its breath as does Michael until Brigitte breaks the silence, 'Why do you have those scars on your wrists? I saw them yesterday.'

'Something—happened in Munich, but I don't want to talk about it,' Michael replies defensively as they reach the river.

'Michael, my father is a veterinarian, but can you believe he loves to go hunting whenever he has free time?' says Brigitte with indignation. 'Besides all the horned trophies, he collects live animals. He has seven hundred pigeons housed in our backyard! My mother collects dresses and drinks. I think it's better to collect love letters from a lover!' Brigitte's voice vapors into the cold air.

'My mom collects golf trophies,' announces Michael. 'It's funny, I've never collected anything, except gum wrappers when I was a kid, and then I found out that I was actually collecting ants. My drawer suddenly had more ants than gum wrappers.' She doesn't laugh with Michael, and his voice hesitates before he awkwardly adds, 'You—have beautiful hair. Could I collect things from you, like a lock of your hair?'

'I guess so, I do need a haircut!' she laughs.

The thin ice crust reflects firm outlines of their shadows, enabling Michael to see their closeness in the mirror of the ice. In her wintry eyes, he imagines the nakedness of her desire for him to come inside her as if into a warm house. Magnetically drawn to her, he tries to kiss her, but she turns her face away. 'Don't kiss me, I haven't got makeup on!'

Their conversation, like everything else in Michael's life, becomes a mine field. Michael shivers as he says, 'I'm getting cold. I think I'll go back to my room. Thank you for the walk. I enjoyed the fresh air. The air in my room always smells so foul. The other guy in there is always wetting either his bed or his pants.'

'Oh, that's wonderful, the guy in your room must have a fantastic sense of humor, or he's doing his therapy. He must have the same shrink I have!' she says, gingerly kicking the snow like a little girl.

Michael silently walks backwards leaving her standing like a small Meissen figurine against the white porcelain snow where she looks polished in the light that spills outward from the trees. As he turns around towards the ward, a high, hard scream like that of a woman in labor erupts from a window of the building on the hill. Michael shivers and grits his teeth. He kicks the snow off his shoes on the steps at the side entrance of the gray four-storied building, climbs the stairs and enters his ward in desperate need of a weekend leave.

Hiding his despondence, Michael marches up to the male attendant with his cold hands in his pockets. 'I want to meet a friend in Uppsala,' he says. 'I need a permit to leave the hospital.'

The male attendant responds so quickly and strongly that he seems to gain height and weight as he replies, 'I'll ask Dr Svensson.'

Standing in the corridor, Michael closes his eyes, and with his back against the wall he can feel rigidity—no straight shoulders, no man. Now, too tired to face an angry psychiatrist or afraid to be denied permission, he senses a pull to surrender and retreat into the depths of the mental asylum.

The male attendant returns. 'It's all right,' he says, without further explanation.

Michael hardly believes it and decides to phone Urban immediately. *God, thank you, now I've got to get Urban's number.* He races to his room and back to the corridor only to find Agnete crying into the receiver, which she then drops, quickly running off. Michael picks up the phone and listens, 'It's three minutes past eleven,' the recording says. The pupils of Michael's eyes meet in the middle, and he dials Urban's number.

After a conversation in broken German, Michael agrees to meet Urban that night at the *Tre Byttor*, a pub housed in an Uppsala cellar. After hanging the receiver on the phone, he pirouettes around and suddenly notices Bjornson standing next to him. His evil, sick smirk of a smile disturbs Michael who speedily walks away. I*'ve got to get away from that creep and this whole damn hospital. I wonder how long that bastard has been standing there listening. Maybe from Uppsala I can try to get out of this fricken place. I need some money but the only way mom would lend me some is if I promise to study business and become the American she thinks I should be.*

42

She can shove it. If I try to hitchhike the police will get me again. One good thing about Sweden. An American mental hospital would never let a patient out over a weekend.

The pub door opens to admit the jumpy vibrations of Michael. He catches sight of Urban, lanky and shy under his moppy blond hair. Joining Urban, who sits alone in a far corner of the smoke-filled room, Michael orders a beer. With the medication he seems already too intoxicated to be distracted by the scent of female paint and perfume in the damp cellar.

'Michael, is Gaby with you?' Urban queries as he looks around.

'No, she's in Munich.'

After a short silence, Urban nervously clicks his fingers and says, 'I'm really surprised to see you here. What are you doing in Uppsala?'

'I came to visit you and another friend,' Michael says with a forced smile.

'When did you arrive?' asks Urban clicking his fingers again.

'Yesterday.' Michael tries to conceal his hospital experience under his nervous, young-looking hide, not knowing Urban works at the same mental clinic. Their conversation makes him feel momentarily back in Munich, but as they leave to drink more at a student pub in the old city where the beer is cheaper, the wailing winter brings him back to Sweden as they make their way through the drifting snow. The cold wind blows and screams like a woman in labor, but even the wind in Sweden follows the rules as it stops waiting for the traffic light to turn green. Michael listens to the roar of the storm raging among the dark buildings as violent gusts of wind tear at his coat. A street light on the other side of the road casts a weirdly distorted shadow on the brick wall next to Michael and Urban, and as the shadow grows Michael suddenly hears a voice shout, 'I'm going to kill you, you foreign bastard!'

Michael quickly turns toward the voice and catches sight of Bjornson's thin lips curved in a cruel grin. Bjornson suddenly slugs at Michael's darker face before he can protect himself and the present he had bought for Brigitte. In shock, Michael hears the crystal flower vase shatter on the iced street. He tries to pick up the broken pieces through the gift wrap, but Bjornson bashes him again in the face. With one eye now red from a cut above it, Michael, with a blurry vision, is overpowered with more slugs against his face.

Urban runs in retreat; Michael, unable to comprehend, staggers as a steer being pierced at a bull fight. Nearly blinded, he swallows the blood running in his mouth. Noticing a group of students meandering down the road, Bjornson races off leaving Michael shaking in the snow; Michael's muscles are the victims of his adrenaline. The students, singing the eighteenth-century drinking songs of Bellman, look over at Michael lying frost-burned and bloody in the snow but pass him by. Their voices disappear in the laboring wind before Urban returns to help Michael pull himself up from the stinging powder.

'Urban—is my nose broken?' Michael asks, shaking and spitting blood.

Urban nervously glances at it, 'Don't think so.'

The snow muffles even the sound of the footsteps as they walk away from the bank of the train tracks. This neighborhood near the train station, as in most Scandinavian towns, is the life stream of alcoholics and outcasts. The parked cars all wear caps of snow, but the snow can't cap the pains inside his skin, pains far worse than those on the outside. *He really wanted to kill me. I can't tell Urban that I know the bastard. Urban was a real coward!*

In the old city, in Urban's old apartment, Michael goes straight into the bathroom where he inspects his sweaty, bloody forehead gleaming in the mirror. He examines his battered face and nose, hoping it isn't broken, one side is sore and swollen. He doesn't want a bent icon nose. His forest-green pupils embedded in puffed flesh reveal his narcissistic fear, that his Latin looking face might be disfigured.

Still decorated with his deceased parents' furniture of the last century, the apartment remains silent except for the dripping noise of the coffee as it draws through the filter giving a flavor of nineteenth century Sweden.

'I'm sorry I ran off leaving you alone,' Urban shouts into the bathroom.

Michael walks into the spacious living room and takes hold of Urban's arm, 'Forget it.'

Urban pulls away from Michael's touch as he announces, 'Michael, it's late, we can talk about it more tomorrow. I'm having a Santa Lucia party tomorrow evening. It will give you a more positive picture of Sweden.'

'Can I bring a girlfriend?' asks Michael tentatively.

'Aha! What about Gaby?—Okay, I won't tell her,' Urban teases.

In his sleep Michael walks from one dream to another with Bjornson bashing him down into a coffin of snow. Urban's words resonate in his head 'possessing a perfectly chiseled nose isn't the most important thing,' but it is for Michael. Thoughts that tomorrow Brigitte will see his beaten features trouble him even more.

The following evening Michael meets Brigitte at the train station and they walk to Castle Street in the old part of the city to Urban's apartment, the top floor of an old wooden three-story house built in the seventeenth century. Climbing the cold stairway to the top landing they remove their shoes and leave them outside with the wet boots and shoes of the other guests. Michael hangs his and Brigitte's coat in the white-walled landing smelling of wet leather and wood in the raw air. Looking out the window onto the courtyard, Michael, for the first time, thinks the snow in Sweden looks beautiful in the porch light. With the first of the four Advent candles lit in the window, light blends with the primitive darkness outside.

Michael opens the door to Urban's old apartment filled with people and scented with the warm, festive aroma of *glogg*, the ubiquitous spicy warm brandy with almonds and raisins. Standing in the hallway, Michael introduces Brigitte to Urban, and as they talk Michael gives the impression of listening to them, but he feels self-conscious and thinks about the swelling on his face. The medicine compels his once active tongue to lie flat on its back. He remembers being beaten up in America because of mouthing back to some kids who had harassed him.

'Brigitte, I hope you like *glogg*,' Urban inquires as he hands her a small jug.

'WHO TOLD YOU THAT?' she rants as her eyes dart around the room.

Urban stares at her and then at Michael, who never mentioned that she is a patient at the mental hospital and was hoping it wouldn't show. He takes the *glogg* and they walk off, leaving Urban standing with empty hands and thoughts. With their stone jugs filled with the hot drink they wander into the kitchen. The low ceiling of the room reflects the heat and fumes of the coffee brewing and the *glogg* vaporizing on the stove turning it into an aromatic sauna bath. Michael wonders what Brigitte will say next in this room full of smiling Nordic faces. Urban rejoins Michael and Brigitte in the warm room.

'Where is the Lucia chick with the candles?' Brigitte asks Urban, as she playfully places a lit candle in her hair.

'You can be Lucia! You know she doesn't come until early in the morning. If you want, you can stay the night. I've got lots of room,' says Urban.

The doorbell rings and Urban leaves them to greet his new guests. In the living room, with its polished wooden floors and windows framed with plum draperies, Michael keeps Brigitte occupied with his conversation, avoiding other guests so she won't make off-the-wall statements.

'The knots in the pine chest look like freckles to me,' Brigitte comments to Michael who thinks he can understand her, but he's sure no one else would. If Michael could hear voices, the walls here would reveal much about Strindberg, Froding, and Karin Boye, writers who all lived on this small street; in the corner of the room is Karin Boye's old oak desk. Michael identifies with Strindberg who, when living on this street, found no tranquillity with the student life and *glogg* tradition.

'Brigitte, what time do you have to be back at the hospital?' Michael asks, breaking their silence.

'They think I'm staying with my mother for the weekend,' she says to Michael, and then gulps down another jug of intoxicating *glogg*.

First she won't let me kiss her because she doesn't have her make-up on and now she wants to stay the night. I can't figure her out. I can't figure girls out anyway and it's even worse when they're crazy. Maybe she's wilder then I thought. I wonder if she has AIDS. I hope she's not a gonorrhea girl.

Later in the evening, the guests all leave into the crystal chill except Michael and Brigitte. She borrows a sweatshirt from the host and changes in the bathroom as Michael sits with Urban in the kitchen until she emerges from the bathroom, stumbling half drunk into the kitchen wearing more on her face than on her body. Michael laughs: her face is painted like an Indian, but she is wearing a Dallas Cowboy sweatshirt.

Urban stands, in baggy pajamas with the crotch extending to his knees, says 'goodnight' and retires back to his room. Brigitte, mischievous, brave and flushed, pulls up her sweatshirt, and Michael's eyes pop open.

In front of Michael, still seated, she stands with the souvenir football jersey of the Dallas Cowboys with no pants on, showing some of the tight curls of her pubic hair. She stands like a quarterback, ready to call the next play. With her long hair swinging and soft breasts swaying under the emblem of a star on her jersey, Brigitte laughs and pulls Michael into the bedroom lined with brown bookshelves holding several athletic trophies. The *glogg* displaces his wariness of doing something with a crazy girl as he gazes into the so familiar yet so strange face.

47

'You have dark green eyes like the dog I have at home,' Brigitte says assuredly.

'What kind of comparison is that? You're crazy, you're beautiful, but you're crazy,' he says. Her skin is covered with goose bumps. The radiator gives no heat but only tuneless exploding notes. She reminds him of Gaby and the pain that had assaulted him in Munich, so excruciating that he had to leave the country. It flashes in his mind that he had found Gaby with her hands on her friend's body; those fingers still fumble in his mind day and night. Their peach skin, their yearning breasts, and their naughty perfume teased the air, and they still tease and torment his thoughts.

Prowling outside the house, windswept shapes of snow swarm at the window, threatening her before dissolving into fine white powder. Lit only by candles and light coming through the window, the room reveals icicles sparkling at the eaves, resembling bars of iron. Brigitte's perspiration gleams on her spread legs and arms as she stands blocking the closed door. His eyes, like those of a caged animal, jerkingly look to all sides. Michael's gaze, under his thick mane, darts from the flickering candles to fasten like saber-teeth upon Brigitte's neck.

'You're an animal and so am I—I want you to take me from behind!' she orders while her long fingernails tear at his pants.

She turns, the sweatshirt whirls about her small waist exposing her haunches. Michael's mouth becomes an oval, hovering on what to say. His stalking, more than cat and mouse games, brings the smell of excited flesh with the swirl of legs, bottoms and arms. His scent declares that this bed is his territory as he throws back the covers and pulls off her sweatshirt exposing her long and lithe figure. In the moonlight, Brigitte, conspicuously white on the inside of her thighs, turns and pushes her strong tigress haunches into the air. A primeval rite takes place—again—this time pervaded with a feral pheromonal flavor, totally devoid of feelings. Exhausted, she turns around and bites Michael on the shoulder. Under a pile of covers they fall asleep on the floor beside the bed.

Waking a couple of hours later to the sound of the doorbell, Brigitte, with her smeared green eyes and upturned nose looks at Michael sternly then yells, 'WHAT ARE YOU DOING HERE? WHAT HAVE YOU BEEN DOING?'

'You're crazy! WHAT HAVE *YOU* BEEN DOING?' Michael shouts back, pulling clothes on over his naked body. *She's crazy! Crazier than I thought. God, this is as crazy as the monastery.* The rest of the apartment is a shambles, littered with dirty glasses, a forest fire aftermath of cigarette butts and ashes from the party. His head pulsates with pain and anger, and he watches the rituals of candles and coffee in this frozen land as the apartment again fills with people and laughter, but he can't laugh with them.

As the doorbell rings and four policemen enter the apartment, Lucia, with candles in her hair, tries to offer the policemen drinks; a uniformed man pushes them away and asks, 'Is there an American named Michael here?'

Michael's heart pounds against his rib cage and sweat rolls down his face like wax from Lucia's candles. As Michael stands, a policeman orders Michael to follow him.

Brigitte walks out of the bedroom and with the telephone receiver in her hand she points at Michael yelling, 'He's the one! He raped me!'

Michael's imploring eyes stare at Urban, seeking help, among protests that he didn't rape her; Urban, embarrassed as the other guests, doesn't utter a syllable as the policemen roughly steer Michael and Brigitte out of the flat and into one of their squad cars. From the apartment windows above, Urban and the guests observe the police cars until they speed away, taking the two back to the mental hospital, piercing the gray morning fog. Like a drunkard, he stumbles to a bed in a locked room, his head aching with the words of the policeman calling him a rapist. He's angry from being locked in and bangs the door with his fists, but he knows that the key he needs to turn is in himself. *God, help me. After a long journey I end up in a mental hospital. Tell me I've been really sleepwalking, or that it's all a dream, a nightmare.* Michael's life now appears to be a Russian roulette; everything he chooses turns into a risk. Brigitte has shot at him with her words and wounded him, and now, like a cripple, he is locked in the hospital.

After a torturing wait two male attendants pull Michael to Dr Svensson's office; inside he hobbles to the psychiatrist's desk yelling, 'DO YOU SEE THESE BLACK AND BLUE MARKS? Bjornson jumped me Friday night when I was in Uppsala with a friend.'

The doctor frowns as though struck in the face. 'It must have been someone who reminds you of him. Bjornson is afraid of violence,' the psychiatrist replies in a dismissing tone.

'Maybe to himself but not to me! He's got to be put in a closed ward!' asserts Michael.

A woman's scream from the other end of the ward blends with the gruff voice of the old doctor sitting at his desk. 'Try to be friendly to Bjornson. He has enough problems without your adding more to them.'

The words bang against Michael's head like a stick against a drum skin, and he cries out, 'YOU DUMB SON OF A BITCH! HE TRIED TO KILL ME AND YOU PUT THE BLAME ON ME! I WANT OUT OF HERE!'

'I'll make the decision when you can leave—. And now you can leave my office,' replies unperturbed the doctor, standing up to usher Michael out of his room.

Michael slams the door and walks to the junction in the ward where he pauses, overwhelmed by the necessity of choosing a direction. The scent of breakfast coffee pulls him along towards the dining room; he feels weightless, devoid of manhood, a victim in motion of whatever pulls at him. He doesn't go, he is pulled; his body, a spaceship out of control. Lena shouts into the corridor, 'Agnete, the phone is for you!'

Suddenly, black-haired Agnete runs past Michael pulling up her panties. *I can't believe this. Do people here act like this because they are crazy or because they're Swedish?* In the

50

dining room the patients sit with their granite profiles. Michael, stretched over the table, holds a coffee cup, his mare's mane nearly hangs into his corn flakes. He sits in this position for half an hour without a thought—until a reflection in the glass door opposite the table causes him to raise his eyes. Michael perceives the image of Agnete, now dressed, sitting with her legs separated, exposing her white thighs and black panties. Starting to stare, Michael is distracted as Bjornson rises from the next table and saunters like a bear down the petrified corridor. *I must start acting more crazy so I can be transferred to another ward and get away from Bjornson.* Gripped by a sharp pain in his penis, he worries if he has contracted gonorrhea; he rises wearily, looking now like someone who has parted with his health.

In his room, after the enervating effect of the pills begins to wear off, Michael shaves, looking into the metal mirror, where he sees a puffed reflection with eye-sores in his face. He fears what Bjornson still might do, but most of all he fears what might happen in mirrors. Thoughts of the reflection of Agnete's thighs still tantalize him, he walks into the common room where he finds Agnete with another patient who believes to be Napoleon, wrapped together in her Palestinian scarf.

'Would you like to play some cards?' Michael asks, noticing that Napoleon's hand is in the wrong vest. She pulls his hand out of her vest, saying, 'I want to play.'

Napoleon, after Waterloo, follows behind her and Michael. They pull up chairs and sit between the other patients already playing cards, and Michael deals out the cards to Agnete and Napoleon between the cards of the other game. *Maybe this will make them think I'm too crazy for this ward.* After a few minutes Agnete says in a flushed voice to Napoleon, 'You're not the man I married!'

The other patients and Michael stare at the man with his hand and cards in his shirt as Agnete continues to say, 'And when my husband comes, he will tell you the same thing!'

Napoleon shuffles his feet under the table, rises and leaves the game as Michael's roommate mumbles in a muddy voice,

'My wife left me, but it's okay, she was so ugly.'

The two card games, intermingled between them, begin to get mixed up. Lena, the nurse, pushes Michael's cards away saying, 'You stupid American! Can't you see we can't play two games on the same table!'

Michael leaves the games. *In hell, Sweden will be in charge of entertainment.* When he reaches the other side of the room, Michael slips and falls on his back. Frantically moving his arms and legs like a beetle, he begs 'Turn me over, turn me over!' The ward aides drag him to a room, belt him down to a bed, and give him an injection which metamorphoses Kafka's beetle into a beaten human being. He loses consciousness, and in his sleep he yells at God.

When he awakens, Michael finds that he is still belted down onto the bed in a strange sterile room. *God, get me out of this place before it's too late.* His eyes, nervously stuck to a frozen juniper branch banging against the window, stick to his helpless hands and then to the floor. Clogs, maroon slacks, white coat, and apologizing face of the male attendant—in that order—come into Michael's view. He unbuckles Michael, announcing, 'Dr Svensson wants to see you immediately.'

Michael, starched, walks down the corridor while his mind flits back and forth in despair. *What is he going to do? Can he put me in a locked ward with the lobotomized idiots?* As the psychiatrist's door opens, Michael, afraid of being swallowed into the depths of the asylum, slides deep into a rocking chair in the doctor's office, feeling he could rock back into another world. The psychiatrist moves around his desk toward Michael, 'Teresia Thorell, Brigitte's grandmother, called—she wants you to visit her this evening. She knows from the police investigation that you RAPED Brigitte.'

'I DIDN'T RAPE HER!' Michael protests.

'Then why did she jump out of the third story window yesterday?' says Dr Svensson, fixing his eyes on Michael. 'She's lucky she's not dead,' he adds as he stands glowering down upon Michael.

'NO! How could she do that?' Michael cries in pain. He shoves his chair backwards away from the doctor. 'Can I see her?'

The old psychiatrist turns red in the face with a loud 'NO!' then he adds, 'I don't want you to see her anymore. I'm her therapist and I know what's best for her. You keep away from her. Do you hear me? You're a lot of trouble. And I don't want you aggravating Bjornson anymore! I don't know why or how, but maybe Teresia Thorell can talk some sense into you. NOW GET OUT OF MY OFFICE!'

The late afternoon ushers in another night. The headlights of the bus, a snow lantern in the darkness, wipe out some of the blackness, but nothing wipes out the guilt in Michael, as Brigitte's jump keeps jumping into his head. Away from the hospital, something cracks further within him, and his pain and self pity creep out even more. The door cracks open and Michael alights from the vehicle in the city center, and he fears the heavy snow will bury him as the flakes cling to his hair and eyebrows. With every step, muffled by the wall-to-wall cars, Michael fantasizes flying away to warm Italy before being buried with snow. The Fyris river, frozen with ice, porous and elastic in places, gives the center of the city different shades of white. Uppsala, with its bridges wrapped in ice, appears to be made of marble like Venice, but it's only cold ice. He transfers to another bus which takes him to the other side of the cold city.

Teresia's residence is on the hillside called Eriksberg overlooking Uppsala's profile, with its distinctive red Romanesque castle and gray gothic cathedral. The spirals of the church, gray on the inside, rise into the sky, the most depressing gray of all. In Teresia's house surrounded with Bauer trees and snow covered rocks, she lives alone after the death of her husband, a composer and painter. Michael walks around the block three times before he dares to knock. Teresia opens the door, and her eyes reveal to Michael pains that her optimistic personality disguises. She is not the typical dry, academic woman so common in this cobwebbed university city of Uppsala, but a woman full of life. Michael enters the living room filled with books and expressionistic paintings.

'Teresia, I like that winter scene. Who painted it?' he inquires, his face still wet from the snow.

'You like art? That was painted by my granddaughter, whom you met at the hospital. Brigitte has been a painter, and her brother Sten, a writer. He has lived for over ten years at the mental hospital. My family has been gifted; yet, because of their hypersensitivity, my grandchildren have both been the victims of psychological havoc.'

As she explains the pictures to Michael, she stands youthful and straight in spite of the weighty problems upon her old shoulders. She seems happy, yet Michael can sense in the old woman a loneliness and a need to talk.

'Teresia, how is Brigitte doing?' he asks with eyes like mosaics, broken into many pieces and reflecting his preoccupation for the girl.

'She is going to live, but what kind of life is she going to have? She's like her mother who has been in and out of the mental hospital since she was just a teenager. My daughter was different when she was just a little girl. After her I was afraid to have another child.'

'You think psychological problems are inherited?' Michael probes, trying to find out more about Brigitte.

'It seems that way; we have a history of it in our family,' continues Teresia. 'My uncle was schizophrenic. I should have known better. I felt guilty and selfish for having a baby. My husband wanted a child so much. He tried so hard with her but it didn't work out. She thinks I killed my husband, and so she is afraid of me. She thinks everybody is out to get her and that all men are out to rape her. She even accused my husband of abusing her. I think all these problems were too much for him, and they finally took their toll. He was a good man.'

After a dinner—very different from those at the mental hospital—and then coffee and dessert of crushed apples and whipped cream over her homemade spice cake, she speaks of

54

her life and pains growing up in Hammarskogen on Lake Malaren, outside Uppsala. This woman of suffering gives Michael acceptance in her apartment, which smells of the Cézanne apples arranged in a bowl made from a tree's knot. She is a woman that a blind person would think is half her age of seventy-five.

'I was with Brigitte the weekend before she tried to kill herself,' he says in a guilty voice.

'Don't blame yourself,' soothes Teresia. 'This is not her first attempt. I'm going to see her tomorrow. I'll tell her you are concerned,' she promises, as her eyes lit up, expressing her happiness for Michael's visit.

In her elegant and cozy living room, like a page from *Better Homes and Gardens*, Michael's mind—lighter without the weight of the mental hospital—begins to move light-footed. They drink many cups of coffee and talk into the Nicodemian night. After this intensive day, Teresia appears quite tired. In spite of her weak heart and frequent stomach pains she keeps a cheerful mood, but her smile hides a relentless depression that allows her no rest. Michael admires Teresia for not running away from life and old age, contrary to many American women who, reluctant to age, don wigs in the hope to fool others for a moment, until they turn their heads and gain forty years in a second.

After the warmth and friendliness at Teresia's, Michael finds it difficult to ride back to the hospital in the empty bus and even more difficult to fall asleep in the smelly room with a snoring roommate. He turns and tosses thinking of his sister Shelly, the monastery, and then Gaby in Munich. His thoughts will not let him relax any more than a parachute jumper suspended between two places. Michael remains awake all night and just as he falls asleep, he is immediately roused by the morning commotion in the corridor with the hospital's ritual of pills and nuttiness.

In the corridor, a skinny patient, wearing a blue and yellow training outfit, tennis shoes, an American baseball cap turned backwards, and fingerless leather gloves, makes golf swings, trying to hit a golf ball with a golf club that only he can see, then looks down the corridor to see where his ball lands.

Agnete warns him, 'You'll get fungus between your toes wearing those tennis shoes all the time.'

'People don't get athletes' foot at my age,' retorts the man, in apparent disbelief.

'Yes they do, especially people who run a lot, like you! The fungus will spread to the crotch and your whipper-snipper,' continues Agnete in a serious, concerned tone.

Snarling, the gaunt golfer holds his private parts and runs for his golf ball in the dining room.

'If you run too fast, you'll get dandruff too!' yells Gunvor, a slender patient, a former photo model. Her smile shows the missing teeth she pulled out herself; and her disheveled red hair, difficult to comb, is sticky from insect poison she sprays on to rid her of her crazy ideas.

The athletic patient yells, 'FOUR!' with gestures directing Lena to duck; she ignores him and yells to Michael, 'It's time to see the psychologist.'

The therapist—a bohemian-looking forceful Swede in rambling jeans and sweatshirt—ushers out of the therapy room a young woman who yells obscenities. She rolls her sleeves back exposing scratches as if she had recently wrestled with a cactus and is now ready to fight with the psychologist who motions to Michael to enter the therapy room.

Michael sits down, uncertainty scatters across his face. For him, there is a Hansel and Gretel path back to his life before the mental hospital, and now the staff are erasing that track. He is afraid their drugs are forcing him into an imaginary landscape and the thoughts in his head slip lower from level to level like the flight of a hawk.

'You sure seem out of sorts,' the young psychologist grunts.

'I feel terrible about what happened to Brigitte,' explains Michael in a sorrowful tone.

'You should feel guilty!' presses the therapist, looking straight into Michael's eyes.

'I thought psychologists were supposed to take away

guilt!' retorts Michael, uneasy, avoiding his stare.

'You're getting uptight aren't you? Don't you tell me how to be a psychologist!' the professional neurotically returns. 'Now, tell me what this Rorschach card looks like to you?'

'It's a Christmas tree!' *Let him figure that one out. He'll probably think I'm longing to be a logger in the Swedish forests. He's crazy trying to be Sherlock Holmes with my mind.*

'What do you see here?' pries the man.

'The stoning of Saint Stephen' answers Michael rather than the obvious bat. He goes on to title the following card the 'Last Supper' instead of a possible butterfly. *If the therapist can see things that aren't there, why shouldn't I. I guess if we all got his cards right, we'd get a special meal on Sunday, reindeer steaks and a kiss behind our ears from lovely Dr Svensson. Why do I have to do this? I miss my freedom, my Mozart music.*

Instead of Mozart, the soundtrack in his brain is the noise of an earthquake run backwards; he shakes his head in discordance, and the result is the inevitable, unmerciful headache. After the Rorschach card game, Michael pauses at the door as Bjornson, dangerous as a male polar bear imprisoned in a zoo, has that same walk back and forth along the opposite wall of the corridor always avoiding the zookeeper, Dr Svensson and his syringes. The ward aides keep him in a state of bubbling, pent-up ravishing rage. He would be a terror if he came out of his drug daze. *God help me, but help these idiots too. They need Your help more than I do.*

In the afternoon Michael meets the therapy group with a beaten somber image. The gray goat eyes of the psychologist with the Rorschach card game move from one patient to the next. 'What new has happened on the ward?' asks the therapist.

The golf player with an arrowhead nose and threadlike mouth without lips accuses a bearded patient with dark marbled eyes of trying to be Christ. 'We don't need him to be our savior!'

The therapist contemplates the bearded man and his rough hands. 'I bet you're a pretty good carpenter aren't you?' he asks.

'Yes—,' 'Christ' answers, a little confused.

'Would you build a bookcase for the reading room?' says the therapist.

'Yes—, of course,' answers the man, in an eager tone and a renewed liveliness in his pupils.

That's interesting therapy. Of course he isn't going to say 'build your own fricken bookcase,' since Christ wouldn't have talked that way. This definitely makes more sense than his crazy cards.

Oblivious to the therapist, Agnete accuses Michael's roommate of stealing Lena's bicycle seat, 'Doctor, this guy needs therapy. He collects girls' bicycle seats. That's a weird fetish!'

'Did you take Lena's bicycle seat?' the therapist frowns at the young man who sits and hides his face under his gray stocking cap.

'Yes, I'm sorry. I'll give it back,' says the patient in a very embarrassed tone.

'Why did you take it?' the therapist asks with a puzzled face.

'It smelled good,' he explains, unperturbed.

There is silence in the group. The therapist looks around the circle of patients; Michael's battered appearance brings the psychologist's attention to him. He presses Michael to explain the scratches and black and blue marks. 'What the hell happened to you?'

Michael wants to disappear into the white sterile walls of the room as Bjornson grins sickly from the other side of the group. Bjornson's filmy and dilating black pupils stare at Michael. A whimper of frustration escapes from deep in Michael's chest, and his eyes close for a second like a man in intense prayer.

'You look like you were in a hell of a fight. Did this

violent experience trigger old, hidden feelings?'

Michael rocks back and forth on his pillow without answering. As the silence grows, he begins to sweat—his coarse Norwegian sweater sticks to his body, his face looks pale and clammy like that of an actor who has just removed his makeup with a greasy face cream.

'Answer the therapist! You are wasting our time!' cries Agnete, staring at Michael with her cold eyes of indefinite color. 'Answer him! You are ruining the group.'

Michael continues to rock, and in the flickering light from the window, Agnete's silhouette seems to strike at him again and again. He feels as though his life in Sweden is that of a man built on sand.

The therapist asks Michael, 'How do you feel about Agnete's attack?'

'I'm sorry she feels that way,' smiles Michael in return.

Quickly, the therapist returns, 'Why are you smiling if you're really sorry she feels that way?'

Michael looks blank. The therapist leans forward towards Michael and continues to probe.

'Do you ever feel sorry about anything? Name something else you feel sorry about.'

'I feel sorry that Brigitte almost died.' But Michael suddenly realizes that he smiles as he says this too. Catching himself before the therapist can say anything, he covers his face with his hands. The therapist blurts out, 'Now answer my question. Do those swellings on your face wake up old feelings?'

'DAMN! GET OFF MY BACK!' *Didn't the psychiatrist tell him that Bjornson jumped me?*

'This seems to be a sore point—; would you like to talk about it?' continues the therapist, insensitive to Michael's obvious distress.

'NO, I WOULDN'T!' cries Michael, exasperated.

'QUIT YELLING,' Agnete shouts at Michael. 'Brigitte would be better off dead. She was really sick. She had all those mousetraps circling her bed, you know!' she adds, with the air of making an important revelation.

Michael doesn't smile and continues rocking back and forth on his pillow as the therapist presses him to reveal his past, a past he has tried to forget and suppress. Michael looks around the room, uneasily. His lips part a little as if to speak. His eyes enlarge and form a tormented expression, but then he shuts his mouth having decided it is better never to say what he intended. Squeezed between his need to talk, his fear of Bjornson, and revealing his past, he breaks into a sweat across his brow. Again, his pupils widen as he struggles to say something. The impatient therapist corners Michael relentlessly, 'Since you're here, you might as well cooperate. You know you have no other choice.'

'All right.' Michael can't stretch these words into a mouthful. *If the police hadn't stopped me from jumping, I wouldn't have to go through this shit anymore. And I thought suicide was accepted in Sweden. Because I tried, they keep me in this place, and because Brigitte tried, they keep her locked in her broken body. I understand her after meeting her mother. I'm like her, I've got nowhere to go. Urban can't have any feelings either, or he wouldn't have run off. He didn't even try to help when Brigitte called the police.*

He searches for support from the group but finds none and keeps control of his tortoised shell. The long-legged Gunvor, toothless, glares at him, Bjornson snickers, and Agnete, wrapped in her Palestinian scarf wears her lost expression, defined by lipstick and eyelashes. Michael has buried his past like a coffin, and now the therapist tries to dig up the grave inside him, his personal graveyard full of goblins and menacing thoughts clawing inside him. The psychiatrist, determined to tear up Michael's whole life with its broken roots, continues to pull at the turmoil inside him; Michael loses control. He begins telling—with gutting words—his story of the monastery, his eyes suggesting a suffering from something secret and burning.

FOUR

VESPERS

Leaving the gray-blue sleeting rain behind on a wet morning, the old train pulls into the emerging sun and mountain station of Ebenhausen. On the platform, Michael queries the conductor for directions, suddenly realizing that his school German bears little resemblance to the Bavarian spoken here at the small station. Standing outside the *Bahnhof*, looking at the town center with his Rorschach mind and Ray Ban eyes, he starts meandering along a road of trees and reaches the village square dominated by a monument dedicated to the fallen soldiers of Ebenhausen. A brief perusal of the inscriptions on the obelisk reveals to Michael the absence of his family name. He continues restlessly across the main road into a cobbled street stretching barely eight feet between the tall houses topped with stone-shingled roofs. Shadows obscure sunken doorways to shops adorned with eighteenth-century windows. Finally, Michael discovers his father's family house with its jigsawed balconies of dark veneered wood recognizable from all the stories he had been told.

Apprehensive about phoning the monastery, he treads over a bridge crossing the Isar river which bubbles through the town and walks past the *Gasthof zur Post* with its blue and white *Rautenmunster* entrance and Maypole decorated with shields portraying all the different professions, but not the monk's. Nerves keep him walking, and soon he finds himself outside the town, where sheep peacefully graze on the nearby fields, but their peacefulness can't reach him. In the distance, under leaden clouds, *Fischerschlössl*, the local castle, stands tall on the hill behind the village. *This is like a fairyland, but what's the monastery like? I wonder where it is.*

In a tangle among the other old houses, Michael comes upon *Café Hubertus*, where he decides to inform the monastery of his arrival.

61

The sun suddenly disappears but not his apprehension as heavy raindrops fall on the cobbled street with a distressing, drumming rhythm. Sitting at a table and watching the heavy rain through the window, he suddenly realizes this might be his last chance for a beer and finishes two before a black Volkswagen parks in front of the old café. From the partly open window of the coffeehouse come nerve-wrecking noises from the car: the engine, the windshield wipers, and finally a horn. At the sight of a robed figure in the car he begins to sweat. Alone in the café, Michael sits, paralyzed, until a monk walks into the café, stopping at Michael's table. 'Are you Michael?' the man asks in a polished German, with a voice in harmony with his lean and wooden gestures, a chess piece with sharply carved features.

Michael simply nods, surprised he can understand the monk with his deep voice after hearing nothing analogous to *Hochdeutsch* in Ebenhausen.

'Michael, I am Brother Gunther, welcome to Germany,' says the robed figure, wearing a discrete smile which contrasts with his piercing steel-blue eyes.

Michael follows the monk to the small black Beetle, and as they ride down the narrow street, Michael leaves his window lowered, ajar like his mind. The wind whips his eyes and blows his thick wavy hair; the cold, wet air stings. They drive out of the medieval town into the Isar valley where wide expanses of tall, dense trees and open grass fields line the river. The three-kilometer jotting road swings by large farm houses, small settlements and churches with bronze-green onion tops.

'Michael, your uncle was a monk here, I was told. He was a pious man, in charge of the beehives in the garden. God called him to Him three years ago, as you know. He was still a young man.' Michael simply nods. The monk continues, 'I have been to your country—many years ago … I remember feeling so small in those wide open spaces … so different from here! You see, I've been fortunate to have done some traveling—most of the monks you are going to meet have never left Bavaria,' he says as they speed down the winding gravel lane. Michael's internal journey meanders through his mixed thoughts, making him reluctant to participate in a conversation, however small.

The thumping rough road and bouncing noises of rocks under the vehicle increase Michael's breathing. Anxiety mixes with excitement, becoming almost unbearable for the young man. 'How far away is the monastery?' he asks.

Brother Gunther points down at the wooden bridge; Michael perceives the stillness of the monastery walls and church tower, ashen in the revealing light. Gunther drives the car deeper into the valley, gradually more deserted, populated only by a few cows whose hanging bells ring as they look up curiously at the intruding car. A gate suddenly appears in the enormous gray stone wall, partly hidden behind pines, shallow shrubbery and vines which resemble a black spider net of twigs and branches covering the granite. As the car swings through the gate, Michael quickly looks back as if to have his last glimpse of the outside world.

Inside the walls, a church steeple juts above a connected series of buildings; the bells start ringing, filling the air with a medieval holiness. 'Schaeftlarn,' the monastery, symbolizes one of the most powerful royal families of medieval Germany with its fortress-like appearance. Michael wonders where the Benedictine wine is. His father had always jokingly maintained that that liquor was the reason Michael's uncle had chosen this order and life.

As Michael steps out of the car, his unconsciously clenched fists relax. He follows Brother Gunther through the rain into a small building adjacent to the church where his steps collide with his shoes as if his shoes wouldn't follow his feet. In the meager cell, Abbot Friedrich shakes Michael's hand while he surveys his rather long hair. In a brown cassock covering his slacks a shade lighter, the abbot speaks with a voice so weak that it wouldn't carry his utterances to the other side of a checkerboard. The tiled squares under their feet resemble the squares of a chessboard; Michael thinks it is the abbot's move. As the abbot turns slowly to his brown-robed chessman, Brother Gunther, he asks his pawn to show

Michael to his cell.

Michael's white chamber has a low ceiling from which protrude large age-blackened beams. The window looks out onto the garden but not beyond the wall; the outside world is not to impinge on his cell. In the austerity of his new abode, the warmth of his bedroom in Denver is a mere memory. Here, the only decoration on the walls is an aged-darkened wooden cross, of pure lines, bare and essential. The robe doesn't fit his physique as the clothes he brought, but with the addition of a rough cord around his small waist, he likes the dark brown robe even without a glamorous cut or famous label on the collar. Reminiscent of the stories about his uncle who lived and died as a monk in this monastery, the robe represents a tie to his uncle and provides him with a sense of family.

Michael's thoughts are interrupted by a bell and a knock on his door. 'It's mealtime,' announces Brother Gunther in his baritone voice.

He directs Michael down the soundless corridor as if sneaking and planning a robbery. In the silent dining room, nothing breaks the monks' routine except curiosity about Michael, expressed only in their eyes. The intense stillness after the hustle of his journey and the ride through Munich fill Michael with a sense of unearthly desolation. To increase his earthly need for strength, Michael eats four hard-boiled eggs, half a loaf of rye bread with strong, pungent cheese and drinks a pot of black coffee.

After the midday meal, the abbot introduces Michael to an elderly monk, Brother Hubert, the spiritual director of the novices, who also speaks in a voice so low that it wouldn't carry to the second floor of a doll's house. Michael quietly follows Brother Hubert to the spiritual advisor's cell, where he is invited to sit on a rickety stool. He sits uncomfortably at the sandaled feet of his new advisor. The old man's brown robe is shiny from wear, his face wrinkled like the valleys around the monastery, and he smells of incense and pipe smoke. Crossing himself with his callous hands, the monk's eyes focus on Michael. 'In this life you are to learn the invisible presence of God.'

'For thirty-four years—,' the old monk begins, bowing his head while he seems to have lost his thoughts for a few seconds, then he continues without stumbling, 'for thirty-four years I have not set foot outside the monastery. I was a young man when I entered the monastery and I had never known a woman intimately. It is a hard life and you will be tempted here, you will have dreams, but you must pray and God will help you in this life. The devil will tempt you in your dreams. The devil inside a woman's womb never sleeps. It will tempt you in your bed.'

The aged, lonesome eyes of the monk frighten Michael, who suddenly almost falls off the stool when a bell suddenly rings. Brother Hubert leads Michael to Vespers in the church, which is dark except for the last sun rays of the day, filtered through the stained glass windows and the candles illuminating the two side altars. The air is fragrant with wax and incense. The psalms for Vespers begin slowly, gently, like the rustling in the wind of the trees on the hills around the cloister, but the monks' voices, though sweet and hushed, produce shrilling and discordant impressions on Michael. Loneliness chokes him as he listens to these men mechanically repeating the words of prayer as if they were dying with the day. The Gregorian chant surges and heaves like a turgid sea; the dense, heavy repetitions slam against his confusion and bitterness as he remembers Laura's unfaithfulness. Michael's mind, plaintive and monotonous like a lamentation and his unwavering green eyes focus on the crucifix as though the whole plan of his life were firmly nailed. After the chanting, the monks sit in silent prayer until the abbot knocks on his pew from the back of the chapel to signal the end of silent meditation. Brother Reiner, asleep next to Michael, responds to the knock shouting 'COME IN!' The monks laugh until the abbot knocks on his pew again.

After concentrating on the German words of Vespers, Michael returns to his cell and stares into the wilderness of the garden outside his window. Soon tired of the view, he unpacks from his suitcase a meager sum of possessions which doesn't include the clothes he loves, especially his favorite white sport coat. Exhausted, he falls asleep on his bed, his athletic body twisting and turning until his nightmares wake him. Suddenly jarred by the bell for the Matins, with a fluttering whimper, Michael battles in the dark his way out of bed, blinking and gasping. His nightmares distress him; he doesn't want to be a monk.

After Mass, Michael walks rigidly into the long and narrow refectory where the abbot sits at the head table with his knotted brow. Brother Hubert, a somber mask with dreamy eyes, takes a seat next to him. *I wonder if the old man is possibly dreaming of some woman's breasts.* In a small elevated pulpit, a novice declaims the life of Saint Benedict in a chanting voice as the monks bend over their plates in silence. After eating his bread and cheese, the abbot takes a small bell standing at his left side and rings it three times. Soon the room fills with the sound of sandaled feet on the tiled floor, the only sound to break the silence of antiquity. Michael abandons himself to this new and foreign world where centuries-old routine replaces individuality.

The monks proceed to the monastery courtyard where grass grows between the cobblestones, and the garden walls are partially blackened by dampness and mildew. An oncoming storm carries the aroma of fruit trees, chrysanthemums and the courtyard's sweet perfumes of roses as Brother Gunther distributes the mail. This is the first positive ritual for Michael who receives a letter from his sister Shelly. Before Michael can open his letter, Brother Ronald approaches him while deeply inhaling on his pipe and exhaling through his nostrils; his hair is prematurely smoke gray, short and meticulously combed. Behind the smoke, Brother Ronald admonishes Michael for tying the cord around his waist wrong. *These guys don't seem very personable or hospitable.* Their personalities are as austere as their robes, sunken eyes and body language which clearly expresses a teutonic fortitude devoid of sociability. *These monks give the air of being the elect of the suffering. They believe that their strict following of religious rules has put them above mankind.*

Noticing Brother Reiner, a huge homely man with a scar on his left cheek, Michael introduces himself then says, 'That was funny when you said COME IN!'

The monk responds, 'I can't understand what you're saying,' and walks away. *What a nice holy man, what a bastard.*

A young monk, with cropped wavy brown hair interrupts Michael's thoughts by unexpectedly extending his hand towards him. With a voice at pulpit volume, he says, 'I'm Brother Dietmar, you're from America, I've heard. I hope you like this place.'

'It's a very friendly place,' observes Michael with all the irony he can summon.

Dietmar smiles, understanding. 'It's because monks aren't supposed to have special friendships. You'll get over it!' The conversation with Dietmar is shortened by the sound of a bell, as in silence the monks begin climbing a stone stairway leading back into the main house. 'It's time for spiritual reading in our cells,' whispers Dietmar.

Michael shuffles quietly down the corridor behind the other monks. Stopping at the lavatory, Michael fumbles at his robe to relieve himself, and finds even this simple act a complicated ritual.

Back in his dark cell, Michael tears open his sister's letter.

'Dear Michael,

I still don't know why you had to leave. I should never have told Laura at the dance that you were my brother. You changed in so many ways. First, you never had any time for me anymore, not even time to listen to me. In fact Laura says you never gave her. a chance to explain what happened. I never thought you would react this way. Laura's pregnant. She is going to have Denny's baby. It will never work out, Denny's too much of a playboy, and he's not smart enough for her, besides she wouldn't stay together with anyone who didn't like literature, that's her biggest love, and Denny doesn't even read.

Michael why did you have to leave me? Now I've got no one to help me with Mom. All she does is criticize you for going back to Dad's old town. If I didn't need my money for college I'd move out. Maybe you were right, but why did you have to move so damn far away? I really miss you! I have to study now, but please write to me.

Love & kisses,
Shelly'

His heart tears at the thought that Laura's pregnant; finding her photo among his papers, he tears it into a hundred puzzled pieces which he throws at the bare floor. *How did I get so obsessed with her? Maybe the sailor was obsessed and raped her, maybe it was a date rape, or maybe he got her drunk or put pills in her drink. I never gave her a chance to explain the situation. I just took off.* Michael searches for explanations to calm his hurting vomitous feelings. *Damn, she's pregnant. Maybe I should have stayed and tried to get her back.* Sitting paralyzed on his bed, Michael remains motionless as a statue; his face stands out positively paler than the white-washed walls enclosing him. A lightening flash tears across his mind, illuminating more than the mountains around him. The window reflecting on his face, the raindrops on the glass give the image of teardrops rolling down his cheeks. It looks like he is weeping, but he won't allow himself to cry even when alone. The rain is the only thing he finds familiar and this realization scares him. After the rain abates, Nature sympathizes with Michael by showing him leaves on the trees weighted with tears, but even Nature's message fails to reach him; he stares frantically out the window as if seeking consolation in a world that knows nothing of his troubles. Michael pulls out some paper to write his sister Shelly a letter.

'Dear Shelly,

Thanks for your letter. It made me happy to hear from you even though you had bad news for me. I'm trying to forget Laura. There is so much happening in my life and I wish I could talk with you. I really miss our talks. This is a real crazy place. First of all it's spooky quiet, and we're in the chapel all the time. I've only been here a short while, but it seems like an eternity. I've made one friend: his name is Dietmar. It's a good thing that you're not here, you'd probably be trying to put a make on him.

Are you getting on with Mom any better? I don't know how Dad puts up with her. The only way he can do it is by drinking. I shouldn't have got mad and yelled at him before I left home. I do love him even though we got into all those fights. He gets drunk and acts crazy. Some day I want to talk it all out with him. I did find Dad's old family house. Great architecture! What I've seen of Germany is really beautiful. Well, I hear the bell, time to parade to the chapel again. Take care, and write me soon. I miss you, sis.

     Love,
     Michael'

In the chapel, Michael opens the book Brother Hubert has given him for spiritual reading.

'Forget your conscience, surrender it to the guiding light of
    Divine Love.
Let go of selfish vain anxiety and the Holy Spirit will make
    you clean and free.
Simplicity and the absence of worldly desires are your daily
    bread.
God's love will give you vision in your dark nights.'

In Michael's mind these words suddenly get twisted with

Brother Dietmar's. *How can the monks learn anything about friendliness if special friendships are discouraged? That's crazy. How can they love God if they don't care for each other?* Michael's instincts and intuitions point to a more humanistic form of spirituality, different from what he finds here at Shaeftlarn with its humorless, aloof, enigmatic monks.

Late in the afternoon, the Bavarian Alps look as if they were crumbling in the rolling fog and the ashen teutonic sky seems about to fall on the monastery. Michael, numb, not knowing whether he is awake, asleep, or even dead, runs through the monastery passages hardly noticing the other monks, running around the sanctum as if bits and pieces of his life were flying apart, much like the rush hour commuters who run for the train afraid that they might be left to spend the night in the cold streets of Munich. He can still hear the dread of his sister Shelly's voice on the phone, informing him of the death of their father. *No, it can't be! God, don't let him be dead! I never worked things out with him. I left with so much hate. No! No!* Michael runs to his spiritual advisor, who can't comfort him. Michael begins to pack everything he needs before his morning flight from Munich, which his spiritual advisor is arranging. As he pulls clothes from his closet to pack, he is like a ragged soldier in retreat. *Dad can't be dead, can't be dead, can't be dead ...* His cell floor is littered with letters for needed addresses of friends like the stubs at the horse track betting windows.

With the appearance of an SS officer in a robe, Brother Gunther drives him to the airport. On the aircraft, Michael settles into a window seat, and finds it is warm and stuffy until cool air comes from the jet stream above his seat. At take-off the jet engines groan as if sharing his pain. Though not hungry, he eats the meal served by the stewardess. When they lower the movie screens, he's relieved at the prospect of occupying his mind with a film, a bob-sled ride on the screen with its purposeless tossing and turning can't keep his attention; he can't identify with the hero of these tinsel adventures. Even though the laughter of the other passengers swirls around him, he is alone with his private pains and thoughts. After the film, tired and crammed, Michael can't sleep as many of the other passengers do—any more than one could sleep in a bob-sled speeding down a mountain. This journey feels more anxiety provoking than the deadly curves of the bob-sled track. *Death isn't really a reason for mourning; it seems one mourns for the living more than for the dead anyway.* After interminable hours, the aircraft begins its descent, and the small spots take shape as long rows of houses and buildings as the plane prepares for landing at the Denver airport.

At the terminal, Michael notices his mother and sister. Shelly's large sapphire-blue eyes sparkle in her terracotta colored face framed with long, blond hair. As she walks toward Michael she cocks her head like an artist about to begin a work of art. Emotion engulfs her, as with shaking hands and body she throws her arms around her brother. Michael's mother, lifting her long Modigliani neck, exhales her cigarette but barely says a word. Being back in Denver feels like a black, black calm, and his old love-hate relationship for his parents comes back in gusts. The death of his father provides no relief, rather his utter absence is worse. The empty space brings more desolation: his drunken father yelled at him, but at least lived and moved. Suddenly, the few positive memories like a fishing trip in the mountains or movies on Sundays seem more important. *I feel as if I too have left the world.* All his chances of talking things out are now gone The pain burns when Michael walks into the living room and notices the old tobacco-colored leather chair his father always sat in facing the sliding patio doors in the afternoon sun ... the chair is now empty. This time he doesn't notice that the sun is shining. His father's death took the sun out of his existence. *I was selfish, I went to Europe and left him with all the company's problems.*

In the evening Michael sits silently in the tobacco leather

chair. *I wanted so much to tell Dad before he died that I didn't always hate him. I only yelled at him because he was drunk and abrasive or felt he never had time for me. Why did he have to die before we could talk this out?*

Michael's family first respects his silence, but after three weeks of hardly uttering a word, they think his grief needs relief, as it only increases their own pains. To counteract the dread her brother casts in the home, Shelly invites him to join her at some school friends' party. Outside the discipline of the monastic life, Michael is robbed of direction and accepts.

Shelly's metallic blue Corvette guns down the wet street with music loud as a rock concert, but only Shelly's head moves to the beat. Shelly has a passion for blue; everything she wears is blue, from her shoes and a belt around her slender waist to a head band in her blond hair, even her large eyes are tinted sapphire over blue. Before entering her classmates' apartment, Shelly announces, 'Laura will be at the party. Denny wouldn't marry her so she had an abortion. She's eager to see you.'

'Shelly, I've made a commitment to the religious life. As soon as the practical things with Dad's estate are taken care of, I'm returning to the monastery. That means I've given up girls. Do you understand?' Michael says, as he peers into her doe eyes.

'Yes, but I don't want you to leave home again,' she pleads biting the weight of her lower lip as they wait at the door.

His desire to see Laura is intense, it burns his whole body, but he also fears that she might reject him; her terrible betrayal is what he remembers with intense vividness. His parting had been fast, and he still feels paralyzed after the terrible blow. If she rejects him again, he fears it could drive him into a mental desolation worse than the one he has already known. He is testing a fate that hasn't destroyed him entirely. What would the emerald of her eyes express?

As Michael and Shelly enter the loft apartment, they notice Laura, with flowing black hair and slender arms outstretched, twirling to the music. The lines in Michael's face tense when Laura bumps into him; nervous, Laura notices that Michael and Shelly are standing with no drinks in their hands. 'Can I fix you both a drink?' she offers. Shelly nods and squints in the gray-blue swirls of tobacco smoke.

In the kitchen, Laura, remembering Michael likes lemon with vodka, starts mixing a drink. 'Got to be careful about mixing this drink.' Her eyes are glued to the glass as she dabbles an ice crescent. 'Too much lemon ruins the vodka. Humm ... Want the same Shelly?'

'A white wine, please.'

Tense, she spills Shelly's wine and pours another. Michael takes his unspilled drink and leans against the kitchen table as Laura, sipping and peeking at Michael above her wine glass, keeps staring and stops talking for a moment. Laura, full busted in a tight, dark sweater, and firm bottomed in black leotards has dirty feet from always going barefoot with the constant need to have contact with reality.

With an impulsive smile, Laura asks Michael, 'Do you want to dance?' She begins rippling to the rhythm of the guitars in the speakers.

Michael just stares at her in religious silence.

'Are you all right?'

Again, no answer. She takes his unwilling hand and leads him where the rock music is louder, outside the kitchen, into the living room. Michael seems oblivious to the music, and Laura's attention turns to Denny, her former boyfriend, a muscular, black bearded young man with a sleeveless leather shirt, who appears at the door. She leaves Michael, saying, 'I'll see you later. I want to talk with you.'

On the other side of the room she starts jumping unrhythmically with Denny. *It's better this way since I don't want to get involved with her again, but why do I still feel jealous?*

Disappointed that she left him, Michael melts through the shifting crowd back to the kitchen for his drink, and moves to a couch in the den near some closed patio doors. All of a sudden Denny and Laura fold their frames next to Michael onto the same soft couch. Denny nods slightly with an uncertain smile, then turns his back to Michael and talks to Laura. Michael hears only the vibrations of the music and the boastfulness in Denny's voice as it drones into the air. *He's a fruitcake, nutty as a fox squirrel, a real cuckoo. I don't know what Laura sees in the bragging idiot.* The room is damned with smoke; a mounting wave of depression and jealousy submerges Michael, who can't help noticing Denny and Laura, crouched up at the end of the couch.

The maddening chatter of the party, and Laura and Denny's conversation jar Michael, who, visibly impatient, turns to his sister, 'Are you ready to leave?'

Driving home from the party, Shelly tries to start a conversation. 'I found out tonight that an anthology of Laura's poetry is being published by a major New York publisher. I'm sure she wanted to tell you about it, but she was really nervous with you there.'

He already feels jealous of Denny and now hearing that her poetry is being published before anything of his makes him even envious. Michael just concentrates on controlling the car as he speeds down the wet, curved pavement.

'I've talked with her so many times after you left. She loves you. She's angry with you for leaving and kissed Denny to make you jealous. She's always talking about how much she enjoyed being with you, she really missed your wonderful talks. She feels guilty about the time you caught her and Denny in bed, but you never gave her a chance to explain.'

Michael's thoughts race faster than the Corvette in his hands, and he feels he has no control over his confusing thoughts as the car goes into a spin turning a corner. Only his thoughts collide as he pulls the car back in line again.

'Slow down Michael! This is my car.' Resuming her regular breathing rhythm, Shelly continues, 'I heard you said some odd things to Denny about your drink.'

'That creepy guy poisoned my drink! He hates my guts, smirking behind my back, but he didn't fool me,' Michael says as he brakes for a red light.

'Why would he want to do that?' she asks with astonishment.

'He's jealous of me,' Michael says as he bites his words.

'Laura does still love you. She wants to meet you at the *Crimson and Gold*, the pub close to the university, tomorrow night. She wanted to ask you herself, but she was afraid Denny would hear and start a fight,' says Shelly as she pulls her feet under her thighs, curling up on the car seat.

'I'll fight the guy!' exclaims Michael with determination.

'Forget about it, what about tomorrow?'

'I'm not allowed to have dates ... but if you come with me it's okay,' he says, looking at Shelly.

In the neighborhood of the University of Denver, Michael and Shelly meet Laura at the *Crimson and Gold*. The pub retains its high roof and rough hewn rafters from whose scored crevices pizza spices circulate, gently drifting down upon the wooden tables and beer mugs, but his thoughts are not drifting gently into his mind, rather, they question his sanity. *Am I gambling God's graces and calling to the priesthood by being here, and allowing my feelings to go free? Could I lose both God's and Laura's love and really be alone? Is my obsession with Laura destroying me?*

Before they finish their first round of beers, Laura says excitedly, 'I want you both to see my new loft apartment and I want to try out my new fireplace.'

As they leave the pub, a heavy wet snow falls and by the time they reach Laura's apartment their heads and coats are brimming with unshaken snow. Laura's new home is cold, and she starts building a fire in the white stone heath. As they kneel before the fireplace, Michael pours some red wine. In the feeble firelight he looks over at Laura and sees the highlights of water mist in her hair; Laura's black hair stands away from her face in disarray as she hands Michael a new log for the fire. The alcohol burns like ammunition in Michael's body as he watches Laura stretch for another log; he senses her bottom will explode in her tight jeans. His ignited eyes circle around the room as if the whole surroundings were burning. 'I'm going to leave you both,' announces Shelly, 'I have to study for an exam tomorrow.' *God, she can't leave me alone with Laura.*

The wine has slowed down Michael's mind, and he can't think fast enough of an excuse to leave before his sister disappears. Now quiet and alone together, Laura wiggles her behind into the warmest spot opposite the fire and looks at Michael.

'I finally get to explain what happened the last night we saw each other before you disappeared,' begins Laura with a nervous smile. 'Michael, when I first met you, you were a man whom life makes drunk. I loved your passion for life, but it also scared me. Something held my feelings back ... you were so impulsive and restless.' She sips some wine from Michael's goblet then continues, 'You touched me with your wonderful kisses and your imagination, but you were so reckless. I had been dating Denny when I met you, and I felt safe with him, his feet were on the ground when he wasn't at sea. He was easier to understand, life was easier with him, not so much fun, but it was easier. But he couldn't make me happy enough. He wasn't sensitive or expressive of his feelings. And after you left, I couldn't forget you, you had stirred the poetry inside me. I was a fool to let you run away ...'

Michael finds he has two minds and two hearts. Her words make him very happy, yet he feels God wants him to be his monk; he's torn in two. Reflections of the falling snowflakes dance in her happy eyes; he struggles valiantly to regain the self control which he feels fast in danger of losing. Michael sits on the floor, stretching his jittering legs. Trying to get more comfortable, she lays her head on his lap and her hair splashes across his legs. The light from the hearth emphasizes the shape of her womanhood, and the swelling inside him reaches an almost unbearable pitch. His mind becomes crowded with qualifications, analogies, consequences, doubts, suggestions and counter-suggestions. The situation fills him with the wildest combination of joy and fear, spurting like the fire. His whole body tingles as he moves his fingers through her silky hair and touches the delicate features of her face. There is a tangy taste in his mouth. Laura unbuttons his shirt and slides her warm, wanting hand upon his stomach. Her fingers are demanding, and his hardness presses against her hand. Michael stops her fingers; Laura sits up. Tormented and silent, Michael gazes into her eyes a few seconds; she pulls off her sweater and shows her candied breasts.

'Stop—I'm confused. I want to make love with you—,' Michael admits with some hesitance, 'yet I also feel God has called me to the religious life.'

'Don't you love me anymore?' she sighs in her sweetest voice.

'You know I do—but I can't do it.' Before Michael can finish his sentence, she pulls off her jeans, and with an updriven tempo, she embraces Michael and kisses his temples. He buries his shuddering face into her fragrant black hair until she finds his lips and kisses them. A few seconds later his lips form a word: 'Wait!'

She runs her finger over Michael's lips. 'Relax!' she demands with a pouting mouth, then finds her way into his mouth.

Confused, he moves his hand to her back, and gliding his twitching fingers he toys with her hair. He proceeds to the small of her back, and smoothes the back of her panties like his conscience. *As long as I don't go all the way, it's okay if we touch each other.* Michael plays with the lacy edges then the elastic waistband, stretching them like his mind. His hand crawls under her silk sheath and reaches her warm skin. With quick hands, Laura removes Michael's clothes, and before he can reflect, she leads Michael inside her. Their bodies, engaged in the rite of carnal knowledge move back and forth in spasmodic motion. When his guilt starts to pull him out it's too late. Michael's face shows calamity and exhaustion from the fight with himself, Laura and God. Laura pulls a quilt and pillows from the couch and they lay covered in the glow of an embering fire. Her heavy breathing begins again, but this time in slumber. Michael can't sleep. His guilty conscience and Tantric flames toss and turn his body restlessly. He reaches for the bottle of wine, gulps it down like lemonade on a hot night in Texas and finally slumber comes to soothe his aching mind.

Shortly before sunrise he awakens, and in the darkness he feels her nakedness. Emotion engulfs Michael; he starts to lavish caresses upon her, to fondle her warm and delicate sleeping body. Entwined once again, he swells with feelings for her. *It already happened last night, so it makes no difference what happens this morning.* His mind becomes inflamed as he holds her breasts and kisses them tenderly. Her warm breath intoxicates him. Her hands reach for Michael, who blissfully traces the contour of her body and tells her how beautiful it would be to see her again. Lying on his stomach, he stretches towards the floor lamp, but her caresses gently stop his motion. As she tries to pull Michael into her, his guilt makes him soft. Her hands and tongue ricochet from one part of his body to another and his mind gets caught in her limbs. *Maybe it's because she relaxes me, but I'm turned on much more now with her than I was last night. She seems much more beautiful to touch, and she's touching me so much better. I don't want her to stop touching me. She's wonderful.* Her knees spread apart, her whole frame surges out, swelling up and bulging away from her body. The muscles of his thighs tighten and loosen like a spring and everything is outstretched. She pulls him into her and violent explosions tear at his sanity.

As Michael lies on top of her and the sun starts to show itself through the frosted window, she tries to push him off her. He playfully holds his position, and in the dawning light his eyes become unsteady, like his mind, when with jolting shock and horror he realizes he's looking into Shelly's eyes. With disgust he immediately pulls away from her. 'YOU ARE SICK!' he shouts. 'How could you do this?! I'm your brother! You—you instigated Laura to seduce me. You're despicable! God, I don't believe it!'

'But, Michael, it was beautiful—I love you,' she repeats

78

as she covers her body with the blanket.

'I love you too, but not like this! You disgust me!' Michael yells as he violently pulls his clothes on. 'Tell Laura I'll hate her forever for this! Damn it Shelly!' He slams the door and walks away.

He jumps into his father's Porsche, driving as though it were the last lap of a race, down through the city, straightening the bends of Denver on the long curved Speer Boulevard. Passing restaurants and office buildings, early risers walking on the sidewalk appear in a flash. Nervous, he keeps driving, trying to catch up with some meaning in last night's events. Finally the end of the lap is in sight. He drives into the iced parking lot of his neighborhood parish. Inside the church, lit with vigil candles, Michael, with the other sheep, wait for the shepherd. With a quick shuffling of feet under his cassock, Pastor Flied, a sea captain's face, stops in front of the sanctuary and introduces his new assistant, Father Clennons, a dark, short and pudgy young man.

'Since Father Clennons is newly ordained and inexperienced, he will take all the people with venial sins—and I will take all the people with mortal sins.'

Michael finds this arrangement rather odd. As he expects, no one lines up at Father Flied's confessional, for that would reveal their mortal sins. All of the flock line up for Father Clennons. Michael notices Father Flied leave the church. *I bet he did that to avoid hearing confessions, probably because there is a good basketball game on TV.*

'Bless me, Father, for I have sinned. My last confession was one week ago. Last night I made love to a girl … I mean two girls.'

'You don't sound very certain. Was it one girl or two girls?' probes the confessor.

Embarrassed, Michael answers, 'I thought it was one girl but it ended up being two girls.'

'You mean you can't tell if it was one or two girls?' the priest asks impatiently.

'No ... It happened, then I fell asleep and the girls changed places. Does it make any difference? I said I'm sorry,' Michael says, frustrated.

'Yes, of course it makes a difference because I must know how much penance to give you. Now, did you know you were making love to another girl?' the priest queries in a louder tone.

'No, I was pretty drunk and it was dark,' Michael answers in a low voice.

'If you had known it was another girl, would you have made love to her?' continues to probe the priest, resuming his patient tone.

'Of course not ... she was my sister,' Michael admits quickly in a sweat.

'You should have gone to confession with Father Flied!' replies the priest, in obvious shock. 'What you've just confessed is a grave mortal sin. If you had been involved in a fatal car accident before coming to confession, you would have gone straight to hell! Only God could forgive you the ugly things you've done!' the priest asserts in his unforgiving voice.

Outside the church, Michael burns with disgust and guilt and fire trucks rage through his blood vessels. Afraid to drive home and find Shelly there, Michael first thinks of calling his friend Jason, but after a late breakfast at a diner he decides instead to attend a basketball game at his former high school. His car creeps into the wide shadowed pavement of the high school parking lot next to the gymnasium. The gym is filled with noisy people in anticipation of the big game and he hopes the excitement will keep his mind on other things. Michael's body is as stiff as the wooden bleachers. His alma mater, the Mullen Mustangs are tied for first place with the Jesuit high school, Regis. This is the deciding game. Like the losing basketball players, Michael desires to expel the nervous sensation in his stomach and the throbbing in his blood. The image of Shelly and Laura changing places while he slept scurries across his mind as a former younger classmate blazes over the court for a basket.

The half-time, even with his school winning, is a dreadful pause. Everyone is heading for the refreshment stands. He is suddenly alone with his disturbing thoughts, images that scare him. With trembling hands he buys a coke, stands looking for someone from his graduating class, and cola rivers run through his fumbling fingers. Scores crowd by him, but no one from his year. Michael feels used and dirty and walks in circles.

The teams run back onto the court, but the jubilation of the spectators is muffled by the panting and groans of his sister echoing loud in his mind. Each time his team makes a basket, he cheers, but he might as well be on the side of the losing team. His lips move, but his heart stands still. *God, I don't know what to think or do. I don't even know what's hurt me most? Laura not loving me and playing with my feelings or Shelly seducing me.*

Suddenly Michael realizes the game has been over for some time, and he is one of the few people left in the bleachers. He is still immersed in the stinging surge of thoughts. He cracks his neck, wipes the hair from his greasy forehead, and imagines blemishes on his skin. As a teenager, tension had always reflected itself on his face with pimples and Michael imagines fluorescent acne breaking out on his olive skin. He can picture all of the pimples crowding on his face.

Shaken, Michael drives along the winding road up the hill toward his suburban family home. Exhausted, he wishes he could roll over in sleep at home, the day would end and nothing could be carried over into the next day. *If only I could fall asleep and extinguish everything and then tomorrow could be totally new ... What happens if Shelly gets pregnant?* As Michael drives up the street, he sees the blue Corvette in front of their house, he brakes, spins around, the big wheels slide on the ice before biting into the street, and he races the German machine back down the hill. Michael's courage to face Shelly is as deep as the grooves in his wide striped hopsack blazer. *I'm afraid and embarrassed to see Shelly again. I've got my passport and ticket which I can have*

*changed at the airport. Right before the flight to Munich I'll
call Mom and tell her the car's at the airport.*

He drives through the foothill suburb overlooking the
city of skyscrapers, which are trying to rise higher than the
surrounding Rocky Mountains. The road to the airport leaves
the foothills and, walled in by the tall Denver buildings, the
roar of car engines and horns start to clamor the ugly song of
his pains. The car floats in the space of the cosmopolitan
city, and Michael's eyes, at first hypnotized by the car in front
of him, keep closing; the incessant reminiscing of his sexual
encounter with Shelly has exhausted him. Reflecting on the
strangeness of the world, he wonders why his life is such a
mess, why his dad died at the age of forty-five. Michael
imagines his own fears began in the womb, when he was
afraid to come out and face the harsh light. If only someone
could have heard his cry in that darkness.

FIVE

THE MOON IS A HARSH LOVER

In flight, the image of his father's casket, buried not very deep in his mind, keeps surging, reminding him of his father's pleas to assist him with the company. Sweating, Michael is apprehensive that the airplane, which is taking him to a runaway place on the other side of this world, is not faster than his heart, not able to take him away from his pains. He hopes the arrival at the Munich International Airport will push his problems far behind him, back in the seclusion of the Colorado Rockies. He hopes the past is not something in his mind alone. Michael tries trampling on his past, tries to crush it, only to find that he is actually bruising himself. His past is not distant, only fragmented; each sharp corner cuts bleeding sores in his psyche.

The train stops at Ebenhausen, buried in a spring snow. Stepping off into the blinding whiteness, Michael is oblivious to the storm and plows through the deep snow in his city shoes. Leaving the outskirts of the village, he walks along the main road until he sees the cold shadowed banks of the frozen Isar river leading down to the monastery, and he hopes the long hike will dilute his feelings of loneliness. Along the river bed and road lined with snow heaped up ten feet deep along the side of the mountain, avalanches of depression crush down upon him. The blowing snow clouds Michael's mind with anguish, and the ice on the river hides Siddhartha undercurrents of peace.

As evening deepens, and with the end of the monastery wall in sight, Michael reaches the stone gothic archway and enters a maze of tunnels which lead to his dark cell. After removing his half frozen clothes, he pulls a woolen robe over his shivering body and walks along the dimly lit corridor to the abbot's cell. His feet sting in his sandals. The monks stare at Michael as he waits for the abbot, their only reaction to Michael's return after a month's absence.

Their indifference, exacerbated by the strict rule of silence, deeply angers him. *I hate this boring, depressive stuck-up place, these fuckin' holier than holy brethren.*

The abbot opens his door which holds back the scent of Benedictine liquor. The abbot's narrow mouth, pointed like a fox's snout, asks him nothing about his family. Always looking straight ahead, the abbot's one glass eye froths gray feelings inside Michael as the pointed mouth opens to utter simply, 'Give the rest of your money to Brother Gunther.'

In the abbot's conclave of bells and rules once again, Michael begins to live the slow choreography of the monastic life, the beginning of his martyrdom again. The brown robed abbot, gray hair unkempt and gray lips drooping, stands unstable, shifting his weight from one foot to the other. Michael excuses himself and leaves the cold cell, while from behind the closed door comes the sound of something crashing onto the floor. *He must have lost his balance and knocked over his floor lamp or something. I wonder if the abbot must drink to live in this place. He's always got alcohol on his breath. Does the abbot and the band of monks here find it just as hard to live in this boring, depressing hole?*

Poured out to the dregs, Michael walks from the two-storied gallery into the chapel. After gently genuflecting, he falls back in his favorite pew in the rear of the choir loft. With a gothic window view over the vapored valley, he begins to talk with God. His eyes then gaze at the marble Madonna standing in a niche—a copy of a work by Pisano, the Italian sculptor. At the side altar, her simplicity breathes through every fold of her robe as the sculpture possesses a combination of natural charm and divine dignity. Michael's closed brown eyelashes flutter, and he slides into a trance. A few minutes later, he opens his eyes. The evening shadows are blending with the light like blue ink dropped in water, and slowly everything turns blue. Stumbling to the back of the choir loft, he finds the switch to artificial candlelight. In the dim, parchment-colored light he attempts to read the narrative of a mediaeval mystic who professedly talked with Moses. The abrupt ringing of the bell jolts Michael's concentration.

In the long refectory lined on both sides with slender columns, Michael stands with other monks along wooden planked tables. The dark oak paneled room, lightened by gilded wood reliefs behind the abbot's table, reflects the last of the twilight through the late gothic windows. While eating, the monks listen to the reading from the book, *The Imitation of Christ,* read in a monotone voice, which blocks the subjective tones of the reader. It's Sunday, and the abbot rings the bell that announces permission to talk, but Michael realizes he is changing, as he has no desire to speak.

Finally Brother Ronald addresses Michael, 'You could be a bit more Christian and share of yourself when talking is granted.' Michael responds with a nod: he has nothing to say.

'Michael, what did you do in the States?' Dietmar blurts out.

Michael's eyes remain glued to the cheese on his plate until one gnome-like monk, with black eyes twinkling in his wrinkled face informs Michael, 'We don't eat meat, in order to discourage sinful thoughts.' Michael nods to the kind old monk, but doesn't say a thing, as talking becomes an additional duty laid upon him like the meeting in the chapel at five-thirty for Vespers.

Sitting silently at the table, Michael delivers a mental dissertation with scriptural logic on the advantages of the religious life, remembering the words of a priest at his *alma mater,* Mullen High School, exclaiming that a vocation to the religious life was God's gift to a chosen few. *God, if I walked out of this place, it would be like walking away from You ... It would be like throwing a gift back at You. God, You've got to help me, I'm not happy here. I feel guilty not being able to appreciate the calling You seem to have given me. I'm doing something wrong, because I'm going crazy trying to be Your monk.* At the monks' table, the conversation about Teresa of Avila fails to reach Michael's ears: he is distracted by a nun's voice from the nearby kitchen. *The nuns are always quiet. It's probably the young postulate, Sister Monika. She probably hasn't learned all the rules yet. It's funny, even Sister Monika's voice sounds so beautiful. That's not good. It used to take a cute tush to turn me on and now even a girl's voice does it, maybe it's the Bavarian accent.* The utterances that reach his ears are low whispers, very soft, like the ones of a childwoman. Trying to block out the nun's words, Michael blocks his own thoughts and feelings, and instead of being the energetic young man he was, he turns into a silent youth, as a yearning, sensuous man disappears in the whirlpools of his eyes. After the meal, he feels relieved to leave the dining room and the nun's voice which reminds him of Laura.

Michael and the other monks enter the florid rococo chapel, and parade to their pews for hymn chanting. The Gregorian chant pulls him into a trance as he focuses not on spiritual matters but first on Laura and their wonderful talks about literature and art, and then on their attempts at ice skating on the mountain lake. In his trance he actually experiences himself holding her hand as they fall on the ice, but these sensations make him feel empty and lonely even though he can still hear her funny laugh. Coming out of the trance he feels a pain in his hip from either the fall on the ice or standing so long in the chapel, and begins considering consciously that it's easier for him to think his and Laura's relationship was only physical, therefore superficial. The end of a superficial bond hurts less than a deeper one. He comforts himself with these thoughts as he vividly recalls waiting for Laura in her dorm room one evening and watching her change clothes before going to the cinema. Laura had struggled out of her jeans and grabbed a white mini skirt instead, peeling off the last layer of clothing—her underwear—to make the skirt fit smoothly on her hips. Freed from the constraints of her white panties, she had thrown them at him like a flirtatious handkerchief thrown at his mind. Now, with the same motion, he shakes his head as if trying to shake that handkerchief out of it. He wonders what the monks behind him think when he shakes his head so vigorously. *They surely think I'm crazy. God, help me get rid of these thoughts.* The contemplation of Laura has petrified his sex under his warm robe. Disgust and jealousy devour him.

Michael realizes that he is suffering from something that never actually troubled him before, jealousy, and he feels frightfully degraded. His parents had always spoiled him; he had obtained everything he ever wanted but his desire to be an artist; Laura had denied him everything, even his own worth. One side of his heart feels a bitter spiteful rage for her betrayal, the other a longing. He doesn't understand why the two sides of his heart can't beat together or why his feelings don't fade and wither, but here no one could understand. He knows he must keep everything inside himself.

A bell rings and the monks fold their robed figures onto the hard wooden pews. As the monotonous prayer continues, his wandering mind tells him that it isn't his choice, but God's, an incomprehensible arrangement for his uncontrollable future. An attempt to leave on his own accord would be a painful ritual. Suddenly, hearing the nun's voice behind him and turning to see if it's the attractive young postulate, Michael's eyes meet the abbot's glass eye, a disturbing sight. No one besides the abbot is behind him. He then turns around and continues in the religious ritual of community prayers, trying to chant louder than the girl's voice which now clearly echoes in his head. Michael hears her call his name. *Am I hearing things? No one else seems to be responding to someone in the back of the chapel. Maybe I'm just tired.* The community prayers in the presence of the other monks choke him; he sits stupefied until he hears, 'Michael—I love you … I want to be with you.'

His eyes quickly scan the pews. In a sweat he turns around: behind him the abbot is sleeping. Michael genuflects, leaves the chapel and walks nervously back to his cell to rest. The darkness is distressing him and he lights a candle. *Shelly could have instigated that young postulate teasing me, but that's impossible. She could convince Laura, her best friend, but never a strange nun here in the monastery. I really need to talk to someone about what happened with Shelly. It must be driving me crazy if I'm hearing voices, but if my sin with Shelly almost gave young Father Clennons a heart attack, it would surely kill old Brother Hubert. And if*

they knew of it, they would definitely kick me out of the
religious life ... I'd feel guilty if I did something to get
myself kicked out and You want me here ... God, I'm going
crazy. God, help me, PLEASE!

To the uninterested and unaware brothers, Michael is
dedicated to prayer with God, but in reality he is shaking in
his cell. He fears the voice as a man on a cliff fears losing his
balance. *A drowning soul needs a raft, not explanations.* The
candle burns out and his cell is plunged into darkness. The
full moon shines through his window, flirting for his
attention. The Luna and stars strike him with the awareness
that he is sharing the same cosmic life; he is participating in
the consciousness of this vast universe. The celestial body
hypnotizes and seduces his mind to think that it is strange
that he exists and likewise unreal that he lives in this
monastery. Michael recalls the beginning of his life with the
Benedictines then tries to think of his past without a
beginning, but his mind is too feeble to grasp it, and he
concludes that the moon a harsh lover.

After a sleepless night, Michael secludes himself in the
library. In his quest to understand the meaning of the female
voice, his mind keeps hankering to explain this obstinate
tongue. In the library loft he finds a book on the mystic who
had heard Moses and other books about men and women who
had heard some saint speak with them. These books confuse
him even more as he sits stiff at an old wooden table, sharing
this room of learning with dusty rows of age and wisdom.
The bell rings.

Startled by the signal for spiritual direction, Michael
drops his books and walks toward Brother Hubert's cell. In the
corridor Michael lays eyes on Brother Dietmar, dancing down
the hallway as if practicing steps he had learned with the
Munich Ballet Company before entering the Benedictine
Order. As he reaches Dietmar, who pirouettes in his long
swaying robe, Michael tries to imitate the dancing turns but
gets his leg caught in his cassock and falls. Dietmar's hushed
laugh and Brother Reiner's abrupt entrance cause Michael to
jump to his feet and Dietmar to rejoin the silence. A

consciousness of Brother Reiner's own strength is inherent in the easy swing of his body under his robe. Brother Reiner's rough, ruddish face has a solemn air as he walks ahead of them and leaves through an open door into a covered, vined passageway leading to the monastery garden. Michael glances outside at the drizzling rain and feels drowned in his distress as he walks down the corridor with Brother Dietmar.

Breaking the rule of silence, Brother Dietmar asks, 'Where are you going?'

'I've got spiritual direction with Brother Hubert now,' Michael answers, almost forgetting he had vocal cords.

'That guy is a bastard with his pseudo-spirituality and spying. Be careful what you tell him,' Brother Dietmar says, as he does a triple pirouette and then walks up a set of stairs.

For Michael, Dietmar's words make the monastery seem like a haunted place full of secret tunnels. Michael continues down the damp corridor, thinks of the human weaknesses in this house and then of his own weakness while he daydreams of Laura's perspiring face as he fumbles at her panties under her karate robe, a fantasy becoming too frequent and therefore intolerable. Why did he for a second imagine he had escaped these painful desires by running off to Europe? He can't deny the passions that twist him so deeply, and worst of all, the hopes he had of their relationship. He left so unexpectedly; decisions are always so difficult as they always involve two dimensions: one conscious and the other unconscious.

After entering the old man's cell lined with old manuscripts and books, Michael sees the spiritual director seated, holding his jaw, either thinking or experiencing a tooth ache. The old man moves his hand and offers Michael a stool at his feet.

'Brother Michael, I want to commend you for your following of the rules, especially the keeping of the rule of silence. You are a good example for the new novices,' he says, thumping his finger in the air.

'Danke Schön, Vater.'

Michael realizes the narrowness of the plank he is treading, and telling his spiritual director about the voice would be like jumping off the plank—and where would he fall? Compelled to continue straight ahead, Michael finds it impossible and too dangerous to proceed backwards in his decisions. After Brother Hubert's sermon, he rises from his subservient position and leaves the aged monk. In the chapel, Michael kneels and prays to the Virgin Mary, convincing himself that he will repress every thought of Laura, afraid he will be possessed again by those tempting thoughts of her. *I'm gonna strive to lead a life in accordance with the monastic rules. I'm gonna be a monk if it kills me.* He almost strangles himself, twisting his neck as Laura's image again echoes through the maze of his mind.

In his cell Michael changes clothes for work in the carpentry shop and wonders if Dietmar is correct about Brother Hubert secretly spying on the monks' movements. Michael waits until the bell rings signaling the beginning of manual labor, and sure enough Brother Hubert enters the room without knocking. Finding Michael standing naked in the posture of a Greek disc thrower, the shocked elderly Brother slams shut the cell door. Michael laughs and then his thoughts blend into the silence. *He does spy ... that bastard!*

It's a warm Friday, Michael and Dietmar have appointments at the dentist's, for their yearly checkups in the village of Ebenhausen by a doctor who offers his services to the monastery. After their late afternoon appointment with Dr Windberg in his old study above the *Apotheke,* Michael, relieved that the dentist couldn't find any cavities, meanders the village with Dietmar. Brother Gunther will fetch them at the *Café Hubertus* after doing his shopping in the village, which includes supermarket wine since the monastery no longer keeps the age-old tradition of distilling its own quality liquor.

Michael and Dietmar ramble down the narrow cobblestoned street shaded by the balconies of the houses decorated with flower boxes overflowing with multicolored early spring chrysanthemums in the fairy tale style of King

Ludwig. They walk past the onion-steepled church, the village shops that sell fresh bread and sausages, finally stopping at a book store, to look at novels, something they don't have at the monastery. Meandering along the river Isar, barely twenty feet wide, which winds its way through the village and the azure grass banks, they walk over a narrow footbridge spanning the river to the road on the other side to *Gasthaus zur Post* covered with paintings depicting the last battle of the Bavarian hero, *Schmied von Kochel.* Michael vividly remembers this *Gasthaus,* even the first time he came to this town it was like a déjà vu experience, as if he'd been there before. The clicking of beer mugs and zither music attract them to a beer garden behind the Gasthaus where a crusty pork roast turns on a spit.

Michael and Dietmar sit at a table next to a blonde curly-haired *Fräulein* named Monika and her dark-haired friend Elke who queries in a friendly tone, 'Why do all the handsome guys become monks?'

'Not all the monks at the monastery are handsome,' Dietmar is quick to reply then continues with a laugh, 'You should see our abbot!' the image triggered in Michael's mind makes him smile.

'What's life like in the monastery?' pursues Monika, unable to hide her curiosity.

'We have dances at the monastery every Friday night,' says Dietmar in an official tone. 'The ugly abbot is the disc jockey!'

Monika glances at Michael's sedate face turned toward the red coals in the fireplace, not knowing whether or not to laugh at Dietmar's words.

'Doesn't your friend talk?' asks Elke, confused.

'Silence is our way of life,' answers Brother Dietmar solemnly.

They talk and laugh till dark, except for Michael, who feels guilty for not meeting Brother Gunther as agreed. *Maybe he'll think we took the bus back to the monastery.*

Finally Dietmar stands up. 'Michael, are you ready to go?' Michael doesn't answer: his mind is three quarters eclipsed as the moon in its last quarter that evening. They leave the café and find their way back to the monastery. Emerging from the woods, Dietmar pants out, 'Hope we don't get a trimming from the abbot for this!'

The monastery walls glow silvery in the moonlight. The two monks climb their way into the fortress then walk along the walls, followed by their flowing shadows, furtive and silent like invaders. Michael tiptoes quietly over the courtyard as if it were a mine field.

The morning is melancholic. From one of the square stone windows in the library tower growing out of the red-tiled roof, Michael notices an unfamiliar car drive over the blue-gray cobbled stones in front of the house. A priest quickly runs from the car through the rain to the monastery entrance, where Dietmar suddenly appears with a suitcase; he drives off with the priest and disappears from Michael's senses. The scene before him is quickly replaced with images of the night before, a sound in his stomach like a toad, a pain in his chest, and utter blackness and emptiness in his head. Michael's senses seem shattered—pieces of a broken beer glass like the one he'd drunk from the night before at the *Gasthaus*. Now his solitude is complete, his awareness stingingly real. *I didn't talk to Dietmar enough, he was the only one around here who was any fun. Are they going to boot me out too?* Michael wants to leave too but can't anymore than a puppet on strings can.

The monastic bell sounds signaling scriptural reading, and Michael returns to the chapel with admirable punctuality to his hard-to-concentrate-on studies of the spiritual life. Obedience is an easier vow than chastity for him as it provides temporary relief from his compelling need of deciding. Inside the dark chapel the faces of the monks appear timeless and blurry, suggesting to him that everything is taking place at the edge of his consciousness. Unable to feel totally peaceful, Michael walks outside into the rain-washed courtyard looking for some peace with Nature, trying to find some sense of it all: but even the rain makes everything blurry. *A peaceful mind is more explosive than a worried mind*. He walks in the garden, listening to the myriad of sounds produced by the raindrops as they fall on the various surfaces of the courtyard: leaves wide and narrow, cobblestones polished by innumerable sandaled steps over the centuries, the tiles on the roof. He keeps picking up the thought of Laura throwing her panties at his feet like a dropped flirtatious handkerchief, and he drops the thought in his head faster than his fingers could have dropped her knickers. His steps take him on a side path, where Michael suddenly slides and falls in the mud. *Damn, if only I had the strength to go back to my cell and throw myself out of my window. I can't stand this anymore.* He gets up, walks back towards the house along a windy path lined by tall bluish bramble bushes on one side and a dropping embankment giving a view of the Isar river and valley on the other until he comes upon a thick forest where the wind, now softer, stirs the delicate smells of the wet earth and pine needles. Coming into a clearing before the monastery he can see two men and a car at the gate of the house. One of the men is Dietmar. The other monk drives off, leaving Dietmar behind. Michael runs to his friend who informs him that he had been reprimanded for returning late to the monastery and sent to discuss his vocation with Father Kleebert, a personal friend of his family. Dietmar had taken the blame and responsibility also for Michael.

On Easter Sunday, the abbot parades to the altar in full liturgical array. He then slowly moves to the side shrine to collect the Blessed Sacrament. When the abbot opens the gilded rococo tabernacle, he discovers it is filled with decorated Easter eggs. In disbelief, he turns around, showing shock and anger on his face which blend with the floral design of the altar. The abbot mumbles through the mass until it is time for his cenobitic sermon. The first few minutes are steeped in silence as the monks think the abbot is ailing. Then, like thunder, down comes a spontaneous doomsday sermon for forlorn creatures. 'God's sword shall come down upon you!' replaces the usual rejoiceful Easter message of a 'Resurrected

Life' surprising the monks on this morning of liturgical joy. Michael retreats deeper into himself.

The sun climbs up the far side of the mountain and runs down the near side into the monastery and Michael's cell window, which lets in the warm mellowness of a spring breeze rich with the fragrances of flowers and the song of bees buzzing among them. The last of the spring snow, which had kept Michael a prisoner more than the walls, now begins to melt around the monastery. Saturday morning after mass and breakfast, Michael discards his heavy robe and dresses in gray slacks and jacket, the brightest colored clothes he has. *I've got to get out of this house. This place is driving me out of my mind. It looks beautiful outside.* He leaves his cell and walks down the corridor, where icons of holy men and women, dark and indifferent on the wall, appear friendlier from the sunlight shining down the hallway. Michael bounces in his walk in rhythm with the old dust dancing in the sun rays.

Once outside the main gate, he stops to deeply inhale the air redolent of pine; then he proceeds along the monastery wall and into the forest of the mountain side which leads deeper into the valley, down a serpentine path that narrows and darkens from the thick shadows of the hedge of brambles and pine scrub. The fragrance in the warm air keeps him in a trance, and, like a dream sequence suddenly changing, he finds himself in a glen covered with small baby-blue flowers, with small blue and white butterflies flickering above them. Here, under the warm rays of the sunflower sun, he can look down into a valley where he sees part of a deep ultramarine-blue lake. The sounds against the silence are different here than in the monastery: here birds—not monks—sing.

Michael starts his descent. At the bottom of the vale, a mountain creek bubbles into the fertile shores of the lake. There he finds the boat the monks use for fishing; between the gathering clouds the red sun glares down on him as he lowers the boat into the water. The clouds, which darken Michael's soul with their memory of winter, play hide and seek as he paddles through the gully where the creek meets the lake. Before finding cover under large pines hovering over the brush, rain begins to pound all around him, but his soul is not splashed clean like the rest of nature. He straightens his highly strung back as the sun returns, drying his face and jacket with a heat massage. As he lets his gaze travel with the water washing over the brilliant rocks, he stretches like a newly hatched bird toward the light and his thoughts stretch towards the horizon. *If the water weren't so cold, I'd love to take a swim.*

Silence reigns except for the running of the creek waters into the lake. A sudden creaking sound of trembling tree branches interferes with Michael's thoughts of his previous life as a student in Denver. A girl emerges from the woods, materializing before his eyes on a rocky rim of the lake. Michael almost drops his oars as he sits silently glancing at her. Behind her, the last of the melting snow trickles through the pine thicket, finding its way into the lake. *Who is she? A local village girl? I thought nobody could come too close to the monastery.* The girl positions herself on top of a large boulder a few feet away from him, and an intense voyeuristic sensation invades his soul, bringing blood to his cheeks in a somewhat guilty rush. A gentle smile on the girl's face as she takes notice of him reaches him with surprise, and in spite of his vows, his heart swells and presses his lungs to the sides of his slender frame. *She is beautiful, but there is no use trying to get to know her.* Frustrated by his present condition of belonging to a religious community, he bites the inside of his cheek. Her sunflower hair reflects in the sunlight as she suns herself in blue jeans and a white sweater. He enjoys looking at her until a hawk flying overhead with its wings outstretched projects on the water the shadow of a cross. Guilt, rising from somewhere inside him, begins to choke him.

Everything seems somewhat blurry and erased in the haze of the steam rising from the lake, yet her simple beauty clearly has taken over his mind on this late dewy morning of early spring as the young grass has taken over the fields. The immediate world is colored light green, but another world now centers around the blue of her eyes. In a trance Michael paddles to the side and pulls himself out of the boat, nervously shuffling his sandaled feet on the ground. The crunching sound of the pine needles rattles him. He turns and glances at her again. *Looking into her eyes is like gazing into a wild frontier forest.* She returns his glance with another smile, this time trespassing his life along with the wooded conclave. To secure the boat on the shore, Michael ties a rope around the trunk of a young pine tree. The rough bark scores the inside of his sweaty hand as he scratches the idea of chatting with her. The pain in his hands give him a sense of being alive as blood and hormones rush through his body until the sound of bells grope through the cool air announcing it's time for community prayers. The cloister is on the other side of the thick forest, and Michael realizes he will be late. He starts to walk back in the motionless air, afraid to look back, but not allowing himself to run. He walks up the hill back to the monastery with his precious cargo of recent thoughts.

Late for community prayers in the chapel with its smell of old wood and stone, Michael kneels in the rear of the church. In front of him, the friars' heads are covered with woolen hoods as if to hide fat necks. Michael joins his hands in prayer and covers his face, feeling the marks of confusing thought on his brow. *Who was the girl at the lake?* Suddenly realizing his thoughts have deafened the abbot's sermon, his dented mind now attempts to concentrate on the rest of the homily.

The abbot hides his arms, crossed in his sleeves, and rocks his stiff body as he orates, 'In the religious life you shouldn't strive to stand out as an individual. It is always the community that matters. God has called you to the highest life. It is a greater blessing to be a monk than to be a president of a great nation. There will be many temptations to deter you from the road to perfection. There should never be two monks together, *nunquam duo*, always at least three; two can be sinful.' At the altar the abbot mumbles the rest of the

Mass.

'Two can be sinful' still rings in Michael's head the next day as he walks outside the monastery walls into the woods filled with blackberry brambles, also never in twosomes. As if hypnotized, he follows the path into the valley again, walking over puddles of melted snow in the uneven parts of the track, his mind muddy with thoughts of the girl he saw yesterday. He reaches the woods by the lake, where he finds her footprints in the remaining patches of snow. He wants to follow her impressions on the ground, but then realizes that he is standing on the wrong side of the world, biting on a balloon of worldliness, hoping it won't pop. The groping gossip in his head convinces him to wait for events to unfold. Pigmentation returns to his skin, along with a renewed impression of peaceful permanence. The wooliness of his garb extends to a wooliness of private thought and a fuzziness of feelings. *God, why did you choose me to be Your monk? Your call is a wonderful gift as the abbot said, and I hope I can love You as You love me.*

Afraid to be conquered by the temptation to follow her tracks, Michael forces himself to walk back to his religious community, to ascending the dark side of the Alps to the cloister, an old edifice of stone clinging to one side of the mountain. Suddenly, the nine hundred foot ridge resonates with the bell, symbolizing the throaty love of God, summoning the monks to a period of monitoring by another monk other than their spiritual advisor. Michael had chosen Brother Dietmar who for the past week has monitored Michael's behavior and his following of the Benedictine rules.

A white-washed corridor spotted with frescoes depicting the life of Saint Benedictine leads to the chapel entrance, dominated by a large pewter chandelier hanging from the ceiling. To his right, Michael enters a narrow dark hallway lit with brass oil lamps. He passes the library where several monks sit, their laps and minds crushed by bulky medieval books. Among them sits Brother Hubert, the small emaciated monk with patches of parchment-thin skin, showing through his thin gray hair. Michael looks for Dietmar and finds him sitting on a stone bench of the courtyard. Two other monks walk in the courtyard in their swaying robes, with the slow rolling movement of saints walking on water in Galilee. Dietmar greets Michael with an ironic, humorous face, weighed down by the hammocks under his eyes.

As they walk around the sacred square of lawn, Michael whispers, 'The Easter eggs in the tabernacle was a funny idea! These monks don't have any humor. Humor brings people together, religion needs to be an interpersonal relationship with God, not individual performances. The way some of these priests take the vow of chastity, resembles masturbation, not a relationship with God.' Dietmar has to hush his laugh. Michael continues, 'Even the holy vow of poverty isn't really a sacrifice since all material necessities are provided. Real poverty is a risk. We aren't taking any risks!'

Suddenly the bell rings announcing the beginning of silence and spiritual reading. 'Michael, I smuggled a novel in with me when I returned from Munich. I couldn't live without novels,' confesses Dietmar, with a wink.

Walking past them, Brother Ronald hears Dietmar talking after the bell. He contracts his wrinkled eyes and forehead into a grave expression, while admonishing, 'It's silence now!'

Silently, Dietmar walks out of the courtyard leaving Michael with his thoughts. Any gesture of friendliness from Brother Ronald would be a gross error of community life, the awful egoism of the pious. In his loneliness, Michael is aware of his withdrawal and stifles his compassion. Professedly a beacon of truth, the religious life leaves him only with impressions of illusions of sainthood. *Is a friendly monk as obscene as a monk with sexual desire?*

In his cell, Michael tries reading a book required of the novices before they take their vow of chastity. The book seems to be talking only of Laura; he closes it and puts it aside, picking up instead a book by the mystic St. John of the Cross. Michael identifies with the mystic's dark night of the soul consisting of pessimism, anxiety, convictions of worthlessness, abandonment by God, rejection by loved ones, thoughts of death and terrible suffering. He feels an utter blackness in the monastery as he contemplates that only a few monks express any friendliness; their facial features seem weighed down by a darkness similar to his own. *Maybe we should wear red robes to cheer us up!. God, are You playing a game with me? You seem to like games, You even played games with Job. Even Christ on the cross felt abandoned.* Only by identifying with Christ's pains can Michael soothe his own. With the bending of Michael's will his anxious straining choices or wanderings will disappear. He looks out his window onto the courtyard, his gaze restricted by the monastery walls. *Doesn't God even take care of the birds, yet they can fly over the walls?* He mumbles something about holding onto the birds and keeping away from darkness when he hears a slight noise behind him: an envelope has been slipped under his door. A note from Brother Gunther instructs him to use the bus for his appointment at the dentist's the next day.

After the dented drilling noises at the dentist, the traffic sounds in Ebenhausen sing of life. From the bridge spanning the river Michael has a view above the houses of the dense woods cutting off meadowlands on the hills with grass colored pink by the sunlight between the clouds. Walking past the village bookstore adorned with red geraniums in the low window boxes and books peaking above the flowers, Laura's book flies into his mind; he wonders if her poetry collection receives good reviews and sells well. The window of the bookstore in Ebenhausen displays only a few books in English—a handful of popular novels for tourists. He's sure there is no chance they'd have Laura's book, still his curiosity draws him into the small shop. In disbelief he recognizes in the salesgirl the same girl who had appeared like a vision at the lake. Friendliness radiates from her big blue eyes framed with long eyelashes; her warm smile and cute chipmunk cheeks seem to invite him to approach her instead of the other saleswoman who disappears into the back room.

'Do you by any chance …' he hesitates, 'have a book by Laura Wren?' *What a stupid question! Of course they don't.* The salesgirl consults the author's guide of *Books-in-Print* where she finds a title, *Red Cloth.*

'I didn't know monks read modern poetry,' the girl smiles with a twinkle in her eyes.

His attention is so focused on her clothes, a mauve sweater and a white pleated skirt that he forgets what he is wearing and wonders how she'd guessed he was a monk. It takes him a moment to realize that he's wearing his robe.

'I'm sure some of them read it,' replies Michael, thinking of Dietmar.

'I saw you in the boat last week, didn't I?' she asks in local dialect. Michael smiles and nods, happy that she remembers him. 'One of my friends from Ebenhausen is a nun at the monastery,' she continues. 'I've been there to visit her, it's a beautiful place, especially the chapel ... I love Gregorian chant,' she admits, her voice lowering in pitch, becoming somewhat more intimate.

'I do too, my room is only the fourth down the corridor from the chapel so I can always hear the older monks singing Gregorian when we novices have spiritual reading.'

The new language rolls off his tongue with ease, although he hardly ever speaks it at the monastery. He suddenly realizes the peculiar effect of his speaking a different language: it instantly gives him another character, almost a different personality, and somehow he doesn't recognize himself. She keeps gazing at his eyes and then his lips with an almost impertinent intentness, as if she were waiting for his next word or mispronunciation in German.

If indeed it all began at this point, he can only remember her asking what kind of literature and art he likes. She presses herself on him like someone pressing upon a bruise; it is as if she wants to extract his literary and artistic feelings. Her smiling face peers under her blond hair waiting for answers, as she gleams in the mauve-lemon light of a spring sun fading in and out of the clouds and store windows.

He remembers reading several biographies of Vincent van Gogh, and now he feels he can partly identify with the man who started life as a cleric, only to realize he couldn't fit in and found his vocation as an artist. However, Michael is determined not to be self-destructive like Vincent. *Like Vincent, I'm mad, I am temporarily insane and must somehow stop talking with this girl.* He looks for a sensible sort of delay when suddenly it's closing time for the bookshop.

Leaden clouds gallop into each other above Ebenhausen, finally crashing and spilling a downpour over the village. After a friendly exchange of 'Wiedersehen,' Michael leaves the store, but feels compelled to wait in the doorway for the rain to abate. While he waits, the salesgirl emerges from the shop, and runs through the rain to find shelter under a linden tree across the road. They exchange a glance through the rain, then Michael makes a mad dash to join her. At his intrusion, her milky cheeks flush a little, and she draws back from her face her dripping hair darkened by the rain. With a sensation of something noiselessly exploding inside him, Michael watches her make gentle and ineffectual movements with her slim hands and long, uncertain fingers as she talks about the music of the raindrops falling on the leaves of the linden tree. He notices a small mole upon the slender stalk of her neck, a sort of cappuccino mark on her satiny skin. 'Would you like a coffee?' he asks.

Suddenly realizing he'll need to use his allowance for the bus to pay for the coffee, the *coitus interruptus* of his thoughts urge him to withdraw his offer, but he is held by her world of books and ideas. From the first moments, maybe because of the genuine blue of her eyes or the radiance of her smile illuminated with a glow from within, he feels he can only be honest with her and keeps looking into her pure cerulean eyes which seem to hold the source of a much desired peace. He wants to keep their conversation alive, even though he knows that, once alone, the recollection of it will fill his soul with an intolerable depression. The sky slowly lightens like a healing bruise, and the watershed begins to fade.

The sunlight emerging among the rain clouds finds its way through a window pane into the *Café Hubertus* and onto the girl's pale cheeks. *She reminds me of a pre-Raphaelite maiden, so pale, yet luminous.* They sit opposite each other, near a window. She asks Michael about the book *Red Cloth.* He doesn't want to talk about Laura, and not knowing what to say except that it's poetry on elusive ethnographic symbols of love, like butterflies, he quickly shifts the conversation on biographical portraits to describe his own writing instead. Somewhat awkwardly, he starts, 'When I use my experiences in a novel, I don't write about them in the order in which they took place—for that is autobiography—but in the order in which they first become significant for me.'

'That's how multiple personalities think,' she jokes, apparently trying to help Michael release his nervousness.

Their friendship begins with an exchange of common literary and psychological likes and dislikes. Despite different backgrounds, their eyes share a common gaze as a butterfly, fluttering its wings of red cloth outside their café window, leads their sight to the ceiling of thick gray clouds above the mountains, yet somewhere the sun manages to shine illuminating the small town and the vivid green hillsides behind the café. The sun steams the cobblestones, giving the façades of the houses an almost erased, blurry appearance. This afternoon seems as mysterious as bread becoming the body of Christ. He stirs his cappuccino, the coffee and foaming milk converge for synthesis; one chamber of his heart feels a calling to the priesthood and the other an inexplicable attraction to this girl, yet the changes taking place in him, unlike the coffee and milk, cannot find a synthesis, although her laugh banishes some of his nervousness. She laughs with all of herself, her eyes close like the ones of a chipmunk, her laughter makes her cheeks even fuller, and her smile is pure sunshine. *I love the way her eyes wet with laughter.*

As he sips his cappuccino, he remembers awakening so restless that morning; he had thrown off all the blankets in the wars of his dreams, and by morning his bed was a battlefield. In his dream he was wearing a camouflage military uniform and was wounded, yet, even awake, he feels he is disguising himself, as his monk robe resembles a costume at a masquerade party. *Who am I trying to fool?* Suddenly his thoughts reawaken old guilts. He also wonders what people in the café think; they do look at him strangely. In the blue light of the café nestled in the pine-green mountains, he feels his experience is similar to a surrealistic painting, but even more like an hallucination, or the momentary happiness one finds in novels—yet she is undeniably real with a profile classic in form, emphasized by a beautiful Roman nose. He likes the way she throws back her hair—now dry as she speaks. Discovering a common passion for fiction, they drug themselves exchanging tales of different novels which one has read but not the other or that they both have read. She acquaints him with a tale of a nun who falls in love with a novelist. He imagines himself the writer and her the protagonist in a black habit, but his visions fade like successive washes of black ink from a guilty conscience. Truly in a trance, his arms too heavy to lift off the table, he appears held by the magnetic pull of this girl—until he thinks of Vespers.

After that day, Michael doesn't return to the bookstore in Ebenhausen, instead he writes about the girl. Later, his impressions and memories of their encounter lie lifeless, in the sheets of his notebook, crumpled on the floor like snowballs. He cannot understand his compulsion to write about that unusual junction of minds but finds it is necessary to explain their serendipitous meeting to himself. He keeps writing, only to tear it up tormentuously when finished. He finds it impossible to describe her ways and the manner in which she had captivated and bewitched him with her smile and chipmunk cheeks. Perhaps as for other artists, death or madness would provide a focus for all the feelings which he now tries in vain to express in his writing, his only form of expression. Her words·resonate in his mind, inspiring him to keep writing. She had expressed her conviction that religious men are close to artists in their spiritual torment and that the denial of worldly possessions is fertile ground to art as well as the means to a deeper understanding of life. 'You can't write the blues in an air-conditioned room!' had once affirmed his psychology teacher turned writer who had introduced him to existential thought at college. Michael's mind travels back to his college days, and his thirst of humanistic knowledge and arts. Was he now being authentic and true to himself as he had sworn to himself he always would be? He does feel a monk's cell is like a writer's attic, the mysterious room in which ideas come to life; everything a man accomplishes is born in a cell.

In his cell, Michael's reading and calm breathing are abruptly interrupted as his door suddenly opens without a knock. The salesgirl from the bookstore walks into his room, and the realization of this develops in his mind like a print in a photographer's developing tray.

'What are YOU doing here?' shrieks Michael, jumping up from his chair, unable to believe she would come into the monastery, his mind shaking like the hand she takes with a mysterious confidence. 'How did you know where my room was?' he continues to inquire, forgetting that he had given her its exact location when talking about Gregorian chant.

This abrupt encounter colors his confusion with a shade of ecstasy. Commenting in a low voice on his meager furniture washed with the last of the sunlight, she compares his cell with a Caravaggio painting. Suddenly, even he could see his wooden desk and bed as a print while this whole experience starts to seem like a painting as the feebler stretching rays of the late afternoon sun smear the colors and shadows across the chalky walls. The five-o'clock bell ushers in the sounds of shuffling brown robed monks down the corridor. Her reaction consists of a mischievous and quick smile full of a quality Michael didn't suspect in her—the power of mischief. Her smile reminds him of the one she gave him when sunning herself at the lake. Michael stands between this forbidden girl and the Gregorian music in the chapel for what seems like an eternity, unsure how to react. With some hesitance, without a word she opens the door and leaves the cell.

Michael watches her disappear around the corner. His impulse to chase after her is restrained by his conscience, and he reluctantly directs his steps towards the chapel, which he enters with a sigh. Dazed by the surprise visit and the hypnotic Gregorian chant, he begins to feel an irresistible similarity with the subject of one of the paintings in the chapel: a saint, his head dropped back, his eyes rolling heavenward, smiling blissfully and extending his arms to welcome bands of angels. Feeling one with this painted mystic, Michael perceives a rush of exaltation and grandiosity in the conviction that God has rewarded him for his suffering. *Thank you, God, thank you, God. Is this a sign from You that I can leave?* But a conflicting thought produces a chasm in his mind: is this God's test of his love for Him? Unable to decide which path to follow, Michael retreats deeper into the fortress of himself, seeking shelter and security. *I won't try to find her in the bookstore.*

Above Ebenhausen's fruit and vegetable market, the wind peels the morning marmalade clouds from the sky like the skin of an orange. Michael's new work assignment entails purchasing bread and cheese for the monastery. For centuries the monks had been self-sufficient, but now with fewer vocations, it is more economical to purchase these items, though they still grow all their own vegetables. Michael buys the crusty brown bread at the bakery adjacent to *Café Hubertus*, where the monastery has a running account. *God, You must always pay Your bills.* This assignment reminds him of a job he dreamed of as a child, working in a pastry shop and eating all the sweet rolls and cakes he desired. Not only the aroma of cinnamon rolls and *Apfelstrudel* intoxicate him as he enters the bread shop, but also the memories of the salesgirl's sincere eyes, the color of a summer sky, and her chipmunk cheeks. He had promised himself he wouldn't go by the bookshop and concentrates instead on the loaves of bread being packed into hemp sacks. Although the aroma of the fresh bread fills his mind, he remembers her faint fragrance and loses touch with his present task. Noticing that he's not paying attention, the salesgirl needs to repeat, 'If you can wait fifteen minutes, you can have fresh loaves of sourdough bread … because of the feast of the patron saint tomorrow we've sold more loaves than usual.'

Michael's throat is blocked, and he can only nod, thinking he has time to run by the bookstore. He only needs to cross the river, walk a short way, and everything in the world would be changed. The novice leaves the shop with the scent of the warm bread in his lungs, the memory of her smile and love of literature in his head. His thoughts intertwine with the abbot's words that morning during meditation about a group of monks in the Middle Ages who on a journey came to a river where they found a young damsel in distress. The monks carried the beautiful young woman across the river and set her down. Later one of the monks asked the abbot if he wasn't putting himself in moral danger and temptation by carrying the young woman, and the abbot responded, 'I laid the woman down, but you are still carrying her!' As he stands near the town water pump Michael realizes that he is still carrying his young damsel in his thoughts, and guilt quickly emerges. The water pump throws its shadow upon the cobblestones, he does the same with his thoughts, collects the bread and leaves Ebenhausen.

Pigeons, like the scattered pieces of a novel, flutter around the monastery steeple as the long pale rays of the late afternoon sun smear light along the exterior stone fortifications and through Michael's window along the cell's chalk walls. At his old desk, holding a pen lightly in his fingers, reverently in his hands like a communion wafer, Michael writes. He needs to put order in his mind—and in his cell whose floor is scattered with pieces of paper. His sense of self spreads far beyond his chair and desk, beyond the crumpled papers on the floor, to the lives of others. He feels alive contemplating that he lives in others, including the Ebenhausen girl's feelings and thoughts, and possibly dreams.

This is a mystic's definition of God: a oneness of life. He senses himself unwrinkling from his former self, as some of the paper on the floor would, and he finds himself not separated from the life outside the cloistered walls, but in a continuum. Suddenly tears flood his moss-colored eyes at the thought that the monastery could be a garden of paradise, and its thick walls don't need to circumscribe his life. A new belief takes root in his mind: he's not committing a sin by looking for her at the bookstore as she is part of God too, a reflection of God's beauty and goodness, which however still remains anonymous. He realizes he doesn't even know her name.

An amanuensis of his own thoughts, he notices how the writing provides a structured analysis to the immaterial quality of his ideas: he feels compelled to put his thoughts in written form. *I didn't like the way she compared my writing technique of putting things in order of significance to the way a multiple-personality thinks. I guess I should have waited after her remark and said, 'I'm waiting for the other personality to speak.'* But then he realizes that multiple personalities are no joking matter, as they survive a terrible loss of love by becoming another person—it's cruel, but life is cruel. Suddenly a blackness in his mind annihilates his present optimism, black dust falls on his desk and black marks scratch his paper. When his mind finally tires and goes blank from the blackness and silence in the monastery, time becomes different, it disappears and doesn't come back until he can actually say or hear something. A black butterfly lands on his desk near a clock; and, realizing that he has been sitting absolutely still for over an hour, he wonders if he himself is even visible or if he's going mad. A red sunset makes the colors of his cell shift from pale-blue to lavender to purple.

SIX

BLUER THAN PALE

After a breakfast of crusty bread, creamy Bavarian butter, apricot jam and strong coffee, Michael walks to the monastery garden steeped in a gray morning light and a vast silence. After the rain, the damp smells of the garden, wet earth and the pine resin permeate the fresh air. After receiving a letter in the morning mail, Michael sits stoically on a stone bench; somewhat tense, almost smiling, he opens a letter from Shelly. As he starts to read, a noisy flock of sparrows sweep up from the ground like pieces of paper and envelopes in a sudden blast of wind.

Brother Dietmar walks over the courtyard, folds his brown robed ballet body onto the bench next to Michael, and asks in a hushed voice, 'Who was that attractive woman I saw you talking with on the road outside the monastery gate?'

Michael's green eyes suddenly widen as he rapidly moistens his lips dried by the constant silence, but before he can utter a reply, Brother Gunther—with puppet-like movements—sits down next to them with a letter. 'Brother Dietmar, I've been thinking, you must know my sister Heidi. She wrote about her dancing at the Munich Ballet Academy. That's where you danced isn't it? Did you know a Heidi Nord?' Brother Gunther asks with more than his words as his piercing azure eyes emphasize his curiosity.

'Heidi's your sister!' says Dietmar, surprised. 'She used to date an ambulance driver whom she brought to tap lessons. He was big and handsome, but really clumsy,' he laughs.

'I—don't know her boyfriends,' Brother Gunther clarifies, with much dignity.

'He used to come to the dance studio in his white ambulance uniform and would dance in them, sometimes dancing into the wall behind him, always dancing as fast as he could. He was always in a hurry as though it was an emergency, and the dance instructor always reprimanded

108

him for leaving tap marks on the wall!' Dietmar says, laughing wholeheartedly.

The laughing comes to an abrupt halt as the bell announces spiritual reading time, the green of Michael's eyes darkens, as it starts to rain; without words and laughter, the quiet becomes disquieting. *The universe must have been silent like this before You created people, God.* The intense stillness seeps inside Michael's head until he opens the door to his cell. With a jump he sees the salesgirl, in a yellow rain coat, sitting on his bed. He quickly slams the door shut behind him before any of the monks can see her, sucking in all the oxygen he can breathe.

Her beautiful skin has been tanned the color of cappuccino by the sunny days since he last saw her, her eyes and hair shine almost as bright as her yellow coat. Without uttering a word she lights a candle, which flickers and skips a beat like Michael's heart, and they look at each other as if each were seeing an apparition; their breathing synchronized; time is measured by their heartbeats.

'I don't believe it,' says Michael, still in shock. 'This is really risky. It's definitely better if I meet you in Ebenhausen, not here. I know you probably wonder why I've not been by the bookstore to see you. That was such a beautiful day—one of the most exciting days of my life—but I've just taken my vows, I've dedicated my life and love to God, and I was very confused after you visited me. I wanted to see you again, but … I was afraid I'd just keep wanting to see you,' Michael stutters fidgeting nervously with the knots of the rope around his waist.

'I liked you from the first time I saw you,' she admits with a warm smile.

'That's crazy! And I thought I was going crazy. Can't you see I'm a monk? We can't have girlfriends! You must leave! Wait a minute … I hear the other monks; you have to wait until it's quiet. Are you sure no one saw you?' he asks in a hushed voice glancing at her pretty legs.

'I don't think so,' she says, smiling in her candor.

'You know, you could get me booted out of this place!

109

Don't you realize that?' he insists, walking to the window then back to the girl, who stands with all the self-confidence in the world, shaking her long blond hair away from her bright blue pupils. She takes off her raincoat, approaches Michael, and gives him a small kiss on his cheek. This simple caress transubstantiates the mere white plastered walls, the heavy oak desk and the olive-green bedspread into white clouds over a grass-green primrose valley. She takes his nervous hand, a captive fish shaking in her grasp, and her touch angles the flesh under his cassock. Confused, Michael sits on his bed twisting his body like a nervous animal to hide his arousal. She kicks off her shoes and folds her slender frame next to his on the bed. *She must really be crazy to enter a monastery to meet me. She must know girls aren't allowed here. Does she just walk in and visit her nun friend?*

Michael's mind reaches, gropes and races from hallway to hallway seeking some light, some understanding; the Order has kept him in darkness, the darkness of the monastery, the darkness of his experiences, and now the darkness surrounding this girl. He senses her gaze trying to reach him as he stretches to his desk and picks up a book as if it were a talisman to protect him from her piercing eyes. She talks but he doesn't listen.

'Why didn't you wait ...' Michael begins to ask, as she leans toward him and takes from his hands a book on the stained glass windows of European cathedrals.

'Gothic architecture is so magnificent. I love the windows in the Chartres Cathedral,' she says, leafing through the pages. 'Have you seen it?' Michael shakes his head from side to side, still dumbfounded.

Placing the book back on the desk, she runs her fingers lightly through Michael's hair and quickly kisses him on the cheek. Completely confused, Michael lets her take his hand and squeeze it while reflections of rain drops on the window dance in her soft eyes as he struggles valiantly to regain the self control he is fast in danger of losing. She kisses him, and Michael takes a small Munchian bite on her soft neck, then traces the contour of her beautiful Roman nose with his finger

110

thinking how much more beautiful it would be to feel the contour of her breasts. She lays her soft face on his shoulder; Michael's eyes move unsteadily. *I don't believe this. This is crazy. Is she after me because I'm a forbidden fruit? God, help me. I don't want to offend You.*

Knowing this girl before the monastery would have been paradise. The unsubstantial life in the cloister is hell. This experience is like a purgatory: Michael's eyes burn. By her taking the initiative he feels less guilty; guilt has kept him away from the bookstore even though he has had the chance to see her everyday after buying bread in the village. He finds this visit really beyond his expectations. Cataloguing his experiences, he recalls that girls had pursued him before, but never to this extreme. The candle light in the window and the passage of time penetrate his awareness only partially; only slightly aware of his physical self, his heartbeat and his perspiration, Michael can still sense the heat on his skin where she kissed him, yet he feels distant to what is happening as if it is occurring at the edge of his consciousness. The girls in Michael's previous life had always been more mysterious initially, before revealing their soul; however, the more he discovers this girl, the more mysterious and eluding to Michael's perceptions she becomes, the more Michael wants to possess her. She seems to like him intensely. What if he loves her too? Can he dare fall in love, take her breath inside him?

Confronted with obstacles and pain, he only knows how to flee as he did, as far away as possible, when he found Laura with a sailor, or Shelly naked under his body. *Why do unbelievable things happen to me?* He remembers his mother admonishing him as a child not to look at the sun as it might burn his eyes, a simple warning to keep children safe. Maybe he shouldn't look at the girl's beautiful smile and legs, maybe he should force her away from his sight, away from his cell, but her radiant eyes make him melt when he looks at her. If Michael doesn't do something quickly, he will smolder with passion; his eyes already burn.

After spending enormous energy, as always when arguing

111

with himself in an attempt to justify his behavior, Michael now wants to forestall her transgression of his life. Sometimes he imagines the worst to help himself accomplish what he needs. *Will I lose God's love if I'm selfish? Am I doing exactly what Laura did? Was she tempted as I, could I betray God the way Laura did me? If I fall prey to my feelings, I have no right to be angry with Laura. Am I using guilt to disguise my anger towards Laura and the monks? Or am I, by loving this girl, loving God like the Tantric Buddhists or Gnostic Christians? Damn, I'm always arguing with myself!*

Still sitting next to him, she slides her arm around him, and his arguments stop. Michael opens the small buttons on the back of her mauve sweater, pulls it quickly over her head, then draws her tight jeans down to her feet. Sitting nearly naked, she hugs her bent knees and peeks with wet, tranced eyes into Michael's until, their mouths joined and her golden hair falling across their faces, she pulls at his robe. Her intoxicating aroma, thicker than the incense in the chapel, breaks against different barriers of his conscience. His comparison of monks with artists triggers in his mind strains of passionate music from *La Bohème* which reverberate in his ears as they consummate the rite of love. Exhausted, they fall asleep. He's oblivious to the bells but awakes when she nudges him. Amazed and ashamed as Adam noticing his nakedness after eating the forbidden fruit, Michael pulls her on top of him.

'Am I crushing you?' she asks serenely.

'You'll flatten me like unleavened bread,' he jokes, feeling as if in someone else's body.

'Only a monk would say something like that, but that's good, then I can bite you,' she whispers, nibbling on his ear.

She continues to tease him and play with his hair until Michael, suddenly realizing what has happened is no secret to God, rolls her off him, stands up and pulls his robe over his naked body. 'Please get dressed in case the abbot should enter.'

The warmth of her presence grows on the side of his

existence like moss growing on a barren rock, but he still feels guilty. Michael walks back to his bed he falls on it, hiding his face deep in the coarse bedspread, half pretending she isn't here in his cell. When he turns over, he sees her smile. Light refracted through his gothic cell window onto the walls is like the light in a Rembrandt painting coming from another mysterious source. He feels as if he's walked into a picture and shut the door behind him.

Her words, like magic, crush his rational thoughts, and his body trembles under the sweaty robe as he feels her hand on the back of his head. Her words almost stop his breath, almost stop his life, and his mind burns with the gravity of the situation. Her hand, stroking his hair, somehow fans a coolness to his burning soul. His vocation threatened, Michael wants to avert as this *Fräulein* maps a new course in his life. His breathing relaxes him, but hers disturbs him as it triumphs over him. She moistens her lips and kisses him, thus threatening his control of the situation, yet only temporarily giving him the extra courage he needs to remain with her. But Michael realizes her cerulean eyes are expecting much of him.

'I want to be with you,' she says naturally, crumbling his confusing thoughts with her words.

Now he can't bring himself to look away from the gestures of this beautiful girl. Yielding to her, he is soon weakened by her kisses and finds his feelings too diffused to take destiny in his own hands. In this time of confusion and the pumping syrup of his masculinity, he stops fumbling after a rational means of escape or the door. They fall onto the bed, their eyelids closed and his back turned to the confusing predicament, as he fumbles to remove her clothes one more time. His flesh is in perpetual torment with pleasure as she removes his robe; as she stretches upon Michael's naked body his contemplation ceases, and his heart starts beating as if it would break through his flesh.

Another bell rings ushering in another world; in five minutes he must be in the chapel for prayers, and already he hears the Brothers file along his cell, bound for the chapel.

Their heavy hustling footsteps, like the running of bulls, stampede upon his heart; he can imagine their bursting through the door, descrying him. Ashamed of having a naked girl in his cell, Michael quickly pulls on his robe; disgusted with himself, he finds his robe threadbare, like the fabric of his life, and the shock of the banging bell resonates in his head.

'I must go to the chapel. Get dressed. Wait till everyone's in the chapel, and then sneak out of here. I'm happy you came but please don't come back! I'll meet you at the bookstore. I must go.' Michael shuts the door and suddenly realizes that his last hurried words were in English. *I hope she understood me.*

Michael is the last to enter the chapel where the monks quietly kneel on the worn wooden kneelers, and rain drizzling outside can be heard until their chant begins. The fervent voices of the men of God rise in the damp, musty air of the rococo chapel like Michael's breath, becoming more intense as he fears that they might perceive the erotic scent still on his body. Michael's eyes dilate: the girl from Ebenhausen walks into the chapel and kneels beside him. He tries to ignore her, but in shock he realizes that the other monks also disregard her. *Don't they find it strange that there's a girl here? They don't even look at her! Don't they see her?! What's happening?* Michael nudges her with his elbow, but she only smiles. Confused, he pushes past her in the pew, and, instead of proceeding to the dining room, he walks back to his cell.

I can't believe this. What's going on? They didn't even react to her. Is it totally accepted that girls walk around this place? What about the chastity vow? The world doesn't make sense any more ... Dad died so young ... my sister has sexual feelings for me ... the abbot drinks ... and now a crazy girl wants me in the monastery. If someone had told me this is reality, I would have laughed. Now I don't know if I should laugh, cry or jump out the window.

Suddenly there is a knock on his door. *Now it's going to happen, the abbot is going to complain about that girl. Oh*

God, help me. Nervously, Michael opens his door, only to find the *Fräulein* instead of the abbot. Michael stretches his head out the doorway to see if anyone else is in the corridor, pulls her quickly into the cell and shuts the door.

'What are you doing?' he asks vehemently, swinging the arms of his robe like flags. 'You could get me kicked out of here! This is all going too quickly, I don't even know your name!'

'Mary,' she answers with utmost simplicity, 'the Virgin Mary.'

'That's funny, but I'm not in the mood for jokes! This is serious, you could really get me booted for this,' declares Michael, exuding anxiety with every word.

'I am serious, Michael. God is showing his love to you in this special way, because you have shown your love by giving up your personal life. God loves you more than you can imagine and so do I,' the honey-hued girl reveals, looking deep into Michael's eyes as if trying to reach his soul.

'You're driving me crazy, Mary, or whatever your name is!' Michael retorts, walking to the window, hoping to find some reality outside his cell. 'Do these monks know you, and that's why they didn't object to your being in the chapel?'

'Michael, you have to believe ... Your disbelief saddens me. Can I wash up and take a nap?' she asks, running her fingers through her blond hair.

'Mary, please leave,' pleads Michael in a weary tone. 'We can talk more about this in Ebenhausen. I'll be there tomorrow.'

'You won't get in trouble. You saw they can't see me,' she reassures him.

Pulling off her sweater and jeans, she stands at Michael's washbasin in her mauve underwear; little drops of water darken the stone floor as they roll down her supple bare arms and shapely legs. With her moist strawberry-blonde hair wrapped in a towel above her Botticelli face, she is a wild flower after a spring Bavarian rain. Michael sits, stunned, as she dries her hair. *God, she is crazier than I am. Why does she say she's the Virgin Mary? I wonder if she could have been a nun here who went totally off her rocker believing to be the Virgin Mary and is receiving therapy here. The atmosphere here resembles that of a mental asylum. Could that be possible? Whoever she is, she sure is a beautiful girl. I feel terrible. I just don't want to think or feel anymore ... it doesn't make any sense!*

The bell heralds the time for manual labor. 'Mary, I must go to work. Wherever you came from, it's best you go back there. I have to work. We can meet tomorrow in Ebenhausen.' *I hope they don't find her here.*

'Can I follow you? I won't bother you,' she pleads.

'I'm sure you are not allowed to go anywhere you want. This is a monastery and there are plenty of rules. I haven't been told that it is okay for girls to run around with us. You must be crazy! You're going to drive me crazy. I must go now. I think it's best you leave.' At the end of his nerves, Michael leaves her, but it isn't long before he hears her footsteps. When he turns around, he sees her running after him.

'I want to be with you,' she insists with loving eyes.

'You're crazy. Please, go,' Michael urges. 'I'll see you tomorrow.'

To seek shelter from the plague of a sudden hail storm, Mary runs behind Michael into a carpenter shop housed in the loft of an old brown brick barn. For Michael the hail evokes images of the plagues sent to punish sinners in the Old Testament. Inside, alone with her and his guilt, he begins to assemble a bookcase, a project he had started the previous month, hoping to chisel away his nauseous feelings.

'Where is the bookcase going to be used?' she asks, feeling the finish on the pale pine.

'In our library—. Now be quiet, I have to finish this today,' he says, beginning to pound nervously with his hammer. Unsteady, his arm can't pound the nails in straight; he can't think straight, nevertheless, he continues to pound pieces together until the bookcase is large enough for the National Library of Congress.

Rising from a pile of rough timber, Mary inspects his

work. 'That's a big bookcase. How are you going to get it out of the shop?'

His imprisoned intellect has lost the sense of measure, and he has been unable to free himself enough to take the necessary measurements of the carpentry shop door. For Michael all the doors to reality are becoming too small: the fresh cut wood scent in the workshop and Mary's presence give him a chiseled sense of being. To escape from his uncarpentered behavior of building a bookcase too large for the door, he yells in an exasperated tone, 'Shit! How'd that happen? Please sit still while I fetch help from the other monks.' Nervous, Michael rushes out of the workshop.

A few minutes later, Michael returns with Brother Gunther and a band of curious monks; Mary moves out of their way as Gunther helps Michael lower the gigantic grained object through the hay loft door with ropes, letting it fall softly onto the thick mud. The other monks help guide it from below, but when it sinks into the mud, Gunther laughs at Michael. Embarrassed and frustrated, Michael can't see the humor in it and notices instead that Gunther doesn't even look at Mary. *The other monks may be celibates and not desire to look at a beautiful girl, but Brother Gunther has traveled around the world and should want to put his eye prints on such a beauty.*

'Michael, don't tell the monks about me. I want only you to be with me,' Mary says, as she wipes the sweat off his face.

Michael scrutinizes Brother Gunther for his reaction to what Mary has said. *God, he didn't even hear what she said. I feel dizzy, I'm going to faint.* Michael runs towards the loft door for fresh air but falls short of the threshold, unconscious. Brother Gunther, taken by surprise by the sudden emergency but quick on his feet, promptly fills with cool water an empty plastic bottle he finds on the work bench then splashes it onto Michael's face, in an attempt to bring him back to consciousness. Slowly Michael opens his eyes and, confused, rises up, quickly regaining some strength, thankful for the brother's help. Brother Gunther then hands the plastic bottle to Brother Dietmar who has just joined them and, placing his arm around the young brother's shoulders, walks with Michael down the old rickety wooden stairs of the barn and along the road to the main house.

'Michael, you really look tired, you need some sleep,' says Gunther, leaving him outside his cell door.

Michael walks into his cell, leaving the door open, afraid of privacy. In the lavatory opposite Michael's cell, Dietmar notices Brother Ronald's sandals in the stall next to his, takes the plastic bottle out of his pocket, squirts the water into the toilet bowl first, then aims it at Brother Ronald's sandaled feet. The brother squeaks, 'It's against the rules to urinate on your neighbor.' He shakes his wet foot and runs from the lavatory to his cell as Dietmar laughs and then cracks his neck.

Awakening in his cell, Michael feels cloister-phobic as he sees Mary sitting next to him on his bed. Every day used to be so similar to the previous one and now everything is different; he closes his eyes for a few seconds to make sure he's not imagining things. When he opens them she is still there. 'Haven't you left yet?' says Michael with pathetic weariness.

'I want to be with you. Don't you want to be with me?' she pleads in a natural tone, pulling his hair away from his forehead.

Feeling her warm, soft hand on his forehead, he relinquishes his defensiveness. 'I don't understand what's going on! The monks don't see you ... they don't even hear you ... I don't understand. It doesn't make any sense. You're driving me crazy. And I don't want to be crazy. Can't you leave me alone?' Michael implores, trying to retain his sanity. She sits up and looks out the window, unperturbed.

He wonders if his eyes could see reality outside where a few monks work in the garden, gathering windfalls of broken branches from the heavy hail. The sun sulks behind rain clouds, and, to the side of the garden, he sees the stone house that in the fourteenth century had given shelter to the knights and their ladies who shared the honor of guarding the monastery. Now there is no one to defend Michael from unbelievable invasions. Unexpected, there is a knock on the door. Teodor, the lumpy infirmary brother who looks like he belongs on a farm inquires very slowly, 'How—are—you—feeling, Brother Michael?'

'I'm tired,' Michael responds as he remains seated on his bed, feeling he must be having a nervous breakdown.

Mary walks in a small circle in the cell; there is a power and vigor to her jeaned hips as she breathes deeply, pushing her mature breasts against her white sweater. She seems impatient for the brother to leave.

'Stay—in—bed—today—, and—you—should—feel—better—tomorrow,' Brother Teodor prescribes solemnly, plowing through his own words.

'Thank you, brother,' replies Michael, moving his mouth like that of a puppet.

As Brother Teodor shuts the door, Michael slowly turns his gaze to Mary, his green eyes hiding deeper in his face. She moves to the bed, pulls Michael into her arms, and the scent of her warm body intoxicates him one more time. Grasping for reality, he embraces her, kisses her almost desperately, digging his nervous fingers into her shoulders and hair, clinging to her as if he were drowning, holding her head against his, as if she might escape his grip.

'Michael, you have lost yourself here in the monastery—and sometimes you reveal the most when you are least like yourself,' says Mary. Michael understands Mary's words: their subconscious take over when they abandon themselves to the waves of their feelings—and their nakedness is complete.

'I am trying not to think anymore. I can't think when I'm with you,' Michael responds as if hypnotized by her blue eyes.

'You are like me—happy for finding the perfect moments—like the rainy afternoon we spent at *Café Hubertus*,' she reminisces with a face full of sunshine.

'I just can't say anything that makes sense. I'm overwhelmed with what's happening,' he says, still looking stunned.

'I love you because you're not afraid of poverty and the drabness of the monastic life. I love you because you're secretly mine,' Mary whispers in his ear as she hugs him.

'There is a fantastic secret between us. I'm beginning to understand—reality exists only between you and me, in our love for God,' Michael says, holding her face in front of his.

'I know you've suffered much in your life. By conquering your pains you created an independence of spirit, a strength that most people will never know. By entering the monastic life, you have found a freedom not known outside these walls.' Mary's eyes reaveal her empathy. Their words, like a revelation of truth, soothe Michael's mind, temporarily at peace.

The next day, a wave of gray organ music from the chapel penetrates Michael's cell. *I've got to get out of this monastery for a few hours and be by myself.* Without saying a word to Mary, who's washing her rivered hair in the sink, Michael shuts the door of his cell and walks to the abbot's room. His voice grown dry from talking with Mary, Michael asks the abbot, 'I need a new pair of sandals. Could Brother Gunther drive me into town?'

With his good eye as glossy as his glass one, the abbot answers gravely, 'Ask Brother Gunther. He also has the money.'

Brother Gunther drives the black Volkswagen to the front of the monastery when Mary suddenly walks through the open entrance. *I can't make a scene here or Brother Gunther will think I'm crazy. Maybe she can explain things in Ebenhausen.* Michael watches Mary climb into the back seat of the car while Brother Gunther sits unperturbed and silent. They drive silently through the wet woods to Ebenhausen and finally reach the cobblestoned town square. The sun, lying on top of the nearby mountains, dries the dampness of the street. Steam from the stones joins with the smoke of the many brick chimneys. Brother Gunther parks the car near the town water pump circled with evergreen trees; on one of the branches Michael sees a butterfly and wonders if Mary is as ephemeral as these beautiful creatures—or if she ever worked at the bookstore.

Once arrived at the cobbler's, Michael agrees with Brother Gunther on a meeting time to return to the monastery. He is pale in his pantomime of the holy life, with his trousers peaking from under his robe, as he and Mary enter the small store. He has always loved clothes and, before entering the monastery, he used to wear the finest fashions Denver could offer anyone who wasn't a cowboy. The leather of the shoe shop fills his lungs like English Leather cologne. The cobbler shop doesn't have much variety and a monk must be content with even less. Mary helps Michael decide on a pair of dark brown strapless sandals. 'You'll look good in these,' she comments, and he feels relieved because he finds it increasingly harder to make even simple decisions.

Michael starts wondering what is going to happen next. *God, maybe You're going to have Mary give me dancing lessons now that I have new shoes.* The sun shines warm, but not in the shade of the evergreens circling the town water pump, as Michael and Mary sit on a wooden bench waiting for Brother Gunther to finish his purchases which now also include fresh bread. Michael was relieved from the duty of buying bread after he started buying Danish pastries for the monks; the abbot thought crusty bread with jam was sweet enough for the monastic life. With that spirit, he knows they would never accept a sweet girl like Mary.

'Do you still have your job at the bookstore?' inquires Michael, in a good mood.

'I was only working there for you, and now we're—,' begins Mary.

'I must be crazy. I'm hearing things,' interrupts Michael, as if talking to himself.

'You're not crazy. You've had many crazy experiences with your family and with Laura, but—trust me—you are not insane,' says Mary in a comforting tone.

I don't believe it, she even knows Laura's name, she's either got telepathic skills or maybe she truly is the Virgin Mary. His eyes gaze straight ahead towards the village market place.

'You're a strong and caring man,' continues Mary. 'Even at the monastery you've met many selfish men, but you're not one of them and that's why God sends me to you, why God gives you this mystical experience. Don't you love me?' purity and beauty exude from her words and countenance.

Michael screws up his half-closed eyes as if suddenly blinded by bright sunlight, and, maybe because truth blinds, he wonders if he is truly mad and she is an hallucination. Maybe if he closes his eyes and opens them again without expecting to see her, she'll be gone. The distortions of reality, besides being disturbing, deeply fascinate and interest the artist inside him, who had always written about confusions of sensitivity. When he opens his eyes she's gone. He only sees the market. *Thank God. How strange. Ever since Shelly slept with me I haven't been sleeping well, it's true that sleep deprivation causes distorted reality. I feel better already even though I'm really tired.* Before, he felt he was becoming breathlessly insubstantial as if he were a figure painted on a canvas, but now his breathing relaxes him. Her breathing had disturbed him, but now he misses her. *God, I'm glad I'm not a full blown schizophrenic. It's better to be lonely than mad.*

'Michael, look at this!' a by-now-familiar voice tickles his ears. Mary's words feel like a fuse burning along his spine—when it reaches his head, his mind will be gone. He turns to look on the other side of the water pump, only to find her brilliant sapphire eyes staring with intense joy into his. She had been playing with a kitten, and suddenly his confusion and shock are overcome by a strange feeling of happiness and peace. He feels weightless, floating, only the weight of his new sandals keep him on the ground. The realization that love and madness only differ in degree makes him suddenly feel heavy, depressed. *I wonder if I'm experiencing a nervous breakdown due to loving someone I can't have? Is my mind playing a trick on me? Other girls' minds have done that. She keeps telling me I'm a good man, really a good man and that I've earned this love, but I don't understand this, unless to love is to feel madness.*

At the mercy of the sound of his pulse, Michael listens for his voice, trying to determine whether he's talking to himself. He soon decides he's definitely not, as she repeats, 'Watch the kitten chase this string!'

Michael keeps wondering if he isn't spinning totally out of control. Looking very pale, he shuts his eyes.

'Michael, wake up!' she shakes him gently.

'I just closed my eyes to help myself think.' He wonders if perhaps he's drifting into waters deep and dangerous. Michael often thinks in images.

'You must stop thinking so much,' she suggests.

'You're just an hallucination or a dream character. I'm crazy. I'm SCHIZO!' cries Michael, exasperated.

'Michael, listen, the symptoms of schizophrenic and mystical states are similar, both break down individuality, but schizophrenia is the disintegration of the personality which, in a mystical state, allows integration with God,' explains Mary. 'Michael, there is much mystery with life, only God knows the real meaning. Your incessant search to fully understand can really kill joy, kill our love.'

He wonders if this is happening to him because he has such a vivid imagination. He had always been told that he has a fantastic power of visualization, perfect for a novelist or painter. Again, images fly into his head, one of a gambler putting everything on her turn of the wheel and another of him standing upon the very edge of a decision like a sleepwalker on a cliff. *Should I go further into the secrecy of our love?* After listening to more of Mary's persuasions he tries with a new self-assurance to be face to face with the sensations that are entirely new to him. 'Mary, what sort of life can we make?'

'A happy one, like our talks, our laughs, our holding hands—and don't you want to sleep with me?'

Michael is confused as Brother Gunther yells from the

123

door of the Volkswagen. Driving slowly through the village, Michael examines the houses and shops with a serene eye, emptying his mind by an act of will of any doubts of her existence, except for one act of checking reality, when he looks for her reflection in the car window. It's there. When they reach the forest, the intense green gives him a resolute peace. They head for the monastery.

After dinner, the abbot tacks on the bulletin board outside the dining room a list of names, cell numbers and work assignments. To prevent the monks from becoming attached to worldly possessions, they change cells every four months, not affording them a chance to become attached to a whitewashed room. The same religious rules apply to manual labor: every four months different work is assigned to them, and this time Michael has the nursery work in the courtyard garden of the monastery. He never saw the bookcase in use and hopes he doesn't ruin the horticulture.

The next day is sunny, unusually warm and, alone in the garden, Michael starts singing to himself songs he loved before entering the monastery. The words he knew so well are now sporadic and spaced so he jumps from one song to the next when the words fail him. Mary strolls into the garden in white cut-off shorts and a burgundy blouse, sits her slender figure down on a portion of the clovered grass that he's already clipped, and pulls a piece of twine for the monastic cat to chase. Michael sees Mary's shadow move seductively over the grass; still in pain, he finds it's better to be in pain with Mary in his life than alone. He has no better explanation than Mary's that she is a gift from God. Seeing how cool she looks, Michael removes his shirt; with manual labor, working clothes instead of their robes are sanctioned. Convinced that no one can hear his singing over the cutting clamor of the lawn mower, he hums a favorite aria of Bach's.

The same evening after dinner the abbot summons Michael into his cell and sternly reprimands him, 'You know it's against the rules to be singing while working. Work is to be done in silence so that we can more easily be conscious of

God's presence.'

'Yes, Father.' *That's ridiculous since I was very conscious of You, God. Music and Mary's presence make me think of You even more.*

'Secondly, Brother Michael, it is wrong to remove your shirt while working. The nuns' kitchen is right off the garden. They saw you and were shocked at your partial nakedness. It gives them impure thoughts, so you must keep your shirt on!'

'*Danke, Vater,*' Michael feels obliged to lower his head in sign of obedience, as resentfulness mounts inside him.

The nuns, who have never heard of the women's lib movement, have the duties of preparing meals, washing dishes and laundry, gathering wood and sticks for the fireplaces in the surrounding forest. Michael finds all this unfair. After leaving the angry abbot, Michael walks the serpentine corridor past the laundry room to pick up his clothes, and it almost excites him to think his muscular chest and arms gave the nuns impure thoughts. Pulling his garments out of his clothes bin, he notices the nuns have sewn legs onto his jock strap. *Damn! Haven't these nuns ever seen an athletic supporter before? They probably thought it was an obscene pair of underwear needing to be modified.*

Still incensed over the abbot's criticism, Michael enters the chapel for the Benediction service, while his thoughts blend into the rococo carpentry of the chapel. He's relieved to be without Mary, whom he left in his cell. Michael wonders if some of the other monks are acting out the psychodrama of a different reality. When the monks open their Gregorian Chant books, they begin to open their mouths as the first sound comes from the organ, but the organ doesn't follow the medieval melody as it screeches oddly in discord. The monks turn around to see Brother Ronald, the organist, visibly irritated. The monk had started playing oblivious to the strip of clear self-adhesive tape running from one end of the keyboard to the other. Michael, confused, turns forward again and looks at the altar where Brother Gunther is assisting the abbot in the religious ceremony; glancing into the sacristy

125

door on the side of the altar, Michael sees Brother Dietmar's shape shake in his brown robe as if trying to hold back a laugh.

After the Benediction, the abbot takes the Blessed Sacrament from the golden monstrance, places the host with the other consecrated bread into the rococo tabernacle and, before shutting the tabernacle door, he whispers 'Goodnight, Jesus.' 'Goodnight, Father Friedrich!' he hears in return, causing him to knock over the ciborium, while hosts spill all over the marble altar. Dietmar quickly shuts the tabernacle door from the sacristy side and disappears into the maze of the monastery, leaving the monk dumbfounded.

It is a drab, windy morning the one that sees Michael meditate outside the monastery walls, in the pine forest where branches whisper in the dry wind, rising and falling over the Bavarian hills. The branches shake in the wind as if fighting with each other, the way Michael does with himself. Coming into a glen he notices the distance dotted with two-storied Bavarian farmhouses. As he approaches them, he sees religious scenes painted on balcony fences over the faded brown timbered entrances. The wind carries the smell of hay before the threatening thunderstorm, and ahead on the small road, sits an old man on a tractor pulling a wagon loaded with metal milk containers. Michael hurries past the buzzing tractor motor as the vehicle stops. A surge of raindrops force Michael off the road, and he takes refuge in the woods until the rain abates. Continuing on his way he wishes for a different route to the lake, as sameness wearies him. Though he needs changes, he never tires of the lake, water always relaxes him, it's his nature to be in water.

From the glen he can see the great gray house of the monastery within its weather-stained outer walls crumbling with dampness in many places, and arcades covered in vines. He realizes that he sees these details because it seems he knows every stone by heart, and the habitual sight of the monastery with its rules and rituals bores him. Here on the rise he glimpses for a moment the ultramarine magnetic mountains on the other side of the valley pulling him away from the monastery. Walking through the well-wooded lands, he finally reaches the lake using his physical sense of direction which proves easier than his spiritual sense.

The wind dispels the clouds and the bright sun shines through the partial cloud cover onto the water. Unstrapping his sandals and pulling his robe to his waist he walks into the water rippling somewhat from the wind. He sees the reflections of the clouds in the water, and he feels that he is standing in the clouds, upside down. His whole world seems upside down; he used to believe Mary's words that he was a good man, but now he feels like a traitor. Has he been a Judas—chosen as a disciple by Christ only to turn his back on him and betray him for selfish reasons? Michael feels God has also chosen him with the gift of vocation, and now he has slept with the Virgin Mary. Was he only being selfish? And even if she weren't real, but only a projection of his subconscious, he still slept with her, and this thought keeps banging in his head as the rain begins to pound on him again. While trudging back to the monastery he recites prayers of contrition, and as he imagines Judas did, he recites reasons for possibly not killing himself.

As is the monks' habit upon entering the monastery, Michael mutters a pious phrase in Latin, like showing a passport when crossing a country's borders. He dashes to the main house, stopping at the dark, dank lavatory on the way to his cell. He attempts to wash his twisting hands in the sink, but the water only trickles out of the tap, while the hand towel falls to the floor, with no clean one in sight to replace it. He can't use the towel, deeming it blasphemous to sacrifice himself to the germs that infect it. He looks at his hands and fears the germs from the lavatory can kill him.

In a sweat, Michael quickly walks to the chapel, making sure his hands don't touch his robe, but the chapel door is closed and he can't open it with his contaminated hands, as this would only spread the bacteria and danger to other places. Running back to his cell, he finds his door shut. As he can't stay still, he quickly walks down the corridor and through the open door leading to the garden, fearing that he is a martyr, a victim called for sacrifice, or that this is his punishment for sleeping with Mary. His arms start to ache as he holds them away from his body, tense with every muscle in a knot. Remembering the shower room where he can wash his hands, he runs back into the building only to find this portal also closed. Breathing heavily, he returns to his cell and manages to kick the door open most of the way with his foot.

Mary sits in his chair, reading. 'Why don't you help me? I'm going crazy!' he pleads with his whole being. 'Mary, you don't give me enough answers. You never say what's going to happen in the future. Am I going to get out of this prison? You must know! You say you're the Virgin Mary. God must have told you. Are you going to age like me or always be a young virgin? You're not even a virgin anymore. We slept together! What is this all supposed to mean? How is it going to end?'

'Michael, you must be patient,' she says, with the determination to quiet him as one tames an animal.

'Shit! I am running out of patience. I can't take it anymore!' shouts back the young monk. But his words fall unheeded into a silence which seems to be eternal.

His heavy breathing begins to turn into an unearthly grunting, his body can't keep still and starts swaying back and forth like the incense burner hanging from the abbot's hand. 'Mary, I can't bear this torture any longer! I'd rather die!' Michael cries, his eyes enlarging as he rapidly moistens his lips to help his overheated body cool.

Now standing, Michael leans over and takes his heavy head into his hands, but immediately jerks them away, realizing he has touched his face with his unwashed hands. His body stiffens and he jerkingly pries the door of his cell open with his foot to run out of the building. At the sound of the bell, the other monks head in the opposite direction toward the chapel instead. With his mind exploding, the prayer signal has neither importance nor reality for Michael. The other monks, racing to the chapel, appear like a flash to his conscious mind. His head is splitting. Michael's sweat glues the coarse sticky robe to his exhausted body. *If this continues I'll sweat blood like Christ. God, help me!* He keeps grunting between his heavy breathing. *God, forgive me for sleeping with Mary.* Passing Brother Hubert, Michael shows no apologies on his face for not going to the chapel as fear, hate, aggression and anxiety explode in his eyes. *Before the germs kill me, I'm going to kill myself. Mary's no help either. I've got to get away from her, away from everything. God, forgive me.* He doesn't notice the sun shining again as he runs through the forest towards the lake.

At the shore, Michael lets all his clothes fall to his feet and runs into the cold water. *This lake gives me peace. God, forgive me.* Michael swims easily, showing he never had to torture his way from the dog paddle to the breast stroke, and despite not being in the good shape he always was before, he swims as if water were second nature to him. His rhythm isn't broken even by the sudden boulders and rocks he needs to circumvent. His figure and the spray of water appear as a blue mist moving over the surface of the lake. Suddenly exhausted, he stops to catch his breath, and in the stillness of the air, looks around and sees Mary drop her clothes and dive into the water. Michael resumes his swimming, heading for the far side of the lake, but before he can reach the deep water off the cove, he can hear her splashes behind him. *Damn it, I can't even die alone.*

'Michael, wait for me!' calls Mary, swimming swiftly towards him.

He dives under the water, racing to the bottom of the lake until, reaching for him, she grabs at his foot. He turns around, looks into her eyes of love, and knows he can't die. He grabs her hand and they surface. Exhausted and gasping for air, they manage to reach the cove, and in the waist-high water, Michael feels washed from the germs and kisses her wet face. Her hair, tangled and darkened by the water, is like seaweed on her pretty face. They wade to the sandy beach surrounded by thick pines and Mary falls straddle-thighed onto a sand dune as if making love to the whole cove. Michael turns her over, and her heavy breathing joins Michael's, like an orgasmic unity. Their eyes meet, and instead of drowning in the lake, he drowns in her blue pools; Michael feels safer kissing her than looking in her eyes, and with his arms around her, he tastes one sweetness in life. After wishing for death, he now realizes nothing frightens him more than the idea of losing her.

Later in the afternoon while the monks have a work period, Michael sits in the courtyard, weeding the rose garden. He picks a white rose, pricking his finger, and gives it to Mary who sits next to him. 'Mary, I only feel safe when we're making love. Then I don't give a damn about the rest of the world, but when we're not—I'm anxious,' admits Michael, like a frightened child.

'Don't worry so much. We're happy together,' Mary asserts, smelling the bouquet of the flower.

Michael talks rapidly and deliriously in a voice not audible to Brother Hubert who sees him sitting idle. Brother Hubert picks up a rake, walks over the lawn towards Michael and drops the rake near him. Startled, Michael stands up, grabs the rusty rake and throws it violently to the other side of the garden where it is stopped by a plum tree.

'Go get the rake, Brother Michael!' orates Brother Hubert thumping his finger on Michael's chest.

'Fuck you!' Michael explodes, pushing the spiritual advisor's hand away.

The movement of Brother Hubert's cassock shows that he is preparing his legs for use, but the brother looks as if he'd encountered the devil and storms off. When he's halfway to the door of the house he turns and says under heavy eyebrows, pointing his finger, 'Go into the house, Brother Michael.'

'Shut up, you fuckin' bastard!' Michael hisses at him.

'I want to talk to you after dinner in my room!' the brother orders, visibly shocked.

'Shove dinner up your ass!' Michael yells, exasperated.

Turning his back on Brother Hubert, he hurries across the courtyard into the citadelled house to his cell. Looking out the

130

window which opens onto the green hillsides, now obscure and unreal, he notices that the wind turns the thick forests into aquamarine waves rising and falling over the nearby hills. Now he is not sure if the angry feelings are his own or perhaps those of someone else. The world has eluded him and even Brother Hubert, who threatens him, is not real to him as his mind searches for some degree of reality inside himself. It is the apostasy of his soul. Michael thinks on the fringes of his mind while his twisted pupils staring at Mary appear moist, longing for peace ...

A storm has amassed over the sky and the now black afternoon suddenly explodes, again thunder discharges and oppressive rain falls. Rain runs on the cell window as though the glass pane could bear all his tears and pains. Angrily, he kicks his desk and yells at Mary sitting on the bed. 'Get out of here, get out of this room and my life! You are just screwing around with me and my mind! Why don't you tell me what's happening?'

She doesn't move and he storms out of his cell, walking down the corridor to the dining room, looking down a long tunnel to an infernal pit. The faces of the monks he passes reveal no secret lights, and the dark hall and shadowed silhouettes move in on him, choking his space for air. The gloomy features of the celibates only exaggerate the silent stifling darkness, and in the corridor, burnt out without a trace of life, Michael fears he has been walking for the last hour down this unfamiliar passage. With his anguish increasing, and feeling unable to continue, Michael turns around and heads for his cell gasping for air as the sounds of the hurrying feet grow louder and the hungry, grimacing faces, now foreign to him grow as they pass him. The moving robes and faces tear open the wounds he received from being pushed down the hallway of his home to the front door by his drunk father, who said he did not intend to support any artists. Now only the ashes are left from the dream his father had burnt out of him.

Back in his cell, he flings open the window and breathes in the fresh air which only adds force to his internal maelstrom. He knows he's at the end of his tether and on the threshold of his own destruction.

'Mary, help me, damn it!' Words shoot out of him as he yells at Mary. Suddenly a panic swells up inside of him, a fear that has no limits. He fears living more than dying, but even more powerful is the anguish of losing awareness of his surroundings, including Mary. He refuses to recognize being on the verge of madness, as it would mean embracing death. Is madness his gate to mystical heights? Running scared inside himself into a tunnel which grows darker and deeper, he becomes oblivious even to the fresh air from the window.

His breathing turns to grunting. His blood races in his veins, which bulge on the sides of his forehead, his heart thumps with a falling feeling. As he breathes jerkingly, he strains his neck, and rivulets of desperation emerge from his deep withdrawn eyes. This disbelieving monk is doubting everything, even the reality of the four walls as the room loses its dimensions. Michael sees his cell without fixed boundaries. Only Mary is real, but he fears even she can't keep him from disappearing in his depths.

In the abbot's cell, Brother Hubert talks about Michael; the shocked abbot drops his book, its pages flopping, appearing like a shot bird falling from the sky. 'Father Superior, I heard Michael speaking to himself in his cell this morning, and then sighs like those of a sick and weary horse came from inside his room,' the spiritual advisor says, as he thumps his finger in the air and continues, 'It doesn't help to reprimand him and give him penance for these things. He's crazy, disrespectful and refuses to understand. Today he passed the limits of decency and threw a rake at me in the garden! He could have killed me! He used disrespectful, filthy language, unfit for a monk ... I think he should be dismissed from his vows and sent away from here as soon as possible!'

'No—, I think it's better if we call Dr Schneider,' the abbot says, fearing that Michael is sick and withdrawing into a deeper, more suffering self.

Suddenly Michael's cell door opens and in comes Brother

Hubert, thinnish and shapeless in his rambling robe. 'Why didn't you come to dinner and to my room afterwards? Do you realize you're breaking the rule of obedience?'

Somewhat stunned, Michael is unaware of this intrusion, being immersed in himself. Suddenly, the monk's presence feels like a whirlwind sweeping around him, then comes the thumping of his finger against Michael's chest, but, in total disregard for defense, Michael sits motionless, his only reaction is the roaring of his breath through his nostrils. A few seconds pass, then suddenly Michael hisses at Brother Hubert like a snake, words begin to gush out on his sour tongue, but he no longer sees where the world with Mary ends and the world of Brother Hubert begins.

'Get out of my cell! Get out! GET OOUUT!' Exhausted from yelling, he collapses into a sort of stupor but still hurts from the pains of mental wounds, the deep gashes in his mind. Brother Hubert and the rest of his cell are only partly crystallized; everything unclear and unreal, he retreats back into himself. Michael doesn't know what steps he will or can allow himself to take. Hardly noticing his spiritual advisor's departure, he sits down on his bed. Before, his soul found peace with meditation, but now contemplation has become the descent of the dark side of a mountain, and Michael becomes lost.

Two hours later and without a knock, Brother Hubert reappears in Michael's cell, accompanied by Dr Schneider, a not-quite-foreign face to Michael. The psychiatrist teaches a course on chastity at the monastery psychologically preparing the novices for their vow. Michael sits with his mouth open, gaping like a polar bear, making jerking motions, turning his head in one direction and then the other. Dr Schneider, recognizing the symptoms of psychological distress, suggests taking Michael to the mental hospital in Haar, outside Munich, to receive professional care. However, unaware of the severity of the young monk's condition, the abbot and Brother Hubert are reluctant to this course of action, fearing this event might damage their reputation, were it to become known. They insist that Dr Schneider conduct his therapy at the monastery and offer to assist him in any way they can. Michael and his anguish must be imprisoned within the monastic walls.

SEVEN

WHO WILL STOP THE RAIN

The following morning, very early, the headlights of Dr Schneider's car swing over the monastery walls as he drives into the valley. The leaves on the trees inside the cloistered garden shine a withered color, a dead silver green as if dying from their isolation. With his body slightly disfigured from a childhood disease, the doctor walks with a limp, making his husky figure lunge forward with each step. The abbot in his well pressed robe and apprehensive face greets the doctor then leads him and Michael through the serpentine passages to the visitors' room. Mary, in a teal-blue skirt and sweater, follows them.

'The doctor will talk with you here' the abbot says looking at Michael with his glass eye, like the eye of a vulture, a pale-blue eye covered with a film.

As the abbot departs into the darkness of the monastery, Michael and Mary follow the psychiatrist into a long and cool room. A small window, framed with flowering plants on both sides of the panes opens on the side opposite the door . Along one wall, a huge bookcase with crowded shelves of old books and manuscripts reveals that the monks deny it nothing while on the opposite side an unlit fireplace opens like a Munchian mouth. Dr Schneider offers Michael a chair; sweating and scared, Michael only finds comfort in his rocking movement—back and forth, back and forth—catatonically. The discoloration on one side of his throat and face slowly disappears but not the terror in his eyes.

Standing next to him, Mary wipes his sweaty hair away from his forehead, whispering, 'Beware of this man.' She sits behind Michael on a bench under the window at one end of the room.

Michael's arms drop listlessly on his sides as he, mute and trembling, stares at the floor. Like a hawk with squinting ink-blue eyes, Dr Schneider circles with his lunging body, cowering in on him, silently narrowing the inches of his flight. Michael grasps the arms of his chair, ready to run away should the doctor pounce on him. A stalked prey, he wants to flee from Dr Schneider and all his predators, but the iron chain of the vows of poverty, chastity and obedience ties him to the cold stones of the monastery. Clipping his lips together he keeps looking unflinchingly at the cobbled floor as if he could find an escape there. Michael despises himself for his own anguish, evident in his thick, dark, unkempt hair and even more in his eyes, glossy, like the ones of the blind. *God, let me die, let me die ...* Dr Schneider asks him about his home in Denver.

'My father died talking to Jack Daniels instead of me because ...' his answer fades into the silence of his mind. In his muteness, Michael concentrates on the psychiatrist's lips and their movements: they open wide apart then come together incessantly again, crushing against each other, only to separate anew. Michael and the doctor, like two frightened animals in the same room, can't understand each other. Michael's mind throbs with confusion. He tenses and concentrates his gaze on Schneider's lips. A sense of terror seizes Michael: with cold perspiration on his forehead, ideas in his mind move on stilts in ebb water, shaking with every step. *I'm afraid my mind is going to crack and I'll never find my way back again.* Water in his eyes surges like a mass of whipping wrathful whitecaps of the sea. The psychiatrist sits forward in his chair. 'Michael, try to relax,' he begins in a soothing voice. 'Let me help you relax as if you're sleeping, but you will still hear my voice, only my voice. Have you ever been in trance before?'

'Michael, listen to my voice, not his,' Mary warns.

'That's all right, you don't have to do anything, your subconscious will do it all for you. Your subconscious knows exactly what to do. I will begin to count, and when you hear the number ten, you will go into a trance, but you will still hear my voice.' Dr Schneider begins to count slowly ... one ... two ... three ... five ... ten.

Michael's breathing rhythm slows down, the muscles in his face begin to relax, and finally his eyelids shut. The doctor's words gently stretch out, tentatively probing, assessing, and helping him proceed deeper into hypnosis to realize the encumbering armor and padding of his conscious mind, which prevent recovery from the overwhelming pain and thoughts of outright destruction. He tries to provide sufficient motivation to ease Michael's resistance to cooperating with him. Michael, believing that hypnosis is yielding control of his mind to Dr Schneider, is frightened by the whole process. Sensing this reluctance, Dr Schneider asks in a calm, steady tone, 'Michael, why did you come to this monastery?'

'I … had to come here,' Michael mumbles.

'You didn't want to come here?' says the therapist.

'Would you like to live here?' returns Michael, slowly emerging from a brief trance state.

'No—I wouldn't,' he pauses. 'But if you don't like it here, why are you here?' the psychiatrist continues to inquire, but this time his logic jars Michael's trance, and he opens his eyes.

Michael remains silent and doesn't answer any more of the doctor's questions for a while. Even without hypnosis, the doctor, intrigued, continues to dig under a tombstone which hides Michael's buried memories, but his doctor's words fall dully upon Michael's mind, filled with meanings he only half-guesses as though they belonged to another world. Michael can't express his incoherent desires mixed with vague longings and fears. He sits, sucking the knuckle of his index finger, listening to the doctor's words and looking at him and then at Mary who sits still by the window. The doctor sees only a blank face, as Michael, leaving blank spaces in his thoughts, sees nothing beyond his own eyes, though sometimes Schneider's hypnotic metaphors resonate in Michael's soul like notes of familiar music.

'Michael, the abbot told me you often play with the monastery cat,' smiles Schneider. 'You like animals then?' *Mary loves that cat and I love watching both play.*

'Michael, do you like animals?' the doctor gently repeats.

'I hate dogs!' blurts out Michael, this time leaving ajar the door to his mind.

The doctor finally gets a foothold in Michael's feelings. Slowly, between pauses, the young monk tells him how a huge black dog bit him when he was a child—the source of his phobia.

'Michael, when you see a dog ... what do you hear?' queries the doctor slowly and determinedly.

'G-Growls,' he whispers hesitatingly.

'Have you ever been to a circus?' says the doctor, scrutinizing Michael's face.

Michael keeps silent.

'Were there dogs in the circus?' pursues the doctor, this time sure of obtaining an answer.

'Th-they jumped through hoops,' stammers Michael, unsure of his words.

'That's right, Michael,' somewhat relieved, the doctor pauses to let the image come to life in Michael's mind. Then he soothingly continues, 'The next time you see a dog, remember that happy, funny circus music instead of the growls, and you will gradually react differently to dogs. They will seem funny to you, not scary.'

The doctor's caring suggestions seem to reach out to Michael to help him ease his pains. Touched for the first time by the therapist, Michael begins to feel his anguish falter.

In his cell Michael crouches next to Mary in a corner of his bed. The orchard trees of the meditation garden cast spooky shadows on his walls, and the pattern created by the window panes on the stone floor is one of crosses on gravestones. Thoughts of his father's death reemerge, only to increase his heavy anguish. 'Mary, I'm suffocating here, I don't feel well,' says Michael. 'I need to take a walk and be alone.'

'I'll wait for you here,' says Mary affectionately. 'Have a good walk.'

Storm clouds crowd outside the main door. Michael grabs one of the communal umbrellas, but barely beyond the front gate hail begins to pound the earth, and he suddenly finds himself holding the bare metal frame and a few shreds of the umbrella. The hail, like a cloud of locusts, has devoured his flimsy shelter which he discards into the bushes. Michael stands shifting his weight from one foot to the other, ready to run in both directions at the same time, but he suddenly steps back as he sees Brother Gunther drive out of the gate. The Volkswagen jerks along the gravel road, while the motor makes a pitiful hacking noise like a dog coughing up a bone. The hail disappears into raindrops which hypnotize Michael, who wanders for an hour along a country road dotted with farmhouses. Muzzled by the artificial serenity of the drugs prescribed to him by the doctor and rehearsing circus music in his mind, Michael looks for a dog.

Back in Michael's cell, Mary bends her long neck gently, as a willow bends to the breeze. She kisses and allures him, as if she were the tree of good and evil offering a tempting fruit. Oblivious to her mood, Michael says, 'Mary, Schneider has so many questions.'

'You're smart not answering all his questions,' Mary responds, sitting on the bed at Michael's side.

'I do the same thing you do. You don't answer my questions either,' he pauses. 'No wonder no one understands anybody!' he exclaims sarcastically.

'Please, don't be mean to me,' Mary pleads, then kisses Michael with her moist lips.

Drowsily stretching out on the bed, Michael, unable to keep his eyes open, falls into a half dream with circus music that plays havoc with their conversation. Struggling to stay alert, he kneels on the bed, but Mary pulls him onto her lap as she leans against the wall. Moving into a more comfortable position and crouching next to him, she wraps her silky, supple arm around him, buries her strawberry blond head against his cheek, rubs her fingers through his thick hair and kisses him repeatedly on the cheek. His thoughts become difficult to synthesize. The effect of her teasing on him is electric. Alternating with his thoughts, pleasure goes in and out of his head, and the swelling inside him reaches an almost unbearable pitch as he yields to her tempting and once again tastes the forbidden fruit.

Brother Ronald's bell in the corridor wakes Michael, and he quickly turns to find Mary's eyes opening gently, like a young bird's, for the first time. Stretching her lithe limbs to the light, she smiles and says, 'Michael, there's a rock Mass in the chapel this morning.'

In disbelief, Michael breaks into a cynic laugh as he geriatrically drags himself out of bed.

'I'm still tired, Michael, so I'll wait for you here. The abbot can't tell if I'm there or not anyway,' Mary continues to joke.

Her humor fails to improve Michael's spirits, and, like a marionette on strings, he walks to the chapel illuminated with candles and filled with the sound of the quick shuffling of feet under cassocks as the monks rush to their pews. Brother Reiner tall and broad shouldered stands next to Michael, chanting in a deep bass voice while his goat-gray eyes reprimand Michael for not singing. In his wrinkled robe Michael quietly kneels with his knotted thoughts and hair, stiff like the fur of stuffed animals. *Every woman in my life has betrayed me. I'll never forgive Mom for throwing my writing in the wastebasket. She told me I was a good writer, but she lied ... I confided so much in Shelly—yet she betrayed me ... Laura was only using me. Mom pushed dad so hard; he had to make lots of money or she'd leave him. He should have let her go, because she killed him. She's happy, she's got his money. I'm not sure I can trust Mary—she avoids my questions and plays with my mind. It was stupid of her trying to humor me this morning. God, You are the only one I can trust, help me.*

Michael sits scrunched on a corner of a chair, elbow propped on the window frame, trying hard to prepare himself for therapy. He's afraid to shut his eyes and allow terrible memories to slide through his mind. He cups his chin in his hand, trying hard to concentrate on the gray stone archway of the monastery. Soon his eyes tire and shut. He sees his mother walking into his bedroom then breaking into a rage against him and his sister—then children—because they lay naked under the covers. He and Shelly were playing grown-ups they had seen on the television. His mother's angry voice still echoes in his ears as he opens his eyes and turns around to see the doctor walk into the room.

The doctor grabs a chair and sits facing Michael. 'Michael, you've mentioned several times these last two months the recurring dream in which you and your sister as children were playing mom and dad when your mother caught you both naked. Does your mother say anything in this dream?' the therapist queries.

'She said it was disgusting and that we could end up in hell for that!' cries Michael, visibly upset by the memories. 'But in the dream she laughs.'

'Do you think sex is disgusting?' asks the doctor.

Michael hears Mary shout from the other corner of the room, 'Don't let him interrogate you!'

Like many times before, Michael sits silent, gazing out the window.

'I know it's painful,' empathizes the doctor. 'But I will help you in this journey through hell.' The psychiatrist waits for a response, but, faced with silence, he retreats to a safer area of dialogue. 'You've also had many dreams about Laura. Do you still love Laura?'

'I love Mary!'

'Who's Mary?' the therapist is quick to ask.

'Don't tell him about me!' warns Mary in a caring tone. 'If you love me you'll keep our relationship to ourselves.' *If I say too much Mary will be angry at me, and if I don't talk enough, Dr Schneider might stop coming.*

'Do you want to tell me who Mary is?' repeats the

doctor. Michael looks at Mary and remains silent. The psychiatrist's face is darkened by his fears about Michael's secrets, and for the rest of the session he tries in vain to gain the young monk's confidence.

After therapy, Michael's back in his cell. The open window lets in a cool summer breeze redolent of countryside fragrances, but Michael seems to feel a winter breeze with his face twisted in exasperation and pain. He looks out the open window past Mary and into the garden, towards the pine trees slightly moved by the breeze. He stares with his anguished expression until Mary breaks the silence. 'Michael, we could get engaged!' she proposes enthusiastically.

'What do you mean, engaged?' Michael asks with a searching look.

'A ring would mean we are committed to each other. You do love me don't you?'

'You're crazy, whoever you are!' retorts Michael, relentlessly.

Ignoring his remark, she continues, 'Since you have the vow of poverty, I'll get the ring, but I want you to pick the one you like.'

'Where are we going to do that? Do I get to come to Heaven and choose one? Maybe St. Peter sells rings!' Michael laughs sarcastically.

'Don't be crazy! There's a jewelry store in Ebenhausen,' continues Mary in a hopeful tone.

Michael swallows, gulping Mary's words in his throat. She kisses him, and before long, Michael's mind gets twisted in her slender arms and legs.

Inside the abbot's cell Michael finds everything colored in gray tones like the abbot's eye. 'Father Friedrich, my tooth is still bothering me. Could I go to Ebenhausen to see Dr Windberg?'

'Yes, but you will have to take the bus, since Brother Gunther will be in Munich on errands,' the abbot says, quickly ushering Michael out of his sanctuary.

In Ebenhausen, the sun paints colors on the old houses and bounces up from the cobblestones to Michael's eyes. The village jewelry store with marble-framed windows, walls paneled in dark wood paneling and bottle-green marble seems out of place in this small village, but it's actually Michael who feels out of place. In his black jacket, Michael's shoulders rise to cover part of his head as he hopes no one will recognize him as a monk. The older saleswoman seems to smile in disbelief as Michael bends over the display of gold rings. 'Can I please see the engagement rings?'

The long sales counter with its gleaming glass surface contains neat rows of meticulously shined rings with cut stones and diamonds, but Michael can't distinguish which of the gems were shaped by nature and which by art. He feels odd scrutinizing the rings and the saleswoman, who probably has never seen a monk looking at engagement rings.

Arm in arm, a young couple enter the jewelry store, and the saleswoman walks to the young lovers. Nervous, Michael whispers to Mary, 'Let's get out of here.'

'Pick a ring first, Michael,' Mary pleads.

'I like that one. Now let's go,' Michael says as he points to a gold ring with a simple carved design.

'Good, I like that one too! Michael, quit staring at that girl,' Mary says, irritated.

On the bus, the corners of Michael's mouth suddenly bunch in a grin. *This is crazy. What if the abbot hears one of his monks is out looking at engagement rings?*

Sitting unconcentrated and gazing around on the bus, Michael fears germs and bacteria on the seats, afraid of contracting diseases that could kill him. Looking at the people, he sees them all as possible carriers of viruses, and his phobic thoughts invade the territory inside the bus, a frame of steel seemingly imprisoning his body, while his mind escapes out the window. *Ebenhausen is beautiful, people walk around and talk, drink coffee in the cafés, have friends. I'm jealous of that guy in the jewelry store. He had a girl he could share with others. No one can see Mary. Even though Mary is more attractive, what good is it if I can't lead a normal life with other people. All we do is make love, talk about novels and art. I miss having friends and fun. The monastery is no damn fun. Dietmar tries to have fun there, but he's only frustrated because we do the same damn things every day. All those rituals. I miss talking with Shelly and going to parties and swimming. Why did Shelly have to ruin our friendship? There are a lot of dead trees out there, probably because of the acid rain. It makes it look like the end of the world and it feels that way. Am I crazy and seeing things? But I'm definitely not imagining Mary. No one could imagine a person as real as she is. She's as real as anyone on this damn bus. There's too much damn pressure on me in the monastery. Maybe l just like feeling sorry for myself and this makes me feel good. God, I'm tired, I feel so numb in my stomach. I hope I don't catch any diseases.*

The numbing buzzing of the bus engine sends Michael and Mary to sleep. After a catnap, they awake and realize that the monastery is only behind the curve in front of them. As Michael and Mary alight the bus, wind moves depressingly around the cloister walls and rain clouds cast dark shadows over the monastery. *God, it rains all the time here.* Mary returns to their cell, while melancholic Michael sits together in silence with the other monks, facing a pot of black coffee, sour dough bread and blue cheese on the lunch table of the community dining room. Michael identifies with the flame of the table candle going berserk with the rhythm of the blowing rain outside. The steaming cup of coffee in his hand fails to give him the whiff of energy he needs for his meeting with Dr Schneider. *I don't have the strength for his questions today. I just want to work on my novel.* Writing gives him comfort from the distortions in his life, according to his belief that writers usually have a curious sense of distorted reality. He remembers how when he lived in Denver he would often take a character from his novel to the café instead of a real person in order not to disturb the world of his novel. He tries to compare that experience with Mary and he knows so well that even though he imagined the character, he didn't actually see her with his eyes, hear her with his ears nor was he able to touch her like a real person. *Mary is definitely real, but it's no good if others can't see her cute chipmunk cheeks. She almost makes me feel more alone than if she weren't in my life.*

When Michael walks into his cell, he finds Mary, in a white woolen dress, sitting at his desk. Her lapis lazuli eyes widen when she sees him enter the room. 'Hi!' she says exuberantly, her face florid like the wild flowers on Michael's desk. Her arms around his neck welcome him like a Hawaiian flower necklace. 'You make me so very happy! Here's the ring. Will you put it on my finger?' chirps Mary.

'It's just like the ring we looked at in Ebenhausen!' exclaims Michael, surprised. He takes the gold ring and slides it on her slender finger.

'Now we're engaged!' she happily announces.

Michael breaks their embrace. 'Where did you get the ring?' he asks in amazement.

'I can't tell you that,' Mary says as she continues to admire the ring on her finger.

'DAMN! Why in the hell can't you tell me something so simple as where you got the ring? I'm tired of all your elusiveness. Can your pretty little head understand that?' yells Michael, frustration filling his eyes and lungs. 'This is all crazy and I can't stand it anymore. I want some answers, like, do I have to be a monk all my life? I've got to go see Schneider, but after my talk with him, I want to know what's going on. You keep complaining about Schneider, so why don't you stay here in the room.' Tears flood Mary's eyes as Michael leaves his cell.

In a dark corner on the other side of the monastery, Michael overhears Brother Hubert speak with Dr Schneider in the doorway of the spiritual advisor's cell. *I hope Brother Bastard isn't trying to change Dr Schneider's attitude towards me. I know Hubert wants to destroy me. He'd be jealous if he knew I was living with the Virgin Mary.* As the doctor enters the spiritual advisor's cell, he looks in the crowded bookcase, where the most recent books are from the Middle Ages.

The aged monk frowns. 'Since Brother Michael is still very unbalanced, it will probably be best to have him transferred to our nursing home.'

'Do you mean the one on Starnberger Lake?' the therapist inquires perturbed.

'That's right, Dr Schneider,' confirms Brother Hubert, unflinchingly, fixing his stone gaze on Schneider.

'But that's a place for old senile monks. You can't put Michael there!' Dr Schneider protests, steadily looking the old monk in the eye.

'Many of the brothers have been complaining about Michael's behavior. He talks to himself in his cell, disturbs the silence and is a general distraction in our liturgies. What's more, our Superior General from Rome will be spending a week here, and the abbot is afraid Michael's presence will reflect negatively on him as director of this house. If Michael does anything too crazy, I'm sure the abbot will have him leave this place for good!' Brother Hubert says as he thumps his finger in the air.

'I think Michael's best interests should be considered here,' recommends the therapist emphatically.

'It's what's best for God, and the abbot represents God's will for us here in our community,' asserts the monk in a paternal voice.

'It's time for me to meet Michael,' announces the Dr Schneider, shaking his head, visibly frustrated by the conversation with Brother Hubert.

'I'll walk with you to the visitors' room on my way to the library,' the aged monk says, shuffling his feet behind the psychiatrist.

The psychiatrist's explanations about the stresses of the monastic life feel like accusations to Michael. *Will it be possible to reenter the world I was born in?* Michael fears he will be locked in his own mind, locked in the psychiatric hospital of his own body. Dr Schneider notices anger and fear in Michael's eyes and aggravates him by stepping on his sandaled foot. Fear of contracting harmful bacteria from

Schneider's shoe spreads in Michael's mind as Schneider grabs him by his robe and drags him from his chair to the floor. Michael wrestles trying to get up from the germ-ridden floor.

Suddenly, Michael remembers Schneider's suggestion about circus music. Now, images of clowns rolling on the floor and somersaulting fill Michael's mind, weakening his phobia. At the rhythm of comical oompah music, like a clown he now rolls on the floor with the therapist in a battle of strength. At first Schneider pins Michael hard on the floor but Michael, keeping the circus scene and soundtrack vivid in his mind, regains his strength and throws Schneider against a table. A lamp comes crashing to the floor. A few seconds later Brother Ronald opens the door to behold Michael positioned on top of his therapist. Soon at the entrance to the visitors' room appear several monks. In shock they look into the room where Michael sits on Dr Schneider, trying to pin his shoulders to the floor. The monks rush in to help Dr Schneider who gets up with a laugh.

The blue sky airs the inside of Michael's abode, where Mary jabs a pencil against an opened book at the desk, and Michael, almost lost in his large robe, stands at the window of his new cell looking over the cloistered wall to the rolling hills.

Mary moves towards the window. 'Michael, don't make demands on me,' she pleads.

He turns around. 'Mary, you confuse me—' his eyes search hers, hoping to find answers. 'Don't you understand that?' he turns again as if to find an answer outside his window.

'Michael, I love you,' she utters simply, opening her arms to him.

Michael turns to receive her embrace. 'Whoever you are, I love you too, but ... I don't understand it all, and that's why I don't want to bind myself to you.' After a few minutes' silence, Michael continues, 'Mary, I think I'm cracking up. Dr Schneider suggested that the pressure may be too much for me here ... If I could leave, would you come with me?'

'Michael, God has allowed me to be with you just because you gave up the world to become a monk. If you leave I can't follow you even though I love you.'

The next day, silence reigns in the Bavarian morning under a cool, pigeon gray sky, washed with rain falling over the immutable landmark of the old monastery. From the chapel come the strains of a Gregorian chant practiced on the organ by Brother Ronald, reminding everyone of the approaching festivity, but there is no celebration in Michael's mind.

Suddenly, the tip-tapping of Dr Schneider's steps echoes from the center courtyard soon followed by the psychiatrist himself in a dark tweed jacket. He walks into the visitors' room, where Michael sits with his eyes turned inward, listening to Mary. Before Dr Schneider shuts the door, Mary walks out of the room. Michael's eyes are focused inwardly, revealing possible hallucinating. The therapist watches Michael drink water from a glass. 'Pretend you are drinking from a glass,' suggests the doctor. But Michael can't. Dr Schneider wants to reach Michael's other world before it turns to total anesthesia. 'Michael, would you like to spend the weekend at my place in Munich?' proposes the doctor.

Michael's dark face shows he's thinking. The wind blows against the window panes; the sounds threaten the little room crowded with rows of manuscripts, between the window and the door, offering no assistance in his decision. 'Will the abbot allow that?' he asks with a mixture of hope and apprehension.

'I'll ask him at dinner. We could leave right afterwards.' affirms Schneider.

Mary lies on the bed, curled up like a snail, her face hidden behind Michael's manuscript. 'While you talked with Dr Schneider, I read part of your novel,' announces Mary with a smile and an intrigued tone. 'There are some passages that are staggeringly moving, particularly the one about your father's death; other parts—for instance the scene with your sister—seem vulgar, almost like dirty photographs. Is it a fear of an illusion about girls that you fight with when writing these crude images?' asks Mary, looking straight into his eyes which find no place to hide.

Michael remains silent, thinking their conversation sounds like two separate echoes from the edge as their two imaginations collide. 'Now *you* don't answer *my* questions!'

'Mary, Schneider asked me to go with him to Munich for the weekend!' he announces in a lighthearted tone, yet aware of a possible conflict with Mary.

She walks to him and takes his hands into hers. 'Don't do that. Don't listen to Schneider—he's trying to trick you,' she warns.

Michael paces up and down the room like a caged animal ready to be released. 'Let my hands go. I want to get out of here for a while. I wish you could come with me—,' he says, fixing his eyes on hers, 'but I know you can't.'

Michael is aware that Mary's watching him from the front door as Dr Schneider puts his suitcase in the trunk of his BMW. But suddenly his thoughts of Mary become disrupted as he sees the doctor placing his bag next to a jumper cable. *There could be battery acid on the cable, and he put my bag next to it. Those acids could contaminate me and destroy me.*

After a long time, as they speed down the highway to Munich, Michael, tense and silent, finally expresses his preoccupation. 'Dr Schneider, you put my bag next to your jumper cable. There could be battery acid on the cable, isn't that dangerous?' His brow is heavy with sweat.

'No, not at all, Michael,' reassures the doctor. 'There probably isn't any acid on the cable, but even if there were, it would be so little that it couldn't hurt anyone.'

This logical explanation satisfies Michael and calms his

fears. *At least Dr Schneider answers my questions. I wonder why Mary won't? I miss her already.*

'Michael, once you told me that you wished God would give you a sign if He wanted you to be a monk or not. You see, if the monastic life is stressful for you ... have you ever thought that ... maybe ...your pains could be a sign from God that this is not the vocation for you.'

The words of Dr Schneider move Michael the way the wind shakes the branches of the pines along the highway. *Maybe Dr Schneider is right. It makes sense anyway. Yes ... I think he's right!* Michael is struck by the lightening of sudden comprehension; his heart stops skipping beats and starts beating regularly. The unexpected relief of a burden that's been lifted off his soul floods his blood vessels, dilating them to the point of bursting with enlightenment and well-being. Leaning back in his seat, his face loses its pallor and slowly regains its olive color. Michael's thoughts race forward as Dr Schneider passes every car ahead of them. *This is a sign!*

A warm feeling of gratitude for Dr Schneider's insight now envelops Michael. 'Thank you, Dr Schneider! Thank you, you're right!' He would have thrown his arms around the doctor, if his driving hadn't already been rather reckless.

He wants to tell Mary about this but feels sad at the same time. *What will happen to us? Does this mean I have to choose between freedom and Mary?* In the late twilight, a bright orange haze outlines the tops of the autumn-colored oak trees between the tall pines. Finally, Munich is in sight. The city glows, and so does Michael, feeling that a new life is beginning. *Maybe Schneider can help me decide between Mary and freedom. I feel free already. I love this!*

The next day, euphoric from being away from the monastery, Michael, dressed in jeans and a sweater, walks in the warm September sun in the *Englischen Garten*, the famous public gardens, with Dr Schneider. They stop at the Chinese tower for cold beers, while a thousand thoughts ricochet through his mind. Shapes crowd toward their table: boys in *Lederhosen*, girls in *dirndls*, businessmen and women in suits, Bohemian women in long skirts. A girl rides her bike past their table, her femininity revealed by her thin white dress, and Mary invades Michael's mind. *God, why do I always have to make these terrible decisions? How can I decide between Mary, so perfect but in a cage, and freedom without her? God, You are teasing me. Is there no way to be happy in this life? You anger me!*

Upon arrival at the monastery Monday noon, instead of heading for the chapel for community prayers, Michael runs immediately to his cell. Wrapped in a long, flowing white dress, Mary runs to hold him. 'I've missed you!' she cries.

'You're more beautiful than ever!' They kiss several minutes without a break. 'I love you, Mary.' Pulling at each other's clothes, they roll naked on the bed; Michael bites the cappuccino mark on Mary's thigh.

Suddenly the door opens. 'Stop that! Get dressed, but not in your robe! You're leaving the monastery immediately!' yells the abbot standing at the door with Brother Hubert. The abbot leaves slamming the door, just as other monks come down the corridor.

Michael quickly pulls on his black trousers and shirt. 'Michael, I don't want you to leave,' says Mary lovingly. But her voice fragments into stuttering sounds, and Michael finds the broken expression on Mary's face mirroring his own anxiety. In his pity for himself and for her, Michael can only hold her body as though it were an anchor. 'I don't want to leave you, but they are forcing me to go. I love you, Mary!'

Her contracting mouth makes mumbling and grunting sounds like a forlorn girl. 'This can't happen this way. I'll never see you again … I love you so much and always will. Michael, take care of yourself!'

Dreadful moments follow. Michael walks out of his cell with flooded eyes. He beholds Mary possibly for the last time and sees her body shake. She returns his gaze with doe eyes, like those of the gentle animal because they share the same helplessness. Dr Schneider, still at the monastery, lifts Michael's unpacked suitcase back into the trunk, ready to drive Michael back to Munich. Michael's heart tears in his chest as the car pulls out of the vined walls of the monastery without Mary.

EIGHT

THE BLUE RIDER

At an outside café in Schwabing, strange Salinger people on the *Leopoldstrasse* pulsate like the alcohol in his head; Michael orders another beer. Picasso leaves, with their bold autumn colors, fall from the linden trees hovering over the tables as Michael sits with his aching limbs outstretched under the fire-leaved trees. He searches in every direction for answers to what happened yesterday but no revelations emerge from the bruised leaves, nor the chipped beer glass, bowl of broken pretzels, cracked little white jar of mustard on his table, not even his bruised mind. Recollections from yesterday of Mary's words, their lovemaking, the abbot's words and shocked composure, and finally his exile, bait and torment Michael like a witness under examination with allegations of his behavior.

With a heavy hand the waiter places a *Weissen* on Michael's table. The former monk stares at the yeasty wheat brew topped with a lemon slice. He takes a few sips and waits for the bubbles to reach his head. His vision blurs as he watches the bartender flail ice, gin and vermouth into a tall glass. The drink clouds with the beating like Michael's mind as the waiter hands the drinks to lovers at the next table. Michael watches the couple as they gaze in each other's eyes, and a mental breeze hits him again. *I wonder, since I'm not at the monastery, if Mary is still there? She knows more than I, and she said she would never see me again. The abbot must have given my room to a new novice. He was probably so shocked that he performed exorcist rites in the cell to drive out the devil. I miss Mary so much. One more beer and then it's time to walk to Schneider's office.*

Michael's green eyes narrow with a throbbing headache as he enters the Jungian Clinic in an old brick building in Schwabing. Two of the walls in Dr Schneider's office are paneled in cherry wood; the other two are wallpapered with depictions of the rugged Alps into which Michael gazes as if they were an escape to the mountains; his eyes reach deep in the valleyed maze of the postered walls and he thinks of Mary in the monastery.

'Michael, how are your new living quarters?' Dr Schneider inquires in a friendly tone. Michael doesn't respond. 'Michael, are you all right?' pursues the therapist in a slightly louder voice.

'*Ja*, sorry … I faded away. You said something about my room?' responds Michael.

'Yes, do you like it?' smiles the doctor.

'Dr Schneider, I'm so thankful to you for arranging the room above the *Gasthaus* and lending me the money,' Michael says, genuinely grateful.

'That's so little! I owe the Benedictines so much. You see, when I was studying for the priesthood with the Order, they financed my education for five years,' Dr Schneider explains in a nostalgic tone.

'You were a Benedictine too!' Michael exclaims, surprised. 'Why did you quit?'

'I left the monastery to have a woman in my life,' the doctor reminisces as he looks out the window.

'I left a woman in the monastery,' Michael reveals, as if words had escaped his mouth. The mere allusion to Mary makes his blood buzz in his head, while Mary's scent drifts into his mind, as do her blonde hair, milky skin, blue eyes, and sense of humor. Without Mary, the other half of him is missing.

The therapist's memories are jolted by Michael's statement and he quickly turns to face him. 'You had a woman in the monastery?!' he echoes in disbelief.

'I had a woman …' Michael begins, but soon stops the flow of words—holding his breath so that truth won't escape—something he often does. To choke the truth about his relationship with Mary he holds his breath until he can't any longer. 'Damn!—you've got to help me! I've got to tell you about Mary.'

With an open mind, Dr Schneider listens to Michael's

pains about being separated from Mary. 'It sounds as if Mary is a truly perfect person,' he comments. 'But—Michael, you realize you can't live with her ... at the monastery ... it's a paradox that tears you apart. There are many wonderful women in Munich. I know, I just got engaged to one a month ago.'

As the therapist works on convincing Michael to accept the realities of the imperfect world, he also focuses on the anger Michael feels towards the abbot, the emblem of all those people that have always stood in Michael's way. Slowly but firmly he begins guiding Michael through an internal journey into himself. 'Close your eyes ... You may want to focus those feelings of anger in one of your arms,' suggests the doctor, 'that will be your 'anger arm'—and as you now squeeze the fist on that side, you can feel those angry and bitter feelings growing stronger, under your complete control.' Dr Schneider pauses. 'Now, release that fist and search for a few moments for another kind of feeling. Think of a situation in which you feel comfortable, confident and at peace ... Begin to feel the strength and peace of that situation ... and begin to focus and concentrate those feelings in your other arm. That will be your 'strength and peace arm' and as you now squeeze your fist tighter and tighter you can experience that feeling of strength and peace growing stronger under your complete control ... Don't go into a trance just yet.'

An hour later, Michael leaves the hypnosis session feeling more in control of his feelings. Dr Schneider sits at his oak desk and writes his therapy notes.

September 28,

Michael revealed his hallucinatory world to me today. He experienced the Virgin Mary and still thinks she's real. I didn't confront his experience. Michael can't be with her outside the monastery; this will make it easier for both of us to eventually work it out. If I can help him through this experience, it can be an enriching one for him in spite of all the pains he feels. He himself will eventually confront this experience of Mary, then we'll be able to go further. He seems very motivated to work things out. His imagination is very conducive for further hypnotherapy.

Michael treks to the nearby Student Center building in need of a cup of caffeine to help ease his headache. The coffee *Automat*, with its complicated German instructions, not only dispenses coffee, cream and sugar, but, in its efficiency the machine withholds the cup and swallows the drink. Michael kicks the macho machine and storms out of the building into a chilly autumn light, streaked with delicate shreds of smoke which rise from the chimneys of the antique buildings surrounding the University of Munich.

Suddenly, blackbirds plunge close to the entrance of the student union building, making swift cobalt-blue shadows on the wall—that same shade of blue—Mary's eyes. Something tells him not to run wild on any subject that pops into his head, especially Mary. Therapy had helped him air out his anger towards the abbot as the Germans air out their quilts on the window sills. The university church bells, like metal mushrooms, ring and spread a sound of pain through the narrow streets. Michael thinks of Shelly and his mother, but he knows he can't go home to them. He remembers a particular instance in his childhood, when on a walk, he had picked for his mother a bouquet of dandelions. He can still remember her face as he handed the flowers to her: after thanking him, thinking he wasn't looking she had thrown them away. Michael's thoughts are broken by child-like sounds as a blackbird screeches diving down to pick something off the street. He looks down himself, wondering if he's lost something.

The room Dr Schneider has found for Michael is situated on the third floor above the *Gasthaus Drei Königen*, tucked in the historic district of Munich. To access his room, Michael has to walk through the restaurant where a few people sit, drinking and chatting. As he climbs the stairway to his room, he pulls a large brass key out of his coat pocket, and out comes also a handful of strange German coins, which he had hardly ever needed while in the monastery. Pushed into a corner of his room an old table still bears the remains of Michael's last meal—bread and sausage in the company of an empty bottle of wine. Michael opens another bottle and pours himself a glass of wine, hoping to extract gaiety and intoxication bottled on the Rhine—but falls asleep instead.

Early the next morning the tip-tapping of the rain against the window wakes Michael who lies under a thick German quilt; reluctant to get up, he ponders his hate for the world that gave him birth as an over-imaginative child, conducive to his artistic self but detrimental to his psyche. He pulls himself out of his warm bed, washes up, gets dressed, then takes the old wooden stairway down to the restaurant on the ground floor. After a breakfast of coffee and *Semmeln* with apricot jam in the *Gasthaus,* he walks into the center of the city hoping the sights and sounds of Munich will soften the pains of loneliness, fear and anger. In the Bavarian capital— the city of stone and red tile—the streets busily reflect the industrious spirit of the Germans, dressed in wool and leather, unlike the double-knit polyester clothes that Denverites wore, which made them all look like airline ticket agents.

Michael meanders to the *Neue Pinakothek,* an art museum where he discovers the Klee exhibit, with forms and colors more exaggerated and striking than any artwork he had seen in Denver. Soon tired by all the images in the museum, he decides to take the streetcar back to the *Gasthaus* where he is to meet Urban, a Swedish medical student from Uppsala, who also rents a room in the same house. Michael walks off the narrow cobbled street into the *Gasthaus*. A handful of people sit at a few tables reminiscing the last *Fasching*, the lively carnival, and Michael imagines himself still costumed as a cloistered monk. Unable to join the others, he settles at a table by a window, snug unto himself as a storm breaks over the narrow street and hailstones the size of cocktail olives clatter and bounce on the glossy ebony pavement. With the onset of hail, the *Gasthaus* rapidly fills with people, emptying the street. Before the rain, the air was humid outside; now the atmosphere is humid with libido in the café, as people sitting together around large wooden tables flirt, lifting their beer steins. Michael remembers his love for social occasions and conversation, now, after living in the monastery, he feels he doesn't know how to converse. His eyes cross in a fury watching everyone laugh while he can't. Dostoevsky's words come to his mind: 'one must almost die before one can experience life.' *I want to talk about this tomorrow with Schneider ... hope Urban arrives soon.*

Urban walks into the *Gasthaus* shaking his wet moppy hair out of his face as he looks around for Michael. Like a wet dog, he walks to Michael's table while still shaking the water off himself.

'Do you want to see a film?' is his greeting.

'*Ja!*' answers Michael, thinking a film will keep his mind off Mary.

'There's a Swedish film in Munich called *Capricious Choices*,' proposes Urban as he sits opposite Michael.

Later, in an old cellar which houses both a cinema and a bar, Michael and Urban order Bavarian beers and sit behind a somber wood partition where they wait for the film to start under the light of old movie cameras used decoratively as lamps. After a Mickey Mouse short, they watch the foreign film about a Swedish scholar in his thirties living a double life with two radically different and fascinating women. The scholar seems to represent the notion that male promiscuity is rooted in a fundamental discontent with the limitations of the opposite sex.

After the film, Michael and Urban head for a small pub around the corner. Their conversation isn't much deeper than the lager in their half-empty steins. 'Well, do you like Swedish girls?' inquires Urban.

'That one tormented girl was a real vampire—she sucked the life out of that guy,' comments Michael. 'It was crazy the way she was devouring him to fill her own emptiness. She ...
'

'He should have stayed with the other girl!' interrupts Urban, 'she was much more sensual, with no dark sides, but even the crazy girl wasn't as crazy as the girls here in Germany! If you ever come to Sweden, you won't meet crazy girls as you do here in Munich.'

'I'll remember that!' promises Michael, bored to death.

'If you don't believe me, we can go to the *Oktoberfest* tomorrow,' Urban suggests, shaking his blond hair out of his eyes and snapping his fingers in a nervous fashion.

'I'd enjoy going to the *Oktoberfest!*' replies Michael, showing some excitement for the first time.

'You know, those are exactly the words my German ex-girlfriend used last year,' reminisces Urban, in the same lethargic tone. 'Every night she went to the *Oktoberfest* and said she really enjoyed it. I knew what she meant afterwards when I got gonorrhea from her!'

Fed up, Michael bids the Swede goodnight, leaving him with the beer and pretzels. Slowly climbing the stairs to the third floor landing, Michael wonders where his life is going. The tasteful paintings hanging in his room—landscapes and portraits of Goethe and Schiller—bring the walls closer together. On one of the white plastered walls a mountain scene reminds Michael of the monastery as he climbs into bed. Mary resurfaces in his thoughts and fills his mind, keeping sleep away.

The next day, Michael wakes with a knot in his stomach. *I miss Mary so much.* Keeping his head still, he scrutinizes his room with a detached look, inspecting its somber character. Suddenly, the memory of a dream from the previous night sneaks into his thoughts. In the dream, he runs off and marries Shelly. He shakes his head to throw the dream out of his mind.

'There is a telephone call for you downstairs!' a woman yells through the door.

Excited, Michael jumps out of bed and hurries downstairs to take the call. His excitement quickly fades as he hears Dr Schneider cancel their therapy session for the same morning. All color leaves Michael's face; his jaw hangs like the telephone receiver. His throat is partially blocked for air as he thanks the woman in the pub for the use of the phone. He drags himself up the stairs to spend the rest of the morning in bed until Urban returns from his anatomy lecture. After their lunch in the *Gasthaus*, Michael and Urban drive to the *Oktoberfest*, an insane asylum where every other person is crazy and arrogant or inebriated. Masses of people swarm into the large meadow in the center of the city where enormous tents, raised by different breweries, satisfy the thirsty visitors. On the other side of the multicolored amusement area is the statue of Bavaria, a female figure standing thirty-five meters tall with a wreath in one hand, a sword in the other and a lion beside her. Oom-pah-pah music blares from every tent, everywhere people laugh, yell, eat and drink. The whole place exudes beer, grilled chicken, fish and sausage.

Hundreds of wooden tables fill the huge *Paulaner* tent, alive with revelers and a brass orchestra blaring from a platform in the middle of the enclosure. The tent's sides, decorated with paintings of Bavarian houses, convey the impression of sitting in a village square. Michael sways in rhythm to the music and after clinking his beer mug with Urban, tries to outdrink the Germans. Everyone seems to sing along with the orchestra: men in *Lederhosen* and women in *dirndls* jump up on the tables and dance to the contagious music. A Bavarian *Mädchen* with tousled dark hair signals Michael to join her and her friend on the table.

After much singing and jumping, she turns to the boys

with a smile, 'My name is Gaby and this is Hanna, would you and your friend like to go to another tent which has a dance floor?' Feeling the alcohol twirling in his head, Michael happily accepts the invitation.

As they step into another tent, Michael notices Gaby's hair which refuses to stay pinned back from her face.

'Your friend reminds me of the main character in the new Swedish film playing in Munich,' Gaby says with an angry profile, looking at Urban.

'I saw that film! You're right!' agrees Michael, with some reservation.

'Hanna and I left the cinema before the film was over. The way women were portrayed really made my blood boil!'

'I think the irony in the characterization was powerful,' Michael says in disagreement. In spite of her argumentive attitude, Michael finds that her talkativeness brings the tongue out of his throat, where it had lain, tied, full of knots.

A man in *Lederhosen* and a loden feathered hat begins to slice what appears to be a chunk of Swiss cheese but is in fact a piece of wax. Slivers of wax fall onto the floor, making it smooth for dancing. As Michael dances a slow song with Gaby, he observes how many men's eyes follow her, but instead of feeling ill at ease, he finds their staring wonderful. The contentment on his face resembles the victory he feels after his short argument with Gaby. Reluctant to open his heart to someone new, Michael still finds that Gaby keeps his mind off Mary.

The next evening, Michael hopes to remember correctly where and when he is supposed to meet Gaby; the previous night at the *Oktoberfest* they agreed on a rendezvous, but Michael was very intoxicated. He finds her standing at the entrance of Città 2000, a massive shopping and amusement center of steel and concrete which contrasts with its historic surroundings. Here in Schwabing, the center for students, artists, and the avant-garde, Michael and Gaby walk along *Leopoldstrasse*, a bohemian street lined with cafés and linden trees separated by grass patches on which local artists display their artwork under spotlights. Michael and Gaby turn into a side street and enter Gaby's *Jugendstil* house. In her kitchen, posters on the wall advertise some old exhibitions—Cézanne and Munch in Munich. He sits at her wormed antique table as she brews coffee for their tired minds. The warm glow of candles on the table and the splash of the street lights refracted through the window emphasize the room's artistic look, and Michael remembers Mary's frequent habit of comparing rooms to paintings.

Clad in a long plum velvet dress, Gaby brings the coffee to the table and sits next to Michael. Without wasting any time, she begins to kiss him with hot lips. *She kisses much more aggressively than Mary—like a snake. I miss Mary's kisses.* Before he can draw away from her passionate kissing, Gaby pulls his hand to her breast. Michael pulls his hand away.

'What's wrong?' she asks in an almost angry tone.

'I just broke up with a girl. I'm not in the mood,' Michael explains, shielding himself with his cup of coffee between them. But he feels uneasy as her disappointment turns into an almost tangible tension.

Dr Schneider's words lead Michael into a trance state almost as fast as Mary's smile did. For an hour twice a week Michael experiences a hypnotic state very easily, aided by his own imaginative power. The therapy is very effective, as the psychiatrist weaves stories together, finds themes that touch Michael's subconscious mind, and leads him to an altered state of awareness with associated distortions of perception. The windows and door to Dr Schneider's office are shut, yet in trance Michael feels a cold wind blow against his face, and his legs feel tired from trudging against the gust—which stops with a new suggestion from the doctor. A wet, cold snow begins to fall on him in the doctor's office. Michael hasn't tried to imagine in any detail what life would be like if Mary didn't exist, he simply tries to hold on to Schneider's idea of going into trance. He knows it isn't time for speculation about Mary, lest his thinking and behavior be paralyzed. Therapy exposes Michael's grief, a 'fisher king' wound, a pain in his stomach, a blackness in his mind, a tunnel he needs to pass through. This tunnel might not be dark the whole way, but could eventually turn into a tunnel of trumpets, a joyful moment of light, understanding and peace.

Suddenly Michael sees an immense flock of birds executing a very rapid, complex dance, expanding, contracting, folding over themselves, changing shape and passing with a whirring of wings close to his head. He ducks and almost falls off his chair, but the doctor is prepared to catch him. The trance state intensifies his experiences and increases his sensory awareness to a degree that he never knew consciously. With time it will become clear to him that Mary was a product of his subconscious mind, but he will still miss the experience of her the way an addict misses his drug-induced fantasies.

Outside Dr Schneider's office a north wind makes the rain ripple across the streets of Schwabing, and as rapidly as his therapeutic trance scenes change in Schneider's office, the sun breaks through the swift clouds, making the wet streets suddenly glitter. Michael walks down a side street past the pub *111 Beers* which he hopes to visit and try all the various brews and finally comes upon the *Englischen Garten*, to a meadow covered with silver grass. He walks slowly toward a line of willows from where he knows he can see the lake scattered with colorful ducks, geese and a distant black swan— he wonders where its partner is. His contemplation is broken by cheerful noises coming from a group of young people running over the grass after a frisbee. His eyes follow the scene, but his thoughts run back to his therapy with Dr Schneider, as he realizes the awakening effect of hypnosis on his sensory perception. After having lived in the anesthetic atmosphere of the monastery, sights and sounds come to him with renewed vigor. Even sounds from a radio strike him as magic, as he approaches the Chinese tower pavilion. However, no new scenes have the power to stop his dark

163

pains. Seeing so many people and social opportunities for him, Michael remembers Schneider's advice to avoid those social interactions that are mere distractions—a means of killing time—because only those interactions that are meaningful and pleasurable become the key to turn loneliness into solitude. He isn't sure what Gaby means to him, but he enjoys her company and decides to turn around and walk back through the park to meet her as planned at a *Gasthaus* nearby.

The *Seerose Gasthaus* is frequented by artists, mainly up-and-coming ones hopeful to eventually reap recognition as did Thomas Mann, who also had a *Stamtisch*—a table permanently reserved for him—at the *Seerose*. Gaby likes the place with its quiet, unassuming, and arty atmosphere. Michael and his *Mädchen* clink their glasses of wine in celebration of their three weeks together. Before bringing the glass to her lips, she pulls her long dark hair away from her face; her hair always seems to hide one side of her face, her dark lizard-green eyes, well-shaped high cheekbones, and sensual full lips. She wears a long, pale-blue cotton dress, pulled as tight as possible at her waist; she probably would be slimmer at the midriff if she didn't drink so much wine. Her opinions are of the extreme left variety, especially on the issue of women's rights; she contends that men are beasts—except Michael of course—and she sometimes sounds like the perfect terrorist. Convinced to be an artist, she finds Michael's artistic bent especially attractive. She is probably a better painter than sculptor, but she prefers forming things with her hands, finding this more sensual than painting.

'Gaby, I finally found a part-time job at the *Volkshochschule* teaching English,' announces Michael, hoping the news will bring a smile on her face. 'The pay is hourly, and holidays aren't paid, but it will be enough to pay for my studies at the University's literature department.'

'A writer doesn't need a university degree,' asserts Gaby, in an serious tone. 'If you quit your studies, you could teach more hours, and with more money we could take trips.'

'And what happens if I don't write the great American novel?' argues back Michael, with ambitious determination. 'I can't keep teaching English at foreign language schools, there's no future in that!'

'Where does Urban get his money?' she inquires in a confrontational manner.

'His family sends it to him!' answers Michael with a tone of exasperation.

'Of course! He is a beast, all men are beasts! Well— you're not,' she pauses. 'Thanks for the drink—but I wish you'd teach more,' she insists, hoping the idea would get into his head.

'My studies help my writing too!' protests Michael.

'Forget writing! Make more money!' she repeats, almost spitting her words at him in exasperation. Briskly turning her back on him, she walks out into the fresh air. Michael sits with the bill.

One afternoon a week later, Michael meanders in the direction of his room in the *Gasthaus* after a purposeless wandering in the old brewery neighborhood. The wind, laden with the smell of hops, blows along *Karlsplatz* to help speed the cars out of the city. Gaby is away to visit her mother for the day in Regensburg, and everyone seems to have somewhere to go except Michael, oppressed by loneliness and anguish the whole afternoon. Urban had left that morning, hitchhiking his way to Unterwesen—a small village in the Bavarian Alps—to spend the weekend with a German lumberjack friend of his.

To soothe his anguish, which burns like acid in his stomach, Michael continues walking aimlessly through the narrow streets where the small shops and coffee houses give him a small sense of security, making his loneliness almost bearable. His head throbs with pain; everything looks dead. Michael thinks of Mary, and it still hurts. After much walking, his legs ache—like his head—and he decides to visit Dr Schneider, even though it is the weekend and they don't have an appointment. *I don't feel so alone when I'm talking with him. He really helps me with my anguish.* Walking by a closed boutique, he looks at his reflection on the shop window but sees a stranger instead. This inconsistent identity drives him crazy.

Lost in the maelstrom of his mind, Michael suddenly finds himself outside Dr Schneider's house. He rings the doorbell, then eagerly climbs up the stairs to the doctor's apartment. Only the scent of the old wooden steps gives him a sense of time. At the door, he's greeted by Dr Schneider's fiancée. At the sight of her, his hope begins to falter, as he senses something odd. She is a slender, pale damsel who could have climbed out of a Dürer painting. Tears running from her eyes make her colorless countenance even more melancholic.

'What happened?' Michael asks, his heart beginning to sink.

'Helmut … a tragedy …' her choked voice manages to utter through the tears. 'An awful car ac—uuhh!' tears and cries storm out of her eyes, as she wails desperately, unable to finish her sentence.

Her words are screeching noises to his ears. 'D-Dr Schneider—d-dead?! No! he can't be dead!' cries Michael in disbelief. The woman withdraws into the apartment, quietly closing the door behind her. Michael, dumbfounded, stands on the landing, facing the stairway which now seems an abyss.

He can't be dead! I don't believe this! But I need him … What will happen to me now? I can't talk with Urban, he wouldn't understand, and I'm unsure about Gaby. But she is the only one I can talk with … I must see if she's home already. Now the wooden steps, mildewed, smell of melancholy as he begins a slow, downward descent into a colder maelstrom.

Reaching Gaby's apartment, Michael lets himself in with a spare key she'd given him. Inherited from her grandparents, Gaby's spacious, renovated loft apartment includes her bedroom, a bright studio with a view of a garden behind the house, a den with an art deco fireplace, and a kitchen-bar-dining area. The plaster designs on the ceilings resemble the ones of the Opera House in Munich, another one of Gaby's ambitious attempts to identify herself with the arts. Walking nervously through the den into her studio, he finds her working on a nude clay sculpture of herself—with a smaller waist. She started this modeling in clay when they first met, but the statue has progressed further than their story of a month.

'Don't bother me now, Michael!' she warns without looking up from her work.

'Gaby ... Dr Schneider ... something terrible ... he's dead!' Michael announces in a barely audible, choked tone.

'How did he die?' she reacts nonchalantly, her eyes fixed on the constant molding of her figurine.

'A-a car accident—'

'I'm sorry ... Speaking of cars, Michael, I think you should buy a car to contribute to our relationship,' she says, starting to work on another sculpture.

Struggling to regain his strength and position in what he feels is the start of an argument, Michael replies, 'Gaby, although I live here most of the time, I still keep my room, but we do split all expenses, including food.'

'Since you're using *my* apartment,' she starts, this time taking her eyes off her pliable work to fix them on him rigidly, 'you could at least buy a car and show me that you contribute to our relationship, which should be fifty-fifty,' she ends, shaking her head to get her hair out of her eyes.

'But Gaby, you know I can't afford a car,' protests Michael—frustration and depression from his recent pain still permeating his voice. 'I'm teaching half-time and trying to study half-time.'

'You could quit studying, teach full-time for a while instead and earn some extra money,' she pursues, keeping her relentless look on Michael. 'Our relationship is the most important thing, and it should be equal.'

'And why should you be able to study full-time, Gaby?' he comes back, irritated.

'If I can study full-time and still contribute to our relationship then I'm doing my part,' she declares self-assuredly and almost strangling her soft clay man with anger flowing into her hands.

'Damn! Can't we talk about this another time? All I can

think about now is Dr Schneider—' replies Michael, attempting to shield his open wound and walking out of the studio in search of a quiet spot to grieve.

The streets of Munich, with its parks, monuments, and architecture, where one epoch follows the next seem to offer him more comfort. Wandering the *Hohenzoller Strasse* towards *Leopoldstrasse*, the center of Schwabing, Michael finds a table at a window on the second floor of a café with a view of the bare linden trees and the sidewalk below. Michael's mind is caught in the web of the café music about heartbroken lovers, and his thoughts run back to stranger but happier times. He misses Mary's soft laugh. Without Dr Schneider, who will help him answer the future's riddles? Looking ahead, his dreams of happiness seem so far behind. He stares into his crystal glass of wine but finds only clouds.

Rather than attending his lecture on contemporary German writers, Michael decides to explore the center of the Bavarian capital, in an attempt to forget Gaby's acid words. Munich offers herself to him, an aristocratic city with wide boulevards and avenues, open airy squares bearing the names of kings and queens; a city of art, music, philosophy and beer, products of the monks who founded this city whose name appropriately means 'monk.' Approaching the city center, Michael beholds the *Frauenkirche* cathedral—with its two steeples reaching into the Bavarian-colored sky—the symbol of Munich and also the icon of his story with Gaby, one of persistent duality, far from the unity he had so much longed for. Michael enters an old beer hall nested in one of the many short alleys surrounding the cathedral on *Marienplatz*. He sits down at a long table. People around him, both young and old, soon draw him into their conversation and, detecting Michael's foreign accent, they buy him a stein of Bavarian brew. After answering unending questions about the American cultural invasion of Europe, he thanks them for the beer and walks out onto the *Marienplatz* which swirls with faces. High from the hops, he enjoys the unusual warm winter air and walks back along the baroque *Ludwigstrasse* to Schwabing. Noises pour out of the pubs into the streets, and a local color tinges the pale cheeks of the former monk.

Outside the university library, four statues of Greek philosophers stand on pedestals at the bottom of a large stairway, ushering visitors into a world of knowledge. He leaves the sun rays behind and enters the massive sandstone building in search of a different kind of light. With some books of Heidegger under his arm, he walks to the Herculean hall, which welcomes him with a smell of books and wisdom. There he sits, opposite a man with thick glasses which magnify his eyes. Reaching the end of a chapter, Michael looks up and notices that another man has replaced the heavy-spectacled figure. Michael, resuming his reading, begins to understand Heidegger's insistence that meaning lies in experience rather than knowledge. Recognizing this truth, Michael ponders that even the experience of God is superior to faith in God because while faith is an attitude, experience is more totally human. Excited about this new acquisition of a truth, a stronger Michael walks back to his room at the *Gasthaus*. The contrast between the silence in the library and the hustle on the street parallels the contrast in his life between the contemplative and the enterprising Michael.

Back at the *Gasthaus*, he decides to stop seeing Gaby. He doesn't need the aggravation her selfishness causes him, besides, as Dr Schneider had said, there are plenty of wonderful women in Munich, though Gaby isn't one of them.

Three days later the phone rings for Michael at the *Gasthaus*.

'Michael, I'm sorry about the other day,' apologizes Gaby in an unexpectedly sweet tone, 'I was in a bad mood and I miss you. Can't you come over?' Gaby sounds convincing, and Michael is surprised and touched by her apology. *Maybe there's a side of Gaby I didn't know.*

Entering Gaby's apartment, Michael is met by the humping beat of jazz music and the sight of her in brown tights practicing jazz-ballet steps in her den. Holding a bottle of champagne he bought on his way here—hoping to celebrate something—he stands watching her gyrations and admiring her rhythmic energy. *What am I doing here? If I had any friends I wouldn't be here, but I don't like being alone. I had enough loneliness at the monastery. She's cute, but everything about her is so pragmatic and functional. She can't appreciate the idea of scrambling some eggs in wine, then talk, just talk without arguing and give of herself and drink champagne together and have it 'romantic.' Her idea of a romantic dinner is quick frozen fish, Minute Rice, and five-minute sex. I hate everything which is so impersonal and calculated. Even the fire in her fireplace is synthetic, she doesn't even burn real logs, but pressed sawdust.*

The music fades away. After the last gyrations, she runs to Michael and playfully bites his neck. If they hadn't already purchased expensive tickets for that evening's performance of *La Traviata*, he wouldn't have come. He wants to see the opera, not Gaby because for her romance is a physical activity and nothing else.

'I'll make some coffee,' are her first, promising words as she cheerfully pirouettes into the kitchen. *Maybe I was wrong. Maybe she can be mellow.*

Followed by Michael, Gaby takes the cups into the den with some mysterious solemnity, almost as if carrying two vessels filled with sacred ambrosia for a special rite. Before the coffee has a chance to cool, she undresses herself with graceful impatience, making a chocolate sundae of clothes topped with her creamy white underwear. Taken by surprise, Michael spills his coffee, and in the confusion, she takes off his clothes. Before he has a chance to protest, she rubs her nakedness against his. Though the sexual experience with Gaby is enjoyable, he misses the closeness, that intertwining of souls he had experienced with Mary despite her elusiveness. Gaby's fleshy concreteness is totally devoid of spirituality. Mary wasn't a sculptor nor did she have Gaby's artistic presumptions, yet she had the soul of an artist. *I wish she had a body like Mary's.* Gaby pulls Michael down to herself to snuff out his indecisiveness. Her hands anchor on his bottom for alignment and pressure, but her restless, impulsive, and demanding technique irritates Michael who grabs her breasts like baseballs. She enjoys the pounding sex but not lying in front of the warm hearth.

At the end of the rite, she rises up. 'I know we fight a lot, but I've never had better sex with anyone else. Your ex-girlfriend must have been quite a woman.'

After their five-minute love session, she pulls him into the kitchen, where they spread on the antique table some bread, cheese and cold cuts. Sitting at the table opposite each other, Michael opens his bottle of champagne. Finding it unnecessarily expensive, Gaby starts to argue about his financial situation. The bubbly elixir soon mellows her spikiness though, and they toast each other before Gaby runs out of the kitchen with hurrying buns and tousled black hair. He sits and compares her personality with Mary's until she returns with her champagne glass which she hands to Michael. 'Try my glass!' bubbles Gaby.

Michael sips from the glass then grimaces from the bitter taste. 'What's that?'

'My pee pee!' laughs Gaby, in a sexy demeanor.

Phobic thoughts urinate into his mind, flooding it. Not appreciating her irony, his mood quickly goes sour like her drink.

The next day Gaby wants to begin painting the den and loft studio in her apartment, but Michael becomes nervous as his phobia of dirt and chemicals invades his mind.

'Michael, before we start painting we must wash the ceiling and walls with this special soap!' directs Gaby.

Standing on the ladder in the den, Michael starts washing the opera house ceiling. Some suds run down the sponge and rubber glove onto his arm. Horrified, he throws the sponge on the newspapered floor, jumps off the ladder then shakes his hands free from the rubber gloves. *If I wash my arm in the kitchen sink, I'll contaminate it, and the same would happen in the bathroom.* Michael paces nervously across the strewn newspapers on the floor, not knowing where to turn, while anguish runs through his tense body.

'Michael, what are you doing?' asks Gaby, visibly irritated by his odd behavior.

Michael has never mentioned his phobia to Gaby nor his

monastic experience. 'I-I got these—chemicals on me,' he frantically answers, hoping to sedate her curiosity.

'Don't be stupid, that wash water isn't dangerous' she tries to reassure him, to no avail. Not knowing how to calm him down, she insists that he keep working instead of walking nervously around the room. Surveying the scene from a ladder on the other side of the room, Gaby complains, 'Michael, I'm doing all the work!'

'Gaby, I can't work!' he cries, keeping his arm stretched away from his body.

'Michael, it has to be equal in our relationship,' she states. 'Okay, I'll wash, then you can do most of the painting.'

'Gaby, I can't paint,' replies Michael trying to hide his phobia of chemicals. 'I know it sounds crazy—I don't feel well.'

'Damn, Michael!' finally shouts Gaby at the end of her tether. 'If you can't help with this painting, then you can fix all the meals and do all the dishes for six weeks!'

'Gaby, you sound so calculating again,' complains Michael while walking in circles.

'Why don't you suggest something yourself?' she yells, shaking from anger on top of the ladder.

'I can't think right now!' he protests as the wet newspapers stick to his feet. Afraid to use his hands, he violently kicks his feet.

'Don't you think it should be fifty-fifty between us?' she insists, relentlessly, this time in a reasoning mode.

'Yes, but doing meals and dishes for six weeks takes much more work than painting this room and the loft,' argues Michael.

'Now who's being calculating? Okay, how long will you cook and do the dishes?' she persists with her righteous tone, waiting for an answer that he can't produce.

The smell of the chemicals mixing with his fears nauseates him, and after washing his hands in the toilet bowl, which he deems safer than the chemicals, he sits alone in the kitchen, identifying with the poster of Munch's *Scream* which stares at him from the wall. He wonders if Gaby can reduce the value of career, material achievement, and intellectual analysis to the detriment of her self-importance. Their interactions are destructive, yet he knows his arguing and secret phobias are difficult for her.

One Saturday morning, after some passion, Michael gets up and partially opens the bedroom balcony doors letting in the blue-gray smoky glow of a December morning. Free from lectures and teaching, Michael enjoys Saturday mornings. He starts a Mozart flute concerto on the stereo, then prepares a pot of tea and some toast which he takes to the bed along with yogurt and homemade marmalade from his landlady at the *Gasthaus*. He wishes Gaby would always be as she is when half asleep or when listening to Mozart. *She must be sexually conditioned to Mozart's music.* Gaby's warm naked body climbs on top of Michael. *It's that music, I know it. Every time she hears it, day or night, even when she doesn't have the time, she wants to make love. I hope I don't wear out before the tape.* Exhausted after another three-minute rampage, Michael's back itches from some toast crumbs scattered on the sheet. Still aglow in his spine, he holds her in his arms and strokes her downy limbs, trying to prolong their lovemaking, but she lacks the patience to linger in pleasure.

After climbing to the third floor of the *Gasthaus*, Michael stops outside his door, places his stiff leather briefcase at his feet—a faithful dog accompanying him—fumbles in his pocket for the key then enters his cold room. He pulls a blanket around himself as he sits at his desk trying to read. His study of a few minutes is interrupted by a brief and nervous knocking, followed by the sudden appearance of Gaby, a most unusual sight at his door.

'Gaby, what's happened?' Michael asks, surprised by her presence and worried, taking her hand into his.

173

'Nothing—it's us. We are through. I can't stand it anymore,' she says sternly, pulling her hand away from his.

'Gaby, sit down,' he says, trying to soothe the sharp edges of her words.

'No, I'm not staying. It's too late for us to talk about it. Can I have my keys back, Michael?' she demands unflinchingly, stretching her hand forward to receive the keys.

'Don't be crazy! Let's talk about it. What about my things?'

'I don't want you in my apartment again. I'll bring them here,' says Gaby resolutely, looking over Michael's shoulder to avoid his gaze.

Hurt and only too aware of the inexorable tone of her voice, he hands Gaby's keys back to her.

'I'll be back with your things,' she promises, her voice like a threat.

Her dark hair hiding one side of her face, Gaby shows Michael only one altogether expressionless eye. She walks out of his room ignoring his stumbling words which thump on the cold floor. With a turbulent intensity, Gaby leaves an empty imprint in his room, and with his inward eye, Michael spends the night trying to see and understand what has happened. In this relationship he had let Gaby peel the layers of his soul down to his heart, like an artichoke, exposing his phobias and leaving him vulnerable. Imagining Gaby as cold as one of her sculptures, Michael experiences some relief from his pains. *Gaby thought she knew everything important, yoga, intestinal cleaning, jazz dance—but she didn't know a damn thing about feelings. She has the heart of an intestinal worm. The only thing I'll miss is her silky skin, better than what any silkworm could produce.* He realizes it's not really Gaby he'll miss, however her unsuspected angry separation from him wakes up his anguish of Mary's absence, which still roars like a nest of wasps in his heart.

With no appetite but in the company of his portable radio, he sits at the kitchen table, his mind a constant wanderer. Gaby's departure still shocks Michael's mind, now flooded with the painful feelings of loneliness he'd known at

174

the monastery. He misses the routines with Mary, walking in the woods, going into Ebenhausen, sitting in the chapel and library, even eating breakfast together, but now these memories trigger only a vomiting pain. It becomes clearer to him that he misses Mary more than Gaby because in spite of her elusiveness Mary was more real to him, a deeper person with more dimensions, both spiritual and physical. He and Mary had meaningful conversations; she was truly an artist, while Gaby only pretended to be one, her character no deeper than her silky skin. *Gaby is a silkworm, a worm.*

Trying to reach for understanding, Michael reaches for a bottle of red wine. After a few sips, he begins to feel that state of grace some poets achieve with wine and monks by fasting and mystical communication. Mary's words echo in his ears: 'touch me, kiss me, lie with me.' When he touched Mary, he felt he was touching another world, entering the portal to another dimension. His eyes squint and his lips bunch together as he still remembers the tangy taste of salt and spices when kissing and tasting Mary's supple skin. Michael recalls one day, when after making love they walked in the monastery courtyard alone until suddenly they heard Dietmar's robe, a little too long for his body, hissing over the cobblestones as he waltzed over the courtyard. Now, as clear as ever, he can hear the sound of her shoes walking over the cobblestones as they attempt to walk away from Dietmar and regain their privacy. The sound of her steps enchanted him then, and they still click in his ears now. He even remembers the ritual of reciting a prayer when putting on his robe and the ritual of removing it with Mary's magic words. As thoughts ricochet between Mary and Gaby, he wonders why he made love to Gaby. Thinking of Gaby and her bitter champagne make him ache in the throat.

Michael had the recklessness of all lovers. His passion blazed with the intuition that the beauty of a girl and the beauty and love of God were related in a way he could only begin to understand. *Doesn't God want his human creations to take pleasure in their flesh? That's the problem of the angels, so much love to give and no arms with which to embrace.*

175

God embraced him with Mary's supple arms. God touched him through Mary and offered understanding through the therapy. As he finally realizes that his subconscious had created Mary and all his present pains, he starts to learn what real love is. Love is giving someone else as much as one gives to oneself; he then realizes that his thoughts about Mary are only selfish, exactly what he hates in Gaby. Like Narcissus, Michael has been eager to catch a glimpse of his soul, but now he isn't sure whether what he hears is the pounding of his heart or the rain on the roof, or even maybe a sound from the radio. From the window he can see how the rain has turned the street below into a slippery undulating black river, and he remembers being caught in the rain with Mary in Ebenhausen; he remembers his happiness and with that memory the rain looks less black and more blue. He smiles remembering more of that day: the sun came out as they walked along a narrow road with even rows of trees on each side arching gothically over the path, resembling the aisle of the monastery chapel. As he remembers the sun shining through the colored leaves like the light shining through the chapel's stained glass windows, he feels closer to God and has a deeper glimpse of mysticism. He used to feel guilty about having had an intimate relationship with the Virgin Mary and even thought about confessing his impurity, but how would a confessor react to this young man describing his impure thoughts about the Virgin Mary? Yes, the Virgin Mary is the Mother of God, but Michael now realizes every mother is the Mother of God. God is not only reflected in a child's eyes, God is in them.

After a week's absence from work, Michael receives a check and a notice that he has been dismissed from his job as an English teacher for an unregistered absence. Receiving no other mail, Michael decides to leave his empty room and moves with a swarm of students under the rainy sky to the *Mensa*, the university dining room which offers cheap meals. Some German students at Michael's table start a conversation about American aggression. Michael is against war, tired of talking about it, and he refuses to defend his country's aggressive mistakes. *I make so many mistakes. I guess I should have called the language school and said that I was sick. That was a good job. Why do things always seem to cave in on me?*

Broke, he finds work in a small medieval-looking restaurant, circumcising chickens—as he imagines it—cutting away part of the chickens' tails. Every morning hundreds of chickens wait for him to give them a massage with salt and paprika, a rough rub he'd rather reserve for Gaby. He thumps the birds carelessly on the spit, their wings flopping as they spin over the grill, a disgusting sight to the boss and the prospective customers. Deemed incompetent in the kitchen, Michael is given a job as waiter instead which he finds much better as his interactions with people keep his mind busy, but he misses his students.

Craving closeness, his thoughts encounter Gaby's eyes glaring at him as he danced deliriously across the strewn newspapers in his mind. *I understand how my uncontrollable behavior disenchanted her.* He feels obsessed to call her—maybe just a need for some form of intimacy—even though all she can offer him is her body. He longs for intimacy in his fantasies, trying to fill the void Mary left by embracing his obsession for contact with Gaby.

Whenever Michael and Gaby had a quarrel, she would always call him after a few days of silence, but this time, not hearing anything—and hoping for a change in her attitude—he decides to surprise Gaby with white carnations, her favorite flowers. Standing in the street, Michael looks up at her lit, curtained window, shifting his weight to his other leg as he muses whether or not to visit her. He feels droopy like the brown scarf hanging around his slender neck. The door is unlocked and the hallway lit, but empty, as he tiptoes down the runway to her heart. At the den door he has to pause again to subdue his heartbeats and nervous stomach as his feet seem to melt into the floor from the heat of his body. Michael sees a light under Gaby's bedroom door. He plans to surprise her with the white carnations and hesitates only for a moment before throwing the door open.

He stands in the doorway facing her bed and writing desk on the far side of the room. The lamp on the desk casts a warm light over the room. Sitting up in her bed, Gaby stares at Michael with her green neon eyes. Her face is a mask, immobile. Around the bed, clothes and undergarments lie scattered on the floor. Her bare breasts seem to blush as a naked body tries to hide behind her—the shape of another girl. Nobody utters a sound. Astonished at the scene before his eyes, Michael drops the flowers, his feet turn around on their own accord, and he slams the door behind him. Outside, he inches, stooped, along the street as if a dagger had found its way deep in his back. Stunned, he walks several blocks towards the university. The round ivory marble fountain in the stoned courtyard bubbles a greeting while Michael enters the pristine university building without a reason, in a vague search of truth and stability. He glances at the imposing marble statues of philosophers that look down on him from their white niches. Only Socrates' words seem to echo in his mind: 'know thyself' ... A most simple and basic among human principles, yet possibly the hardest to satisfy. He sits on the steps for a while, pondering those ancient words of wisdom, then he leaves with a new, liberating thought: moving to Sweden.

The following morning, remembering the many things Urban had told him about the famous old university, Michael buys a one-way train ticket to Uppsala. Everything in Munich reminds him of the things he and Gaby have done together. *I can't imagine what Sweden is like, but Munich stinks with its waxy white sausages and sweaty chubby girls.* Leaving the *Hauptbahnhof* with his train ticket clutched tight in his hand, Michael walks back toward his room to gather his things. The sight of the anonymous faces of people hurrying in the streets fills him with the same emptiness and desperate solitude of the time when he left the monastery.

178

NINE

TUNNEL OF TRUMPETS

A frigid breeze blows through the partially opened window into the therapy room of the mental hospital, but no sound comes with it, because the wind, which howls in other countries, moves silently through Uppsala. The padded peacock-blue fabric walls and matching pillows of the catharsis chamber create an ambiance of calmness, but Michael's mood, like an unknown color, slowly fades away, after an intense upsurge of memories of Munich. After the blizzard of rage and hate that had shaken him when first brought to the mental hospital, a temporary calmness pervades Michael, now sitting in the group lead by a Swedish therapist. Although his mind plays the past and present over and over, he lives in neither. And the silence grows louder.

'Michael, what were you thinking about?' queries the therapist.

'Nothing,' replies Michael with a blank mask on his face.

'Were you fading away from us?'

'No,' he asserts, with the solemnity of a monk.

'Stay with the group here!' instructs the therapist.

Oblivious to their words and gazes, Michael stares at their mouths instead; he used to be obsessed with mouths, but not anymore, he's learned much from his obsessions. Convinced that eyes cannot be trusted because they always change depending on the lighting in the room or the time of day, Michael finds mouths more honest, unable to lie, consistent in revealing any insecurity, trickery or other character dimension. Like words, eyes can be deceiving, but mouths always shape or color a definite feeling. The jeaned therapist turns his attention to Agnete—the woman who had earlier accused Michael of ruining the group.

'Men have only one thing in their heads!' she snarls, spitting her words venomously.

179

Agnete is really a bitch. I hope Shelly has not become as bitter as this girl. Unable to listen to her, Michael's thoughts wander with anticipation to his planned meeting with Teresia a few hours later that day, but his thoughts are soon interrupted as Agnete brings the attention of the group back to Michael.

'I hate guys like you who always talk about their sex lives, especially when you try to make it sound poetic and intellectual,' continues Agnete, her anger increasing with every word. 'You fuck even your fantasies. A fantasy fucker, that's what you are!'

Michael's slender fingers shake and his voice reveals a premature control, like all Swedes who appear to have decided along the way that nothing in the world is worth raising one's voice about. As the woman's threat falls on the floor, ignored, with a slight smile on his face he swallows what would be his angry reply to her. His dark hair falling loosely over his young, smooth forehead, his body sits expressionless like the rest of the group. Michael speaks in a still, confident way, playing with a pencil as if it were a hockey stick he would happily swing across the face of the uptight girl.

'You're a poet yourself, aren't you! I like your alliteration 'fantasy fucker',' retorts Michael, sarcastically. After a long drawn-out silence he smiles, showing his small, even teeth, a smile possessing the sly assurance typical of Scandinavians. With the stare of an eagle, he seems to see not only the girl opposite him in the therapy room, but also Gaby. Michael's moss-green eyes, inexpressive, and without the tiniest crease of experience visible at the corners, hide his angry core until he explodes, 'Get off my back, you bitch!' Slamming the door behind him, he storms out of the therapy room.

Later that day the psychiatric team decides to give Michael the chance to live outside the hospital.

It is nine-thirty in the morning. Michael stares at his new surroundings and it seems to him hardly possible that he

180

could have slept so deeply all night. He covers his face with his hands to shut out the scene of the mental patients sitting around him and Agnete's harassment. Now he has at least one reason for not being depressed: he's been allowed to live in an apartment which belongs to the mental hospital, according to the Swedish de-institutionalization and normalization scheme. *It felt great yelling at Agnete, but I feel sorry for her. She's got worse, she never used to have all those pimples, she looks like she's been awakened with an ice pick.* Michael jumps out of his IKEA pine bed and walks over the wooden floor to the window where he can see the bare boughs of the trees dropping like bars of silver under a blue sky free of clouds. *I'm out of there. I'm out of there, thank you, God!* He looks forward to meeting Teresia and taking a long walk in the Haga Valley, which stretches from her apartment to the depth of the Swedish forest of gnomes.

In spite of her frailty, Teresia finds the strength to walk in the cold, windy valley, where the trees, losing control of their branches in the wind, appear weaker than the old woman. Detecting Teresia's heavy breathing over the sound of the wind, Michael persuades her to stop and take a rest, guessing that her smile hides her suffering. Among unbearable stomach pains, she tells him of her recent visit to the doctor, and how she ended up comforting the doctor more than he did her.

'Teresia, you must look after yourself more,' says Michael in a caring way, as they walk back to her home.

Her apartment is moderately elegant and at the same time cozily decorated with handsome furniture probably as old as she is. Two colorful Persian rugs on a highly polished parquet floor lead his eyes to two tall windows which open on a panoramic view of the frozen forest. She is a cultivated woman who speaks four languages fluently, something unusual for a woman her age. Michael notices the contrast between Teresia's wrinkled and withered face and her slender body which possesses the quickness of youth. She disappears into the kitchen, then returns with a pot of tea and a homemade apple cake. Teresia is talkative and visibly touched by Michael's visit. He tells her about his passion for writing.

'Michael, I'm happy to hear that you have a passion—and such a meaningful one!' smiles Teresia, then she continues, changing her tone to a more intimate one, 'I have a story to tell you—a sad one.' She stops to pour their teas. 'You see, Hans, Brigitte's brother, wanted to be a poet all his life,' she begins, in her calm tone. 'He had saved his money and rented a small studio in Stockholm. One day, someone he knew published his verses—his work of many years—under his own name,' she pauses and takes a sip of her tea.

'That's awful! How could anyone ...' begins Michael.

'There are such people, Michael. Hans was a young man like you, sensitive, creative, with that desire—typical of the artist—to sink his teeth into life. He tried to seek justice, but not even the law had been able to shelter him from what turned out to be a real blow to his faith in humankind. Seeing his most intimate thoughts in a stranger's hands, printed under his name was too much for his sensitive mind. He attempted suicide and was placed in the mental hospital you know. But even there he managed again to jump out a window, like Brigitte, and consequently he was placed in a locked ward. His suicide materialized with his shutting himself inside his mind, refusing to communicate with the world that had rejected him through injustice.' *I wonder what miracle saved me from that living death in the mental hospital. The suffering of Teresia's grandchildren really batters my mind.*

'That's terrible, Teresia. But where's Hans now?'

'Still inside himself, in that locked ward you'll never see. Brigitte doesn't know. She's too absorbed in herself to even wonder where her brother is!' In spite of her sadness and weariness, the old woman continues, 'For Hans, writing was not an art, but breathing, living—'

'There are no words for such pain' interrupts Michael. 'Did he keep writing?'

'Yes, but he shared his writing with no one. He doesn't know I have some of it. Reading his poetry is my way of reaching out to him to share his pains, his madness. I'd rather be mad so he could be sane,' says Teresia.

'Don't you think it would be better if he could find peace without your losing your sanity?'

'Michael, I'm an old woman. I have lived a full life. I am now willing to accept the disintegration of death, which at this stage of my life I see as a profound peace, more profound then the joy of living and creating.'

In a contemplative mood, Michael lights some red candles on her coffee table. 'Could I read some of Hans's poetry?' he asks in a hopeful tone.

'Of course. Some of his work is being published again—this time the right way—but Hans doesn't understand this although I told him. He's in another world.'

Michael is suddenly in another world as Teresia's cake in front of him reminds him of an apple cake he had bought for Gaby once and which she had clumsily dropped on her kitchen floor without saying so much as a 'sorry' or 'thank you for the gift.' Michael talks about his broken relationship with Gaby and the crumbled cake he gave her.

Teresia slides closer to the table scattered with books, tea cups and cake crumbs. 'Michael, in spite of the pain it caused you, the crisis you had with Gaby was good for you,' she smiles. 'You cut that destructive bond. You survived!'

The next day, Michael hangs some of his artwork he had produced at the hospital in his apartment located in the old part of the town, not far from Urban's. Although it's cold outside, he opens a window in the small living room to let in the sounds of reality, voices of all types, the buzz of engines and every once in a while the barking of a dog somewhere. Feeling all his senses waking up, Michael turns on the stereo, puts on a pot of coffee and looks at himself in the mirror after shaving, he feels like an artist. A burst of sunlight brightens his small, fir furnished apartment which still smells of pine. Suddenly, Vivaldi's Spring blossoms out of the radio filling his room with the radiance of rebirth. In a fresh burst of energy, Michael resumes his writing of the story about the monastery and Mary. After reading the manuscript he'd produced at the mental hospital, Teresia, intrigued and touched by his story, had inspired him to continue writing. As

Michael describes his relationship with Mary, he is drawn through it one more time, but now those obstacles have turned into stepping stones; the disappointments that used to crush him now seem to have made him a stronger person. Just as one can't write the blues in an air-conditioned room, his pains have enhanced his creativity and expressiveness.

That afternoon Michael briskly walks to the language school located by the river, where he learns Swedish in the Berlitz dialect. After hours of tiring mouth gyrations, Michael and the other foreign students in his class move to the smoky student lounge for a break. Mohammed, a young Arab with the eyes of a Moroccan burro, kills his cigarette on the birch table.

'In this country one has to go to the movies to see the sun!' complains the angry Arab. 'But one good thing about Sweden is that it's a neutral country, none of that aggressive American colonization of the world you see even in Morocco!' continues Mohammed, staring at Michael.

Michael, who disapproves of his country's foreign policy, races through his thoughts for something funny to say. His sweat increased by the steam of hot coffee and cardamom rolls, Michael's face gleams as he retorts sarcastically, 'Why don't we try to guess which of us is a CIA agent?' he proposes cheerfully.

Quickly enthused by the idea of a game, everyone drops in an empty jar a slip of paper carrying the name of the person they think is a CIA agent. The students plan to have a party at the end of the course and give a badge to the person most often named. Everyone laughs in order not to be the suspect except Mohammed, who relentlessly bombards Michael with questions about American imperialism. Though he is against all aggressive politics, wars do not make much difference to Michael, who has always been at war with himself. Slowly, the cafeteria room empties and his mind with it.

Michael catches a bus on the snow-lit street in the late afternoon. The city lights, electric smears of white, are pale against the snow. In the bus there is a cliché of warmth as the

Swedish passengers, wrapped in their warm leather coats, hold their arms crossed on their chests as if to insulate themselves from the possibility of verbal weather, shielding themselves from their co-passengers. But the insulation goes far beyond the double windows and graffitied upholstery as Michael tries to converse with a bearded sociology student next to him, only to find that his sociology ends with the covers of the books on his lap. As the bus stops in front of Teresia's house, the door opens, and the wind fills the bus with even more silence. Michael leaves the vehicle and the invisible treatment of his co-passenger who ignores his departure. Outside, Michael shakes his head as if shaking the silence of the bus out of his hair.

Michael rings Teresia's bell, but no one answers it. He opens the door with the key she had given him. *She is probably shopping at the grocery store nearby. I'll just wait for her inside.* Hanging his sheepskin coat in the stale hallway, his gaze runs along the parquet floor in the direction of her bedroom. There he finds her on the bed where she often reads in a relaxed position due to her high blood pressure. A foreboding of something tragic grabs him. Approaching the bed he sees part of his manuscript beside her, and the bedside lamp shines warm over her restful face.

'Teresia, Teresia!' he cries, but the peaceful figure lies unstirred.

He touches her hand, but its stiffness shocks him. Then he realizes it's too late. *No, God, don't take her too!* He desperately tries to shake life back into her, refusing to believe she's dead. Reverently peeling her eyelids back he hopes to find her there—but it's too late. Their almost daily conversations, walks, and coffees together now flash in sequence before Michael's eyes. As he holds her, he realizes how much she had touched his soul, understanding his pains and joys. Despite their short-lived friendship, Teresia and Michael had touched each other's lives. She had given him the gift of her warmth and strength, while he had impressed her with his unshakable faith in God, in spite of the thorns in his life.

The ambulance he calls arrives almost immediately. He walks outside, under a sky suddenly narrow in an atmosphere too heavy for him. Teresia had made every day special for him with her contagious love for life, wisdom and caring words; she always kept Michael from dreaming too much, and her sheltering friendship had been his final refuge which had made him calmer and more rational. His eyes blurry from wet snow and tears, beaten by yet another blow to his battered soul which was starting to heal, Michael walks towards his home fearing that he might again disappear into the black hole of his mind. Thinking of Teresia lying on her bed, he remembers noticing that the lines on her face had faded away; those same lines which told of the experiences in her life from which she hadn't run away.

The day after the funeral Michael wants to disappear, and with one small suitcase he takes the bus to the Arlanda Airport, hoping to buy a cheap ticket to anywhere in the world. *It doesn't matter where I end up, just as long as nine hundred and fifty crowns are enough. The farther, the better.* Disappointedly, Michael wanders for three hours between the check-in counters of the large blue and yellow hall and the sterile cafeteria where he drinks cup after cup of black coffee. Inside the building, visitors are given an even more dismal view of Sweden than the country merits, as the traveling Scandinavians appear to share his grief with their somber and silent countenance. *They all look like suicidal candidates.* Yet he remembers a doctor at the hospital once stating that contrary to popular belief, Sweden doesn't have the highest suicide rate in the world and that Swedes who attempt suicide are more talkative than the average Swede—just the opposite profile of depressed people in the rest of the world! *Being talkative in Sweden wouldn't be culturally acceptable.* Finally, he gets a canceled two week ticket to Marrakech, Morocco.

Leaving the cold darkness in Sweden, after a three-hour flight Michael lands in Agadir, where he can't smile at the sun but instead breathes in deeply the new, warm air and the scent of mandarins as he walks down the platform steps of the plane. *A brand new place!* Leaving the beach behind in Agadir, Michael's restless procession continues farther with an air-conditioned bus which takes him into the desert to Marrakech. After traveling for miles through arid lands, the bus reaches a mountain pass where hungry goats climb up trees to eat dry, stringy leaves. Leaving behind the Atlas mountain range, the bus creeps into Marrakech, where it is suddenly surrounded by groups of colorful robed people. With their carts and donkeys, Arabs travel as fast as the super-modern bus coach inching through the crowds. Looking around, Michael's face is rejuvenated with impressions of another world. Tall minarets stand, etched on the cerulean dust-powdered sky, while everything in sight has been sun-baked.

When the bus reaches the entrance of the Salem Hotel, lined with pushcarts selling strange orange sausages and *couscous,* the sunlight begins to decline over the mountains. As Michael gets off the bus, he is swarmed by brown-faced boys who in broken English offer themselves as guides around Marrakech. They insist they know where to find bargains, but Michael pushes his way to the main door of the hotel—not in the mood for shopping, he just wants his room and bed. He collects his key at the desk in the Arabian lobby and takes his bag to his room. Once there, though, the scene from the window entices him to explore his surroundings. Walking through the narrow dirt streets, he doesn't allow himself to be hypnotized by all the people trying to sell him everything from a camel blanket to hashish.

Michael orders mint tea at an outside café under trees burnt by the sun to the color of coffee and watches people fill every inch of the marketplace. He sits at a wobbly wooden table next to an old man with a patriarchal beard and weather-beaten eyes over a straight Berber nose. The ascetic-looking man slurps his soup from a large clay bowl as he stares at Michael, and a one-legged beggar on crutches approaches Michael's table, but the waiter chases him away. The *garçon* disappears, leaving Michael to himself for a few seconds, and, with the quickness of a mosquito, a young boy with a clean-shaven head approaches him. In a handful of English words the boy offers his sister for the night in exchange for a small sum. The prophet, standing up from the next table, grunts a few words to the boy, who runs off into the crowd. Another pair of eyes from the other side of the small café direct themselves toward Michael. They belong to a terracotta-faced young man sitting and staring absolutely still like an Egyptian statue. Leaving his unfinished herb tea, Michael rises, almost knocking over the rickety table, and walks toward his hotel.

In his room he throws himself on the bed and immediately falls asleep, only to be awakened some time later by the strange waving voice of the *muezzin* calling the faithful to prayer in the mosque. After much struggling to fall asleep, he wanders again into the unconscious.

As he wakes the next morning, he's welcomed by the view of sunny colors from his room on the fifth floor overlooking the yellow stucco houses which stretch up to the mountains. With his habitual ablutions he prepares his body for the day, then, full of vigor, he walks into the dining room for breakfast. *It's almost nine-thirty, I hope I'm not too late.* In the restaurant, most of the guests have eaten and have already secured their places by the swimming pool as he can see through the large windows.

The head waiter leads Michael to a table where an alluring sandy-haired woman with cantaloupe-colored complexion sits alone surrounded by Moroccan decor. She greets him in a friendly way and starts describing all she has seen that week in Marrakech. The woman begins to enter his life in more ways than he suspects. He enters her life at a distance, describing himself as an American who has been living in Sweden, leaving out the monastery and hoping his experience at the mental hospital won't show. Caught up in each other's conversation, they don't notice that the waiter is ready to leave and finally approaches their table announcing that the dining room is closing.

'By the way, what's your name?' Michael casually asks his breakfast companion.

'Sandra Andrews, and yours?' she says with a sunny smile.

'Michael—yesterday on the bus I read a brochure describing the Marek Palace. Do you know where it is?' he inquires with puppy eyes.

'Yes, it's steeped in beautiful Islamic art. I'd like to see it again. I can show you,' she replies enthusiastically.

Outside in the sunlight, Sandra's eyes as blue as the Sahara sky twinkle with a wonder and childlike liveliness uncommon in a woman who's obviously past her 20's. The radiance of that ultramarine blue possesses both a physical and mystical quality that sanctions Michael's heart to swell as she smiles with such candor, so lightly and effortlessly. Her easy, sociable American way made him feel at ease immediately, something he had forgot the feeling of.

He runs his finger on the café-au-lait colored skin of her arm. 'How did you get this tan with all the sightseeing you've been doing?'

'I don't need to bask in the sun for long, I tan easily,' she smiles warmly.

Michael keeps thinking that he burns easily as his hand still feels hot after touching her. He is intensely taken aback by her bewitching beauty and is struck by his eruptive emotions as they walk the narrow brick path between the houses. Michael wants to grab Sandra's hand, then, realizing how the flaring of feelings have always disarranged his life, he tries to remain calm, but finds it difficult. Her smile is like fireworks of light, and he guesses Sandra's eyes don't disguise the truth that she likes him as they continue the road up the hill which takes them to the citadel of Marek.

In the lavishly decorated palace, they proceed through the sensuous harem quarters and enter the sultan's favorite wife's bedroom, an exquisite example of elaborate Islamic art—turquoise and bottle-green tiles and colorful mosaics offer a feast to the visitors' eyes. Sandra shows Michael her favorite painting in the collection, describing it with the knowledge of an art critic. After admiring almost as many bedrooms as paintings in the collections of the sultan, Michael and Sandra walk into the palace garden. Memories of the monastery garden rush to Michael's mind, but the scent and appearance of the Moroccan foliage reach his senses and alter the image in his mind.

'Michael, what are you doing here in Morocco?' Sandra asks gently, with a slight hesitation in her voice.

'A very good friend of mine in Sweden died—and I had to get away. Why are you here alone?' returns Michael, reciprocating her interest with a bit more curiosity.

'I also had to get away. I've just concluded a long, exhausting divorce. My husband, that is ex-husband ran off with one of his students at the University of Hawaii. She was probably about your age. How old are you?'

'Twenty-three,' Michael answers, embarrassed of his young age.

'Well, I'm closer to 35. When I was twenty-three I already had my second child. That's what made the divorce proceedings so difficult. He had Hawaii's best lawyer, and he almost got my kids. Thank God, one can't buy everything with money,' Sandra remarks, looking around at all the precious artwork of the princely palace.

'Where are your kids now?' asks Michael to regain her attention.

'With my parents at our old wooden house on the beach near Honolulu. We had two houses. Jack kept our home in the city near the University, and we got the summer house. But in Hawaii it's always summer, so it's a great place. And the house has class. It was built way before they started building so many modern places around us.'

'I want to hear more, how about talking over lunch?' suggests Michael, while his stomach contracts with hunger.

On their way to a café their attention is caught by Arabic music, exotic to their western ears and carried by a hot breeze. On a small sun-filled square nearby, a group of local street performers in colorful robes and leather sandals play steel-stringed guitar-like instruments while others dance. The cinnamon colored dancers move sensuously as if inebriated by the rhythm of the music.

While watching the performance, Michael and Sandra exchange frequent glances as their own thoughts dance in their minds until Sandra says, 'Michael, this music reminds me of a special Moroccan show tonight at the Casino Club.'

It sounds like fun, it seems that anything would be fun with her. That place must be expensive, but I can't give her the impression I can't afford it. Taking her eyes off the players, Sandra notices the hesitance in Michael's eyes and guesses his feelings. 'By the way, the treat's on me. My husband pays a very expensive alimony, you know, so I am, or I should say, he is treating.'

While they eat *couscous* in traditional clay dishes before the show at the Casino Club, Sandra begins to talk about Islamic religion and compare Islamic prayer with western meditation. Contemplation for Michael has now become the ascent of the sunny side of the mountain, and in an inspired tone he describes to Sandra his experience at the monastery near Ebenhausen, carefully omitting any reference to Mary. 'Sandra, it was especially beautiful in the winter when snow flakes fell in solemn silence on the monastery, veiling it in a mystical light. I think you would have loved it.'

'I'd never met a would-be monk before,' Sandra replies, deepening her stare. 'It sounds fascinating—but why did you leave that peaceful existence?' she asks, intrigued.

'I had to. It was too peaceful and I realized I wanted to be a writer,' explains Michael. As he begins to describe that holy place, he listens to his own words which sound as if they came from a different source. Rather than a melancholic ancient dwelling, the monastery comes to life as a castle in Michael's description. Mary had made him feel like a prince.

'Michael, one year I skied at Aspen, and we went to a church in the mountains which had a similar atmosphere. As we drove into the valley we could hear a choir singing: and it felt magic. The Gregorian chant must have been truly enchanting.'

'It was—but the monks' voices were like the chant of caged birds,' says Michael, his voice pitch dropping.

'That sounds sad, as if incarcerated,' remarks Sandra, with

a compassionate look in her eyes.

'Some of the monks did look like prisoners,' explains Michael. 'Others had bland, haughty faces wearing sanctimonious expressions—as if they had been holding some superior secret—and looked down on the world.' Sandra's idyllic image of the monastery seems to change before her eyes, as Michael reveals the less enchanting aspects of cloistered life. 'But there were some interesting monks too,' continues Michael. 'One of them, Brother Dietmar, had been a ballet dancer and was funny, but he finally left. The monastery was like a beehive. In the monastery garden, the bees and the monks all knew what they were supposed to do, except Dietmar.' Michael's curious details of a different world keep him safely on the surface of his monastic experience. Unable to speak openly and spontaneously about the monastery, he's conscious of a certain inflexibility in his speech which makes it sound like recitations of a rosary.

Suddenly loud African drums signal the beginning of the show. The room seems to shrink, as Michael is conscious only of his and Sandra's presence. The semi-naked muscular black drummers and the virile beat of their drums stir Michael's primordial spiritual energy, yet inside him shadows of memories and sensations of Mary, like dark creatures from the jungle, prowl and attack him. He fends off his feelings and thinks of Sandra. Fighting the idea that she is much older than himself, he moves his gaze from the black drummers on to her, smiling as he takes her hand. The fingers of her smooth, pretty hand squeeze his hand and then lightly play with his fingers, before moving her hold to his strong forearm. Looking at her legs, he notices they have a shiny tanned sheen, as if varnished. Afraid she might notice his staring, he directs his eyes to the exotic belly dancers.

The show comes to an end, and they attempt to leave the dark club through what appears to be an opening between curtains, only to find a wall of stone and mortar behind them. Surprised, they break into a laughter and a waiter appears from behind them to show them the curtains which hide the exit. Outside the club, heavy rain has turned the narrow dirt road between the houses into thick mud. Jumping and laughing hand in hand, Sandra and Michael try to avoid the deepest puddles. *Wet Moroccan mud is different from Bavarian mud, it reeks of ancient times, sand, carpets, brass, camels, spices and oranges.* The mud won't reflect back any light. It's late in the night, the streets are dimly lit and long robed figures flicker fearfully ahead of them. Sandra, somewhat apprehensive, holds Michael close to her with her arm around his waist, tighter than the knots in a net. The figures disappear around the corner ahead of them, and they come to the marketplace, hardly recognizable without a million people in its night time emptiness. In the shimmer of light hanging upon the stone houses they see their hotel. With a sense of relief they approach the mosaic steps of the Arabian lodge.

'Michael, there's a little village on the cliffs where they make much of the silver jewelry that is sold here,' says Sandra, excitedly. 'They also have a bazaar of course. Would you like to take the bus there tomorrow?'

'Yes, it sounds interesting—but what time does the bus leave?' he asks, secretly hoping to sleep in.

'At nine-thirty. It's a local bus and stops at every little village. The bus comes back in the afternoon, but we could stay there for the night and return the following day or stop on the way back in Tiznitz, a pilgrim village in the mountains.'

Finding her idea exciting, Michael agrees and walks Sandra to her room, one floor above his. On her doorstep, they exchange a kiss. Holding her tight, Michael fills the emptiness left by Mary. Breaking their embrace with her pretty fingers on his mouth, she bids him goodnight.

The next day they arrive at a postcard town on the coast. Situated on a cliff overlooking the sea, the village is crowded with stucco houses painted in hues of yellow and topped with red-tiled roofs. Opposite the bus station stands a French Catholic Church, a symbol of the earlier colonization with its western architecture. As they walk to the church perched on the cliff's edge they pass through a small, neatly clipped park, an oasis of green punctuated with lamp posts topped with coronets symbolizing the monarchy. Sandra wants to visit the church and then do some shopping, but Michael feels uneasy around churches—and statues of Mary—which disturb him. He would almost feel more comfortable in a mosque, if he didn't miss the presence of Christ in the tabernacle.

'While you visit the church, I'll walk down to the beach. I feel like writing,' says Michael, feeling a sudden surge of creativity.

Beside the church, a flight of small white washed steps leads Michael to a path which ends on the beach. The waves rise rampant upon the beach, and a keen wind carries a fresh and fragrant spray. Walking on the sand near the foam racing in bubbles to his feet, air bubbles race in his head as he ponders this new story of Michael and Sandra and its meaning. But his mind finds it all too obscure, too vague. Seagulls swim in the air under the hottest, brightest sun he's ever known. Finding shade under a cliff near the water, he soothes his eyes with the sight of the water, deep blue and cool. He quickly undresses and runs into the waves. The sun bleaches the blue with light. Refreshed, he walks back to the shore and leans against a rock, enchanted by the beauty of the water and the cries of the seagulls. Michael resumes his writing of the elusive story of the monastery and Mary.

On the wave-sculptured floor of the sand dune, quiet except for the pounding of the waves, Michael lies down on a blanket and starts to write how such a guilt-ridden experience, a sexual relationship with Mary, could feel so much like a gift from God. Lying on the white beach waiting for Sandra, Michael feels his life safe from the undertow. His life before knowing Teresia was like living under water, and without her help, he might never have emerged. *Most people would never have guessed that I was drowning.* Thinking of Teresia, Michael finds it difficult to start writing, but the image of Sandra moves the pen in his hand until the thought of their age difference interrupts his flow of words. *How could she be interested in me? She must think I'm only a kid.* He starts scribbling again in his notebook, and after writing a bit and reading it, he runs his thumb up the pages of his notebook and hears them fall as his main character has done many times. Suddenly, Michael hears his name called, he stops writing and turns to see Sandra running with gazelle leaps, landing her slender body in the sand next to him and stretching her bronzeness on her towel. They spend the rest of the afternoon splashing in the water and then reading Persian poetry. Between the Arabic images of the beautifully written verses, he glances at her figure hardly wrapped in a bikini, while his emotions burn more than his over-exposed skin.

The next day, the bus ride to the pilgrim village is like a voyage from the Arabian Nights. To Michael the Arabs in their long robes and sandals look like monks that the bus picks up here and there along the dusty road, in the middle of nowhere. Michael and Sandra can see for miles over the desert without a single house in sight. They haven't met even a single camel caravan—the dwellers of the desert seem to materialize before them like mirages. The Arabs bring a hot dust storm with them as they climb into the bus.

'Sandra, I'm tempted to wink at one of the veiled women,' Michael says with a mischievous smile.

'You'd get us both killed!' she says, worried that he might do it. She distracts him from his idea by pointing out a doll dressed in native attire hanging in the bus driver's cabin, which is decorated like a bedroom with photos and numerous colorful knickknacks.

Arriving at a village below the old citadel, the sight of the walled town on the mountain is breathtaking. After a procession of grinding gears, the bus, followed by its thick black exhaust smoke proceeds through the open gate in the yellow wall with fortress towers on each side. Michael feels he's entering a lost world. They get off the bus and with a few steps reach a dark, narrow street off the marketplace, lined with shops overloaded with gold and silver.

They find the sightseeing half as arduous as responding 'no' a thousand times to the Moroccan salesmen who try hard to pull the passers-by into their tents on the marketplace or into their shops along the narrow streets. Sandra walks into a small shop. A few minutes later she emerges from the jewel loaded store front, overjoyed by her finding of a silver bracelet and snake-shaped ring, which she bought after some bargaining. From what looks like a hole in a wall, a pompous Arab sits selling his kaleidoscopic kilim rugs, ancient and new, which Michael stops to admire.

To celebrate her purchases they decide to eat a local lunch outside the market square in a noisy restaurant. On its doorstep they see many washbasins for the local customers who use them after eating with their hands. The food is spicy, and they need several glasses of ice water to extinguish the *couscous* fire in their throats. From their table the busy street, the domain of money, is dominated by the spiritual symbol of a minaret.

'Why don't we sneak into that mosque?' proposes Michael with a smile, pointing at the temple.

'Females aren't allowed in there!' replies Sandra, scared of being stoned to death if caught.

'They'll know we're tourists!' Michael insists, boldly.

'Michael, that's something for people your age—' she begins, shying away from the idea.

'You can't stop living when you're a certain age!' he interrupts, 'Anyway, you look like you're in your twenties!'

'You are a charmer. Okay, but you go in first,' yields Sandra, flattered by his remark.

Climbing over rows of sandals, they easily penetrate the gray stoned hall of echoing prayers. Suddenly they hear steps behind them. As he turns, Michael's eyes meet the rebuking expressions of male pilgrims, the same expressions that were on the monks' faces. A thought flashes in Michael's mind: he remembers the way he always avoided the austere faces of the monks by keeping his eyes glued to the cloistered floor, but he always recognized Brother Dietmar, whose feet usually peeked from under the robe, in the first ballet position. Feeling unwelcome, they immediately leave the mosque, but find the sun outside even brighter than before.

As the glaring sun starts to set with the promise of the

cool blueness of the evening in the air, Michael suggests, 'Before it's too dark, let's look for that colorful hotel we saw on that busy pathway near the village gate.'

Full of self-confidence, Michael books a double room on the back side of the fourth floor. Their dark panelled room with red velvet chairs opens on to a small balcony overlooking the massive city wall. Sandra lies on the bed nearest the balcony doors, while outside Michael gazes at the black mountains as the star of fire slowly rolls down behind the peaks.

'Michael, you're blocking the sunset,' gently complains Sandra, suggesting more than her words.

Michael backs up to the bed. He lies down next to her and they watch the blushing sun sink into the earth as they sink into each other's arms. The evening becomes an interchange of tenderness and intensive conversations on various subjects, until they find a common interest in French impressionism.

At the bar of the hotel, Michael and Sandra order tea. The Arab waiter pushes mint leaves into the Aladdin lamp of a tea pot. Continuing their previous conversation, Michael asks, 'Sandra, do you think Gauguin should be considered an impressionist or an expressionist?'

'An expressionist, definitely!' answers Sandra energetically. 'His scenes of island life exude freedom from the conventions and shackles of our so-called civilized world! His own innermost wish for freedom and search for a way of life most congenial to him are splashed on his canvases with expressive energy. Just think of the serene faces of the women, a way of life close to nature.' *How interesting! She's so liberated in her way of thinking. Maybe this means she wouldn't mind our age difference!*

Their conversation meanders through most of the French impressionists, then the expressionists, the surrealists, cubists and finally to a painting Michael had been working on back in Uppsala. At first he hesitates, thinking it might shock her, but, encouraged by her seemingly open and creative

197

mind, he continues, 'It is a depiction of Christ on the cross. A nude female figure with long hair extending to the waist is nailed to him.'

After a moment of silence, 'Very interesting!' she smiles, obviously impressed. 'Does the female figure possibly represent the human race—with Christ sacrificing his life out of his love for us?'

'Right on!' Michael is happy to see her understanding of his ideas. 'I'm not sure a gallery will show it because it could be interpreted as blasphemous, but, in fact, it's just the opposite.'

'If any place would show it I'm sure it would be Sweden,' replies Sandra. 'But where did you get that image?'

'I've developed many of my ideas in Sweden while studying Nordic mythology. You see, the Vikings didn't separate sexuality and spirituality the way the Greeks did,' explains Michael. 'Our western culture has been so influenced by the Greeks, and the Vikings were always considered barbarians, but I think they had some brilliant ideas.'

'I'd like to see the painting,' says Sandra with genuine interest.

'You'll have to come to Sweden to see it,' replies Michael in a hopeful tone.

Sandra doesn't answer, but, leaning her head on Michael's shoulder, she listens instead to the native band playing in the lounge. Michael finds it difficult to concentrate on the music as he imagines holding Sandra's naked body and exchanging love. He shudders at the thought of their togetherness coming to an end when she flies back to Hawaii and he back to Sweden, yet he senses their relationship is as unreal as his story with Mary.

They stand on their balcony eating the mandarins they had bought at the market, while the sights and sounds of Tiznitz begin to fall asleep. The sky darkens and purples across the village, sucking them into the night blindness. The full mandarin moon is hypnotic to him here as it was back at the

198

monastery, but, in Morocco, nearer the equator, the night is a darker dark. Sandra pours two glasses of white wine while, entranced, they gaze at the last lights of Tiznitz. Michael almost forgets how Sandra's divorce must have affected her. *Separations, for whatever reason, are always painful.* He wants to say something empathetic but feels this isn't the right time and keeps quiet. In the moonlight she appears a little older, maybe just tired, and though he can see how the expression lines on her face would become deeper, she looks radiant in her honey tan.

'Did you have many lovers before you married your husband?' Michael asks, his restraint loosened by the wine. *I must be drunk to ask this question!*

'No, I was never really in love—maybe I've never been in love,' answers Sandra, quite naturally. 'How about you?'

'I thought I was once' Michael says, escaping her prying words and thinking of Mary. His face assumes a cat's look of detached self-absorption.

Respecting his reticence, she announces, 'I'm going to take a quick shower.'

She walks into the bathroom in her pale blue cotton dress tied at the waist. Simple things like her dress remind him of Mary while his mind feels twisted to a screaming point as he remembers her lips, of the fairest, purest pink. Silently in his mind, he screams as he clenches his hands on the balcony rail. The sudden splash of water in the shower makes his head turn towards the open doorway; Sandra's blurred silhouette through the glass shower is like the impressionist painting of a nymph. The sight of her slender figure draws him into the bathroom. *I would like to join her in the shower, but that might make me an intruder and scare her.* He turns, and, smiling into the mirror, he brushes his straight white teeth. Over the years he had unconsciously mastered a whole register of smiles, and now he recognizes the nervousness in his smile. She is older, more experienced and probably less obsessed with the physical side of the yin-yang junction of their relationship. Back out on the balcony with the awning that something wonderful is about to happen, Michael is impatient, but a bit frightened. He hasn't been this happy since Mary. The wind on the balcony sounds like a sigh, a deep breathing from Sandra who calls his name.

'Michael, come to me!' her voice is the song of a mermaid.

Slowly he walks towards her. He gazes at her beauty carefully and timelessly as a cat. She is beautiful from her sand colored hair to her toes. A tide of kisses slowly rises over her body fragrant with sand and sea. Staring at her captivating body he suddenly realizes that he's not comparing her with Mary. In his attempt to please her, he gazes at her face as his kisses move up her leg. Expressions of pleasure on her face appear to Michael as grimaces. As if an insect were crawling on her face, she squints and twists her mouth, turns her head from side to side and finally screams as if she's just been bitten by the insect, but it is only Michael who bites her. As he finds and kisses a cappuccino birthmark on her breast, lights flash in his mind like torches in the night outside the tents in the market place. Michael moves inside her like waves on the shore and kisses her lips, ears, and eyes. The momentum continues, and comparing with his past experiences, he notices that this is the longest time he has ever made love. As he reaches her depths, he has the impression of reaching God. Her fingernails dig into his thighs, and she sighs the breath of life while he splashes life inside her.

'Michael, I like you so very much,' she exhales. Sandra weaves her fingers through his hair, and the tightness he'd noticed on her face has disappeared. The quiet of the lovers' quenched passions is broken only by the sound of their breathing and the whispering wind from the window as Sandra lies on Michael's chest. After making love with Sandra, Michael makes another comparison, not with Mary, but with Gaby. With her, sex was like ramming a wheelbarrow into a darkness without God in sight.

The next morning they walk in the marketplace taking in

the scents of Moroccan coffee, perfumes and strong cigarettes. In the line of narrow shops, the hungry shopkeepers wait and watch in their cages of business surrounded by wares begging to be bought. Sandra buys a camel wool blanket in the shop of a young couple, who then invites her and Michael to sip the traditional mint tea in the small back room. Sitting on a pile of Berber rugs, the young Arab's mother doesn't understand English, and remains huddled in her corner of the world drinking mint tea made on the small black kerosene heater in the middle of the chamber. As she drinks, she sucks her lips in back over the gums and then smacks them out again. The wife spreads newspapers over a table, smoothing them out as if they were the finest silken tablecloth and then offers a small dish of grains, carrots and pieces of chicken, only recognizable by the skin. Michael and Sandra learn a few Arabic words from the young Moslem husband whose jaws resemble a rabbit trap.

Outside the small shop, Michael asks, 'Sandra, would you like to spend one more day here in Tiznitz? There are fewer tourists here.'

'Love to, Michael—You've brought my life out of a rut!' *And I've escaped the living death in the monastery!* 'Michael, it will be sunset soon, let's watch it from our balcony with a glass of wine,' says Sandra with a twinkle in her eyes.

'Sandra, you're like a girl—and I love it!' observes Michael cheerfully, unaware of her possible misinterpretation of his words.

On the balcony Sandra contemplates the skyline, but some thought has cast a shadow over her face. Michael's remark alluding to age has stung her though he hadn't meant to hurt her. In their silence he tries to comprehend how Sandra came into his life like the wind from the Sahara, while his mind is bursting with urgency, thinking that she will soon be leaving. Even the sunset seems to last longer that evening, as if the sun, on the verge of departing, still were hesitant to do so as usual, slowed down by some uneasiness in the burnt air.

Early the next morning, on their way back to Marrakech, Michael is still unaware of her changed mood. 'You're so quiet today,' he says, tentatively starting a conversation.

'Michael, I've got many things on my mind,' replies Sandra, seriously.

He accepts her solitary mood but fearing that she'll slip away forever after Marrakech, he tries to think of ways to keep her in his life. After the long dusty bus ride back to Marrakech, tired and tense, they enter their limestone hotel next to the marketplace. Behind the reception desk sits an Arab wearing a robe like a Sahara tent. Michael decodes the expression in Sandra's eyes, and her mouth lets out words which are an echo to her eyes. 'I want to take a nap alone, Michael,' she says, quietly.

He kisses her but feels estranged. In his room Michael drags his feet to the window which opens to a view of the lavender mountains which had been the background to their erotic journey the previous night. The dry breeze animates the draperies which flutter and obstruct his view. The room is dark, and Michael falls asleep on his bed, images of Sandra fluttering in his mind. He wakens two hours later. He pulls open the drapes and sees the sun about to set over the mountains. Thinking of Sandra, he feels a gold rush to hold her and make love to her before the sun makes love to the mountains. He quickly dresses and runs the flight of stairs to her room. After a brief knock on her door left ajar, he enters her room; the last light of the day filtered through the drapes gives the room a bluish-green aquarium appearance. Looking out the window, he hopes to see her lying by the pool below, but there's no sight of her. A plane lifts west over the ocean, catching his eye and rumbling in his ears. His skin turns blue like his thoughts with a sudden, tragic intuition which tears at his heart.

In Sweden, the air is blue with sleet, as Michael, devastated and despondent, enters the Uppland fraternity wine cellar where he is to meet his friend Urban. In the vaulted cellar Michael sits and waits for Urban, who's always late, and hopes to find some comfort in talking; he still finds Uppsala empty without Teresia. The trip had not removed the pains of missing her, and now he endures more pains sitting in the darkness of Sweden, thinking of Sandra walking in sunlight another world away. His thoughts are startled as Urban makes his brisk, uncoordinated entrance knocking over a chair. Michael feels less alone seeing his friend, the only audience to the narration of his Moroccan trip and love affair with Sandra. After a thorough explanation, he regains a capacity for quietness, a stillness in his mind soothes him after all that thinking about the way Sandra disappeared, momentarily banishing the painful aching in his bones.

'Michael, you seem to meet a lot of kamikaze women, who dive right into you and destroy you. You have to admit you seem to attract crazy women,' Urban notes, with the tone of someone making a revelation.

But Urban's obvious words offer Michael no comfort, and he is left to console himself with waffles, strawberries, whipped cream, coffee and brandy. Images of Sandra crowd his head, vivid at first, then melting like the wax of the lit candle on their table. Michael tries to relax as he laughs thanks to Urban's crazy sense of humor, but Urban's loud laugh suddenly catches the attention of a young blond woman dressed in electric blue. She walks to their table and the colored inks of a sensitive memory spread like a Rorschach in Michael's mind as he recognizes in her Brigitte, in a skinnier body. Her eyes smile, but her mouth reveals her confusion as she nervously invites Michael and Urban to a Viking party at Gotland's fraternity house. 'Since it is a masquerade party you must dress up as Vikings,' she chirps emphatically.

Carrying some gunny sacks found in the local grain silo, Michael enters Urban's old apartment which smells of cherry pipe smoke. As they play discs from Urban's jazz collection, they drink beer and dress themselves in the cut out gunny sacks, large leather belts, sandals, helmets with horns and dark makeup, all of which reminds Michael of the Viking party in Denver and Laura.

Only a few snow flakes fall out of the partially closed sky as Michael and Urban reach the fraternity house near the Fyris River. It is late in the evening but the white light of the moon on the snow gives everything a quality of daylight as bright icicles dangle on the frozen silver branches and trees in the garden enclosure. The moon bleaches a path leading to the quarry-stoned building where Michael and Urban remove their overcoats outside the entrance. The wind and snow have turned Michael's hair into a desperate tangle, like his mind, twisting with thoughts of Sandra.

With horns on their heads Michael and Urban storm the house like invading Vikings, only to find the other guests dressed for a formal party. Michael's eyes sparkle with surprise and bewilderment, while Urban withdraws into his embarrassment and turns to leave. In an attempt to stop him, Michael grabs his arm as Brigitte, in a dazzling blue dress, hurries across the large room toward them. The guests' warm laughter draws them inside and, after a few humorous remarks, everyone accepts their strange attire. When dinner is served, Michael, as the Viking chieftain, is invited to sit at the head of the table. Pleased and surprised by this honor, he is even more startled when served a breaded lamb head for dinner. After the Viking dinner a band starts playing pounding music in the adjacent hall which has aged black beams protruding from the ceiling. Dancing to the loud music, Michael and Brigitte lose themselves among the noisy notes.

'Why did you tell me and Urban to wear these costumes?' yells Michael, louder than the guitars.

'I wanted to spend a night with a Viking,' she yells back, as the music stops in the middle of her answer, making her voice stand out. She blushes as the other guests stare at her.

With some hesitation, remembering their last evening together, Michael says, 'Brigitte, let's go to my place?'

They leave the building while Urban is still running around in the tenth century. It has stopped snowing, and the wind shakes the silver ice hanging from the frozen branches of birch trees. The cold vibrant sky seems as naked as he guesses she is under her windblown long dress and blue coat. They run into his nearby apartment house, in the old city, giving the impression the wind is chasing them. Her body dances out of her clothes, and his face lights up as she steps from a pool of underclothing. Moonlight spills into the living room as the weak light and shadows fall upon her. Brigitte's thin body is a flash of blushing color in the wine-dark night as Michael walks toward her in his Viking gear holding a bottle of strong wine and two glasses. Her red nails scratch his skin as she pulls off his plundering costume. Michael takes her with quiet determination.

The following morning Michael continues writing on his manuscript at his desk under the mansard ceiling, occasionally looking at the sun which reflects off the old houses across the street. As he writes about Sandra, tears fill his eyes. *The sunlight now means so much to me, and I wonder if the sun in Hawaii reminds her of me.* Unable to write, he takes a break with a cup of the mint tea he brought back from Morocco and, as he listens to his favorite Vivaldi tape, visions of Sandra running along the sandy beach flash through his mind. The scent of the suntan lotion mixing with the salty fragrance of the sea vapor-locks his thoughts. As his headache disappears so do his mental images, and he decides to walk the icy sidewalk to the *Apotek*. Outside the pharmacy, he runs into Brigitte among the many Saturday shoppers in the old city.

'Michael, you remember Agnete?!' Brigitte asks as if it were a statement.

'Of course,' Michael answers, surprised.

'I've heard she's pregnant, but no one knows who the father is, not even Agnete!'

Michael can't tell from Brigitte's face whether she expects pity or laughter, and he isn't sure himself what he feels. After a pause, Michael says, 'Thank you for that wonderful night. I have to go now. I'm meeting Urban.'

'I knew you were a Viking!' smiles Brigitte with a sexy wink.

Michael meets Urban for a cup of coffee at *Ofvandahls Café*, a continental café built by an Uppsala writer of the eighteenth century. For once he can peacefully sit at the window, talk with Urban, watch the world go by and be content.

'Michael, that party was embarrassing. I tried to get out, but you stopped me and then you left. What kind of friend are you? Let's pull some stunt on Brigitte!'

'I did already, I told her I was Erik the Blue,' Michael says with a nervous smile.

'It's Erik the Red!' Urban corrects him.

'Not for her!' he laughs.

'I don't get it, but I must leave now. I must get back to work,' Urban says wrapping his scarf around his neck.

'Urban, before you leave, I've finally finished my manuscript and since you're going to the main library in Stockholm tomorrow, could you leave it at the Lundberg Publishing House next to the library? It's very close for you. They will be expecting it.'

'Sure, this sounds interesting. See you tomorrow evening, Michael?' asks Urban, slurring his words in his rush to go back to work.

'Sorry, Urban. I can't tomorrow. Run along, I want to stay a few minutes longer and finish *Sorrows of Werther*. Thanks—for everything, Urban. Good-bye.'

Michael watches the sun disappear over the main university hall at three-thirty in the afternoon. After ensuring no one is watching him in the café where only a few students sit, he swallows half a bottle of sleeping pills with a glass of water. Sometimes Michael feels he's acting in a play, a tremendous play, or that life has become similar to a myth, a Viking myth, and in the face of all his unconquerable obstacles, he is to be simply courageous in spite of the fact that he can't win. What lies ahead is a metamorphosis of his life like the substantial change of bread and wine into the body and blood of Christ. *I don't think I have disordered thinking, impaired judgment or tenuous impulse control as they told me at the hospital.* Yet sitting in a posture more rigid than a Viking's, he feels a tug to another world and can feel his mind drifting like the snow outside the window. This world has become bland, even the cinnamon roll he bites into is tasteless like a communion wafer. *Maybe Mary was a repressed part of myself, maybe I found the shadows of my hidden self in her eyes. Even when Mary looked at my face, I feel she saw desperation in my eyes. I probably covered her face with expressions and masks of my subconscious that represented the unknown parts of myself. My conversations with Mary were critical contacts with the cold inside myself.*

He can already sense his mind is rambling. In the manuscript he gave Urban he wonders if his character descriptions are blurry, if he's really writing about other people, or if he's trying to touch the true source of his feelings. He simply cannot know or guess the answers to his doubts, answers which he feels are trapped inside his subconscious. *Even the moon which always keeps one side of the truth hidden from me is after all a dead planet, shining not of his own light but reflecting the fire of a living star.* His ability to control his thoughts is fading. Events in his life crowd his mind with their lack of sequence and coherence. New compulsive ideas obfuscate his mind, and the attractive girls in the café appear powerful, lithe, like animals in clothing, and his thoughts overlap each other, like crabs crawling over each other. Moving his eyes to the closed double glazed windows which isolate him from the outside world, everything appears and feels like a slow motion film. *If I die I'm not surrendering. I have control, I decide. After the monastery experience I learned that You want me to take responsibility for my life. God, I've suffered enough, grown enough through this passion and if You, Christ, chose your death, so will I, and my book will be the testament of my love for You. But do I have the existential right to decide when I want to meet You?* In this maelstrom of confusion, the only certain, rock stable choice is unconsciousness, not yielding to craziness. Everything turns very dark all of a sudden, a tidal wave of blackness breaks over his head, and all he can see is the white snow and the rest of the white pills. He washes down the remaining tablets with a glass of water, pulls on his coat over his blue shirt, stained violet at the armpits, and leaves the café because the darkness of the room only adds to the darkness in his head, making it unbearable.

Michael meanders to Eriksberg, past Teresia's old apartment, and continues the wintry walk into the lucid stillness of the Haga Valley where he saunters off the plowed path through the snowscape and trudges into the frozen forest free from footprints in the deep snow dust. Snow-mantled trees rival with him for possession of the silence. Feeling very tired from sinking deep into the powdered snow at every step, Michael takes off his thick sheepskin coat and flings it haphazardly at a large blue-green boulder covered with crystallized moss. He lies down in a snow bed, waiting for the wind to cover him with a blanket of snow. *Once asleep I will freeze to death very quickly. God, help me in this hard choice. Stay with me. My time is running out. How can I love you best?*

He lies on the ground for what seems like an eternity. His whole life flurries through his mind like the stinging snow squall: *Dad froze the life of an artist in me, the monastery almost destroyed me, and so many women have tempted me with their bodies and destroyed me with their minds.* His faith in and love of God blow between his nodding moments of consciousness. The wind slaps him in the face with wet snow, temporarily abating his slumbering. *I miss Mary more than Laura, Gaby, Sandra or anyone, even though I know it was all in my mind. She really was a gift from You. She taught me to look at clouds from both sides, taught me to find music where I never heard music before. I remember Mary talking about the music of the raindrops falling on the leaves.* Although his thoughts of Mary tranquilize him, his sense of sound seems more acute as the bitter breeze blowing through the woods becomes a woodwind choir carrying faint notes of a Gregorian chant. Sounds from the cloistered forest chant nature's love for God. *I can't be God's monk, but I am a writer and a painter ... I can express more love by living, writing and painting than dying ... I don't want to die ... I want to live!*

In his silken repose there is an ebbing sense of consciousness, an abeyance in the control of his own thoughts. Michael can feel his skin freezing, while his mind is thawing with the idea of living. As the snow man senses he's about to faint into unconsciousness, he struggles to rise. In panic, he reaches for the icy boulder, grabbing a jutting rock and pulls himself up, staggering, trying to gain strength from the rock. *I don't want to die!* Michael loses his balance, falls into the snow, and now in a desperate struggle to live, he crawls through the thick immaculate blanket hoping not to fall asleep. Lying in the snow drift, he jerks his face against the cold crystals to keep himself awake. Crawling farther he reaches his coat, now part of the snow line, and pulls himself up again holding onto a purple pine. Fighting to overcome the pills and nature, he continues to move, now running helter-skelter, staggering like a wounded deer back towards the city, his face a contorted mask. His quarrelsome soul will never shrink back into the body of a slender sulky stripling. *God, help me, don't let me die. I do love You.* As he reaches the edge of the frozen forest, he falls unconscious. In the snow storm a young man driving a car sees him fall, stops, then pulls the half-frozen body out of the snow bank.

The following day, the air is pregnant with sadness. Michael lies, unconscious, his hand warm and heavy in Urban's. In the sterile white hospital room, Michael's face seems to struggle for consciousness. Under Urban's eyes, a sequence of expressions shapes the pale mask of his face: the helpless raised eyebrows when he was arrested by the policemen after Brigitte's phone call, or the bunching of his lips at the time of his attack on the street by the young drunk. Sitting by Michael's stainless steel bed, Urban mumbles words he wishes Michael could hear beyond the incessant radio waves coming from the end of the corridor. Nurses cloak the odors of death in the ward with their serene movements and mystic whiteness. Michael's café experience is now intravenous feeding. His hand twitches. Urban can't make himself stay as tears appear in his steel-blue eyes. The few minutes of his stay seem like hours. Unable to announce his presence to Michael's ears, Urban stands wearing the expression of a mummy, mirroring the look on Michael's face then leaves, slowly walking down the hall. The faces of the dying peer at him above their sheets. Outside, the blue air is freezing to death like the snow-covered conifers which stand at the entrance of the hospital. The parking lot has been cleared of snow; the sun loses its grip on the hospital roof, bounces into the sky, and burns sores on the icy pavement. It's a black winter day, still the sun makes the snow sweat on Urban's Saab sports car.

The following day Urban visits Michael at the hospital where he is met by a rally for his survival as a young nurse explains that Michael had regained consciousness shortly before daybreak. Michael sits up energetically, and begins to talk and smile, happy to be alive. With the doctor's permission, Urban pushes Michael in a wheelchair towards the visitors' room. Spotting a young, blonde nurse wheeling a patient down the hallway, Urban bends over his friend with a cheerful 'Michael, look at that beautiful girl!'

'Urban, there is something—very familiar about her,' says Michael, staring at the pretty nurse.

With a few laughs Michael and Urban lighten the atmosphere in the visitors' room as if it were a café. Suddenly, the young blonde nurse enters the room and walks towards them, offering a tray of pills and cups to Michael.

'How are you today? You had it pretty rough last night. We weren't sure you were going to make it—I'm really happy you did,' she says with a warm smile, as she hands the medicine over to Michael.

'Thank you for the help. I really appreciate what you and the doctors have done for me,' replies Michael, touched by her words. 'By the way, this is my friend Urban, and my name is Michael,' he announces, looking intently into her blue eyes.

'I know—my name is Mary.'

TEN

VALHALLA

It was growing dark in the *Blue Period Café*—a popular meeting place for students. The place had a stylish, smart look, with walls painted bottle-green and cobalt-blue and sliding doors leading out into a garden closed in the winter months. Outside, in the still air, a quiet drape of snow fell slowly and inexorably in straight, thick lines. Ice crystals upon conifers and bushes sparkled white against the dark green hues. Inside, Christmas decorations were already in place. Silver stars and angels hung from the ceiling, crisscrossed with glittering red and green ribbons. The blank portions of the walls were filled with canvases of student artists. I remembered when one of Michael's paintings hung here—a Modigliani-like portrait of his sister—and on each table made of rough red wood stood a vase with a silk sunflower that reminded me of the van Gogh's flora which had inspired one of his paintings. The Christmas lights and ornaments glowed in the wintery twilight, while most of the light came from the wide window I sat next to. Looking out, the heavy snow obstructed my perspective of the university museum, but not my view of Michael's world. I was amazed and entranced—and then it struck me—I had to know if my perceptions about Mary were correct. The sheer unexpectedness of the ending had made my hair stir, while my hands were warm and clammy. When the café door slammed, it startled me so that I dropped the pages of the manuscript across the table.

Michael's manuscript had screamed silently and from all the pages at once; fire must have led his hand, as his words exuded an intensity that had thrust me into an evasive and burning silence. What was the meaning … of the nurse's words? As far as my eyes and ears were concerned, the rest of the world had ceased to exist: all I could think about was Michael and his precarious grip on reality. The café filled with its regular customers, and the noise in the room seemed

212

to rise and fall with the blues music from the speakers. At the next table, a young man seemed to be eating to the rhythm of the music while performing a primitive ritual. His face had a rugged quality like an unfinished sculpture hewn from wood, and I couldn't help but think of Bjornson as I watched him. I had been drawn into Michael's story, totally immersed in his emotions—I had to find my friend.

I suddenly remembered that I had the phone number of his sister Shelly whom I had met several times after our first encounter at the Viking masquerade party. With the hope she could shed some light on Michael's experience, I called her. She explained she hadn't seen or heard anything from him since he was in Denver two years before for their father's funeral and that she saw Michael for the very last time when she left him and Laura alone early one evening and went to the library. This was strange, maybe Michael was already hallucinating—but why seductive hallucinations of Shelly? Michael and his sister had always been close, aside from her blond hair and his dark hair they looked like twins. They had given each other love and support when they received none from their parents. Maybe he did have special feelings for her? I know I did. Shelly was an attractive young woman, and of all her qualities, the one that stood out the most was her passion and love for life. Michael demonstrated a similar passion for life in his ability to write a bewildering, illuminating and pulsating stream of dawning light after a journey into the unfathomable darkness of himself. Shelly and I had been looking for Michael, but now I realized Michael had been looking for Michael. I knew I had to talk with him, and decided on the spot to fly to Uppsala. It was my Christmas break, and I hadn't made any plans. Besides, I could use the opportunity to gather data on my research on Nordic rune stones—but what I really wanted was to talk with Michael.

As I approached Uppsala in a bus from the airport, I could see the skyline of the town outlined by the golden pencil of the morning sun. I checked into a room on the third floor of the Linnea Hotel. From my window I could feast my eyes with the sight of the famous botanical gardens showered with the ivory petals of the flowers that grow in the white weather. All around, the medieval city of Uppsala pulsated with life in spite of the cold air. Old houses frosted with ice were backed one against the other in a tangle of small silver streets, walls and roofs. I was tired, but felt a compulsion to find Urban from the address on the manuscript envelope. I finally found his apartment in the old city.

Urban's pale face appeared from behind his door with questioning eyes. After introducing myself he relaxed and invited me into his apartment. It was an old, spacious place, with polished wooden floors and tall windows framed with ancient plum velvet curtains. Urban's home exuded an atmosphere of old bourgeoisie, of better days, with servants busy polishing the numerous silver pieces that lay, tarnished, in the various niches of the heavy, dark wood furniture which crowded the rooms. Taking vigorous draws from his pipe, Urban satisfied my curiosity on Michael's whereabouts, then retreated into his thoughts for a while, giving me a chance to talk about myself. Then he suddenly revealed, 'After writing his novel, Michael burned it, but he forgot that I had a copy—I decided to send it to you since you are a good friend of his.'

I sat with my thoughts while Urban made coffee in this strangely familiar old apartment whose rooms and furnishings evoked scenes from the novel. After talking about Michael and drinking our coffees, I was eager to leave and surprise Michael. Urban spread a city map on the coffee table and drew a route to Michael's loft apartment at the edge of the city, near the Haga forest. I left Urban and prepared to surprise Michael.

Shortly afterwards, I found myself standing outside a renovated old warehouse with recessed windows opening out of thick brick walls. In the cold motionless air, I rang the doorbell of Michael's apartment. From behind the door appeared Michael's face, at first frozen in surprise then melting into a hearty laugh, as he jumped from joy and gave me a bear hug. Michael had hardly changed since I'd seen him three years before. He looked slimmer, his hair was a little longer, and he had that same energy, maybe more. Overjoyed, he invited me into his living room whose main features were brick walls and beams of rough Nordic pine, kaleidoscopic kilims colored the wooden floor, a tawny worn leather sofa and armchair faced an old fireplace. The room was lit by a partially opened balcony door at the far end of the loft. I felt cold. Michael led me into his studio, bright and as large as the living room but with taller windows, overflowed with painted canvases, empty frames and loaded bookcases. The scent of pine turpentine mixed with the smell of oil colors, suggesting long hours of creative work. There was light and color everywhere. I stood next to him with my hands sunk in the pockets of my Mackintosh, pleasing my eyes with Michael's paintings, absorbing the colors, shapes and emotions that came from the canvases.

'You're a better painter now,' I observed with admiration.

He reminded me that it still was all in the groin of the beholder and laughed. I smiled remembering that conversation, and he took my coat. We sat with a cup of strong coffee at an old pine table in his dining room, while warm sun rays shone through the windows onto a wall filled with icon-like paintings in a Modigliani style I had not seen before.

'Are those yours as well, Michael?' I asked, trying to absorb as much from my friend as these paintings were absorbing rays from the sun.

'Yes—, I've been inspired by Modigliani and Gill—their expression of intertwined eroticism and mysticism in their art stirred me deeply,' explained Michael in a both inspired and spirited way.

I tried to follow Michael's ideas about spirituality and sexuality and the feelings in his voice the way I follow a line of music, and, as does a writer in a narration, he connected apparent gaps in my understanding with interpretations of his own, bunching these ideas together for me. His theology was both Christian and Buddhistic, yet Nordic. As he gave me this synthesis of vision, I started understanding that time and place were fused creatively for him, that time ran in circles, not in a linear march of seconds, minutes, and hours. Time and place became compressed in the way maps compress the world onto a flat sheet of paper or novels compress reality on two-dimensional pages. Talking about novels, I found that books were mystical creatures for him; he read novels with amazement, and art affected him in the same manner. Even though I had started dissecting Michael's book and the monastery, I had to resist the desire to intrude upon the hidden sides of his life, I had to cloister my curious eyes. I noticed that every time he spoke of his girlfriend his breathing quickened, and ideas scurried in my mind as a mouse behind a wall.

After a light lunch but a heavy conversation about Gnostic theology, Michael left me briefly to brew some coffee in the kitchen. I looked through the balcony door windows and suddenly recognized the snowscape and frozen forest. My mind rapidly moved outside the room as I remembered Michael's movements in his novel. He walked back into the dining room with the hot drinks, and his enthusiasm brought me back into the apartment making me realize just how much I'd become involved into Michael's manuscript, and even into writing like him.

'Join me and my girlfriend this evening!' Michael proposed, smiling.

'Thanks, but I'm still tired from jet lag—I'll join you tomorrow,' I said, even though I was very curious about his girlfriend and would have liked to meet her then and there.

'Tomorrow we can go cross country skiing, and I'll show you some Viking rune stones,' promised Michael enthusiastically.

The following day, golden gleams of light lancing through the trees drew us deep into the woods. It was difficult for me to keep up with Michael's vigorous pace, and he frequently had to pause and wait for me, but finally we came to the edge of the frosty forest where we came upon a Viking burial ground. Several massive stone monuments stood, beautiful, powdered with snow. After spending some time on a rune stone, I finally deciphered the symbols of an inscription which told of a Viking warrior who had built his house on this land. Another rune stone nearby was dedicated to Odin, a Viking God. We skied deeper into the forest. The ski trail suddenly followed along an icy river which shone among the trees from the sun splashing down upon its frosty surface. The steep bluish bramble banks were also part of the whiteness.

We stopped to catch our breath and admire the scenic snowscape. Breaking the silence all around us, Michael said, 'Could we stop a few minutes to meet my friend Urban? He works at the mental hospital across the river.'

We skied across the frozen river, through some woods of conifers laden heavy with snow and finally into a glaring golden glen where I suddenly perceived the mental asylum hanging on the side of the snowy slope. The hospital walls and church tower shone silver in the frigid air. From inside the church steeple which jutted above a connected series of medieval buildings, bells abruptly broke the stillness. The snowscape was too steep for our skis, so we carried them on our shoulders along the hedge of brambles and pine scrub. The redolence of pine in the air and the intermittent views of the hospital carried my mind back and forth between Michael's novel and the view before me which I realized was disturbingly similar to the buildings and landscapes described in the novel.

'This mental hospital used to be a monastery in the fourteenth century,' announced Michael, with the detached tone of a tour guide. But his words shook me to the core. Had he ever been at the Benedictine monastery in the Alps?

In the sun the church sparkled like a fabulous piece of quartz. We stood our skis in a snow bank along the church wall, and we walked into the old building sunk in the snow. But my thoughts were far from there, trapped in a snow blizzard in the Alps. The depressing atmosphere conflicted with my excitement: I was comparing what I had before me with Michael's descriptions of the monastery. In a déjà vu experience, I followed my friend down the fluorescently lit corridor to a visitors' room where several patients sat in silence and gloom. Amazingly, their faces lit up as Michael entered the room. He approached a young man with a gray ski cap who seemed especially happy to see him.

'Are you still wearing that old ski cap?' Michael asked, in visible surprise.

'Yes, I don't want to grow my father's hair!' replied the man in total earnestness, convinced of his words which however threw me into total confusion.

I didn't pay attention to what Michael said to him, I was wondering if he still collected girls' bicycle seats. Suddenly they both laughed, and even though I had been distracted by my thoughts, I joined in their contagious cheerfulness, wondering if they were reading my thoughts. Michael went searching for Urban, and I waited in the kitchen opposite the ward therapy room where patients were gathering for a therapy session. I peeped into the room, hoping to be able to recognize some of the patients from their descriptions in the novel—but Bjornson didn't seem to be there. Someone then closed the door. Suddenly, a row broke out inside the therapy room, and the door swung open to let out a young woman dragged by an orderly. Blood gushed from her left arm—she had slit her wrist. There was confusion and noise in the therapy room. A young nurse hurried to help without saying a word, as silent as a nun. A thought quickened in my mind: are there nuns in a Benedictine monastery? The patient and orderly then disappeared in the maze of corridors searching for bandages. With the door to the therapy room left open, I could now unexpectedly hear the conversations of the patients inside the room. I wondered if I'd recognize anyone from their words, if they didn't speak too fast—the only Swedish I knew was the old Norse needed for my research on rune stones. I quickly felt an unexpected wave of fondness for the crazies.

'Everybody here thinks I'm ugly! In fact, the whole world finds me ugly!' a deep male voice erupted.

'So what if you're ugly!' another male voice answered. At first I thought this was the crazy comment of another male patient, but as I soon learned to recognize the voices, I realized it had been the reply of the therapist.

'Women will never go to bed with me,' the patient whined on.

'All right, I want you to act out being a sperm. All sperms are ugly. I want you to talk as a sperm to all the eggs,' proposed the therapist in a steady voice.

'I'm a sperm!' the patient yelled, cheerfully.

'That egg isn't going to answer, she hasn't said a word since she came here over a year ago,' observed another man sarcastically.

I heard a shuffling of chairs, followed by ten minutes of complete silence. Intrigued, I shifted my position to one where I could see the room from its reflection on the glass door. On a chair facing a catatonic woman sat the therapist. He pulled a cigarette out of his breast pocket, then patted his coat in search of a matchbox. Unable to find a match, he looked at the petrified figure, 'YOU GOT A MATCH?' he suddenly yelled at the top of his voice.

'DON'T SCARE ME LIKE THAT!' she screamed back, jumping to her feet as if hit by lightening. Later I learned those had been the first words she'd spoken in over a year, and that they had marked the beginning of a slow reintegration of her self with reality.

Michael and Urban arrived just as the session ended. Michael didn't know we'd met before and was surprised to see Urban recognize me. A young, pretty blond patient in the group ran to Michael, put her arm around his and gave him a kiss while crying, 'My boyfriend is here!'

Michael kissed her on the forehead, then he and I left the hospital without Urban, who couldn't leave his work. Outside, Michael and I pulled our skis out of the snow drift near the hospital entrance, and headed for the frozen river. This whole time I felt as if I was living in Michael's novel, it seemed easy for me to fuse the real world with Michael's fictional world; his story had moved me more than I had realized. Tired after skiing a distance along the river, I was relieved to hear Michael propose, 'Let's have a picnic here in the snow.'

Sitting on a deerskin Michael had carried in his backpack, we drank the warm *glogg* and ate the smoked reindeer we'd carried with us. In the warm sunshine, I forgot for the moment that it was Michael—the young man before me—who had experienced the things I'd read in the novel. 'Michael, I—have read your novel,' I started with some hesitation.

'Really?' interrupted Michael. 'But ... I destroyed it! How did you—'

'Urban sent me his copy,' I explained. 'He was concerned about you—and so was I. I just had to see you, my friend.' I gazed fixedly at Michael's face, hoping to perceive the slightest positive reaction. But Michael kept silent, his eyes turned towards the hospital in the distance. 'Your story drew me inside your world, moving me with incredible force,' I continued. 'I feel I know all the characters as if I'd met them today.'

'I had forgot all about that copy ... of course!' Michael's words uttered with a smile and a sense of wonder relieved me like a balm on a wound. 'I am glad at least it reached somebody!' he laughed. I could tell he was happy, he was his old self.

'Michael—when we were in the visitors' room and that young woman ran down the corridor half naked without any panties, was that Agnete?'

With a smile, Michael admitted, 'Yes—she was always doing that. One day when I was a patient there, she insisted on showing me the freckles on her bottom. When she pulled down her panties, I could have told her they were beautiful freckles, but instead, I asked her if I could take a pencil and connect the dots. She let me until the tickling made her giggle, and the nurse came.'

We laughed and continued to speak of Michael's previous experiences and painful relationships until the blue shadows of the pines slipped downhill and enveloped us. Our warm voices began to evaporate in the cold crisp air, and we decided to ski back to town. Before us a marmalade sunset spread across Uppsala's horizon. At the edge of the town, we kicked ourselves loose of our skis, and I realized Michael had kicked himself loose of his past pains. Undoubtedly he still faced struggles, but not with himself. He had stopped wrestling with his passions, and no longer was consumed by them in his search for acceptance and love. It was the most exciting discovery I could have imagined, his wrestling without the great fear of rejection—it was Michael's belief in his own self. Michael had understood Albert Camus' conviction that at a certain age one was responsible for one's own face—one's own life. And becoming a person meant exactly that: making choices and accepting the responsibilities that were intrinsic to them. He had chosen his own life thus rejecting death and anything between a full life and death. In a form of ultimate wisdom, Michael knew that his life was part of God's.

The next afternoon Michael invited me to join him and some of his friends, including Urban, at a student café. Michael and I meandered along a cobblestoned road, following the Fyris river which runs through Uppsala. We walked past a bookstore which displayed only a few books in English and several shops and houses which had an almost blurry appearance as I kept thinking of Ebenhausen. Finally we came to a narrow footbridge spanning the river to the road on the other side. When we arrived at the café, Michael's friends— half a dozen young men—were already sitting around a large table eating food from a Smorgasbord that included all types of herring, fresh salmon, smoked meats, and cheese. Although the food looked delicious, the view from the window had caught my attention as I could see the white hillside and the castle on the ridge. It was a déjà vu experience. Michael soon brought my attention back to the conversation on socialistic politics; the quest for a better society poured out of these students as did the beer from the many bottles on the table. I identified with their reaching for the future—and the strong beer for that matter. The bubbles from the amber drink dissolved some of my inhibitions, and I excitedly accepted their invitation to join in on what they called their 'invasion.' The time came for Michael's friends to leave the café. Michael and I stayed to have some coffee. I asked him about Brigitte.

'She has a fresh lease on life, and now she has her own apartment. I used to visit her a lot when she lived in the old town. Her apartment used to be a bordello during the war—fancy that! But—the same women from the war were living there!' explained Michael, with his lively sense of humor.

I laughed, and he continued, 'We started seeing each other, and maybe I expected more of her than I did of myself—we were both crazy. Soon I learned that every time I wore blue clothes she wanted to make love, it was unbelievable! I painted my whole apartment blue, but I soon realized I wasn't the only guy wearing blue clothes! Our encounters were wonderful, but I knew that her romps with different guys were not fabulous—because I wasn't the lover. Before, I never was able to explain to myself why men and women should have the same freedom, but now this doesn't threaten my masculinity anymore. We broke up because we had difficulty talking with each other. Eventually her personality didn't change every time she wore a blue dress—though sometimes it did—yet she couldn't concentrate on anything for very long. We'd be talking and suddenly she would run into the kitchen or start talking about something else.'

I understood Michael because I learned from my stories with women that a good relationship is the weaving of a communication fabric of memories, dreams and goals. Poor communication weakens the weave, and the result is a distance widened by a not knowing the dreams, perceptions and hopes of the other, eventually a drifting away, a growing away from each other. A real lover enters the worlds of the loved one, but maybe Michael's painting the walls of his home blue had been the exaggeration of a superficial trait.

With a warm color on his face, Michael continued, 'With my girlfriend, I'm not merely infatuated with her body, I am profoundly in love with her soul, her complex personality excites me and incites my creativity. You'll see. She would have come tonight, but she is working at a bookstore over the Christmas holidays. Tonight, let's call it a day. Tomorrow's the invasion!'

This Viking town had been invaded by the Christians of Birka and tourists by the thousands but never before by half a dozen socialist Santas running down the street along the river in the direction of the market square. Dressed in red and white, we evoked the imagery and emotions of a fire as we rapidly spread down the cobbled streets of Uppsala, alarming the pedestrians as if everything were burning. We continued running down the street with our bouncing bellies and disappeared into the different department stores. I followed Michael into a large department store detouring around a long sales counter at the entrance with its gleaming glass surface containing perfumes and colognes, then continuing past a whirlwind of scents, we ran into the toy department, whose shelves were cram-jammed and sagging with toys. Unable to stop in time, Michael collided with the shelf, uttered his 'ho-ho-ho!', while children looked at us, startled. Randomly reaching toys on the shelves, Michael started handing out gifts to every child he saw, and children's broken dreams were repaired with play tool kits, while galloping fantasies were fulfilled as wide-eyed children received rocking horses. Michael grabbed a bike and handed it to a blue-eyed boy with a Merry Christmas wish. I lifted a doll from the shelf and handed it to a little girl. The surprised parents thanked us jolly Santas as I handed a mother a rattle for the baby she held in her arms. All this was interspersed with joyful Merry Christmas wishes.

It wasn't long before a saleswoman ran towards us ordering us to stop and put the toys back. Turning a deaf ear to her, Michael tried to give the saleswoman another doll which he had in his hands. She didn't dare grab the toys away from the happy children, and the youngsters surrounded us with reaching arms as two policemen suddenly appeared from nowhere and tried to drag us away. The children came to our aid, pulled and bit the guards' legs, and with their help and Michael's strength, we managed to get away from the two men, slaloming among the hundreds of last-minute shoppers on the crowded snow-covered street. We ran towards the old part of town, where we crossed an ancient walking bridge that seemed to be floating on clouds. The fog was beginning to enshroud everything.

I felt out of breath as we ran into a archway and walked into a courtyard which I suddenly realized belonged to Urban's apartment house. After climbing the creaking wooden stairway to the third floor landing and entering Urban's apartment I felt somewhat safer. From the window we could see a grocery store on the other side of the street, but no policemen. Urban and the other student friends were already there. There was also a dog, a large black Newfoundland which belonged to one of the students. We had clearly and cleverly won the chase! Michael and I pulled off our red clothes to remove all evidence of our protest against the materialism reigning in Uppsala, but he put his Santa costume on the dog, who then ran through the apartment in protest himself. This scene irritated Magnus, the dog's owner, who pulled the costume off his dog. Magnus was an anxious-looking student, the typical intellectual radical with his long blond hair, thin, metal-rimmed round spectacles, and the lips of a koi fish. He stood out from the rest of the celebrating group like a book at a party. He sneaked out of the apartment while the rest of us sat in the kitchen with sandwiches and beer, cheerfully commenting on the children's faces. My thoughts and fears were still in a turmoil, but I started to relax after a few sips of beer.

Late in the evening Michael and I walked back to his apartment. The sidewalks and roads were now clear of snow, and the glassy black cobblestones shone under the house lights. It was one of so many Uppsala nights, as Michael informed me, snowless but cold under an unreadable sort of sky devoid of stars. We walked down some steps past the twelfth-century cathedral with its spires that towered over the town and along the river whose icy bridges reminded me of the ones described in Ebenhausen. He'd had something to say, and he'd written it. He had stepped over the edge, fallen into the psychological maelstrom from which he had emerged, thanks to his faith. At the end of his tumultuous journey, Michael had found himself with a new perspective on life—an affirmation that his loud cries, his silent screams, the blows he'd endured had not crushed him after all. His experiences had strengthened him and given him a deeper mystical dimension; he was now even more alive and passionate than when I had met him in Denver.

On the next day, the end of my holiday, Michael drove me to the Stockholm International Airport, taking the old highway through the Uppland forest.

As we walked to the yellow and blue ticket counter, Michael said, 'Jason, now that I'm happier, the Swedes look happier too!'

I remembered his description of the airport in his novel. I checked in, then Michael glanced at his watch and said, 'My girlfriend will be here shortly—I want you to meet her. When you see her—you'll know what I mean.' Michael's eyes sparkled with excitement.

We had a coffee together, my last Scandinavian brew for some time, and we reminisced on the experiences of the last few days.

Suddenly, a young woman appeared from somewhere, running toward Michael. 'Michael! I'm sorry I'm late! I had to work late at the hospital.'

Michael introduced us. 'I'm sorry you didn't get to meet her sooner—this is Mary.'

Dressed in a nurse's uniform, the young woman struck me with her rare beauty—she had a serene expression, and warm shades of genuineness lit her face framed with fair hair. Her sapphire-blue eyes looked at me and then at Michael; her glance was friendly, full of sunshine a reflection of her feelings for him. There was a glow about her, and I was impressed that she had such a wonderful effect on Michael as the glamour of manhood enveloped his face. I admired him, perhaps even envied him. We exchanged smiles as she said,

'Michael has told me so much about you and about all

your escapades together. I feel like I really know you.'

I couldn't help thinking I knew much about her, but I wasn't sure. Unfortunately, it was time for me to depart. We hugged and promised to meet again soon. Though the sun was shining, the cold air kept visitors in the enclosed section of the departure area, except for Michael and Mary who went outside to the upper level of the observation deck to watch my takeoff.

The engines of the aircraft were roaring in preparation for a long journey. From my window seat a sudden sadness dampened the cheerfulness Michael and I had shared just minutes before. I knew I was going to miss Michael and Mary. Without exchanging many words, I had intuitively understood Mary. Her radiance exuded a joy and spirituality that had affected me in the space of a few minutes. The glow between them was almost tangible. It was easy to see why Michael loved her. Michael's manuscript lay on my lap, the only way to take them with me. The aircraft began to move. As I looked out of my window, I could still see Michael and Mary waving at me—the only people on the observation deck.

'Aah!' now I could close my eyes, exhausted—but serene. I was aware of the pain of this special journey numbing my body throughout, yet I felt the sheer ecstasy of a swimmer who had just finished a race.

A realization quickened in my mind, against the background of the increasingly roaring engines. I froze with an intuition, a question, and a strange mixture of terror and ultimate pleasure flooded my body and soul. With great effort I opened my eyes, looked out the window, and nudged the passenger next to me as I felt a compulsion to ask, 'Excuse me, miss, this may sound crazy—but could you tell me how many people are standing on the upper level of the observation deck?'

THE END

Reviews of *Double Journey,* from which *Echoes from the Edge* evolved.

'This is an intensive novel built around a passionate search for wholeness and a thirst for spiritual freedom. It is well worth the reading and invites dialogue and debate.'
Dr Dennis J Steik

'He is guilt-ridden, phobic, sexually obsessed, egocentric, not a person one would immediately like to have as a friend…'
Nils Schwartz
Expressen